To my family.
And to everyone who listened to me talk about
Spider-Man for the last decade.
I appreciate you.

CHAPTER ONE

Peter is incessantly scratching at his leg, but the darn bug bite (not *the* bug bite, but *a* bug bite) he got the other day is under his spider-suit. Which is under his trousers. And it is a *problem* for him. He's sitting in his science-and-engineering class – not an opportune place for him to be distracted. His foot is tense against the linoleum tile, and he's leaning pretty far over to the left, and someone is bound to noti—

"*Mr Parker!*"

Peter immediately stops scratching and looks up at his teacher, Dr Shah, who has his hands on his hips and is glaring at him. Peter wonders, not for the first time, why his spider-sense doesn't work as well in the classroom as it does during a fight with Doc Ock. Peter slowly brings his hand back up and rests it on his desk. Slowly, because even though he's been doing his night job for a bit of time now, he still likes to be extra careful about trying to look normal when people are paying attention to him – despite his… powers? Reflexes?

"Sorry, sir. I missed the question?" His voice lilts up at the end, as if he is unsure if it was a question he'd missed or something else.

Dr Shah just pinches the bridge of his nose and lets out a big sigh. "It's fine, Mr Parker. I know it's Friday and the weekend is calling, but please try and pay attention. I asked, based on the reading I sent home last class, what we can surmise the impact of easily accessible video manipulation might be on society."

The reading! I forgot to do the reading. He tries to focus, but he is so tired, and his leg still hasn't stopped itching. He stares at Dr Shah, as if doing so will pull the answer straight into his brain. Without Peter realising, his hand inches down to scratch at the bug bite again. *Video manipulation?* The bite's tender and swollen now, and the pain of his own scratching seems to break him out of his reverie. "Um…"

"*I* think it means I can put my face into whatever action movie I want and become the star, and that is freakin' *sweet*." Flash's voice breaks into the silence, and Peter would send a thank-you up to whoever made that happen, but he already knows what's coming next. "Parker would probably just use it to be in a chick flick so he can pretend to have a girlfriend."

Peter rolls his eyes, and his shoulders straighten; he's resisting the urge to put his head down on his desk. "Shut up, Flash," he says wearily, hoping he doesn't sound as tired as he feels. Mostly he tries to ignore Flash Thompson, but sometimes his mouth gets the better of him. Someone walks by the classroom doorway, cutting a shadow across the light from the hall.

"Thank you for that, Mr Thompson," Dr Shah says drily. "But that's an interesting thought. We're here today to talk about the ethics of technology, and wouldn't it be unethical to trick people into thinking you've done something you hadn't?"

"And you'd be taking credit for someone else's work!" Liz Allan interjects. "You didn't make that movie; someone else did."

"Not that Flash does his own work in real life, anyway," Randy Robertson says with a laugh from the back of the classroom. Peter cracks a grin.

"I heard that, Robertson!" Flash makes as if to stand up.

"Hey!" Dr Shah has his hands around his mouth to amplify his voice. "Mr Thompson, please stay seated, and *everyone*, keep your comments to yourself unless they are about the ethics of video manipulation." He looks at the class, thoughtfully. "Now, Ms Allan brought up a good point. Is it fair to pretend you're something you're not?"

Peter sucks a quick breath in through his teeth. Sometimes he feels like *pretending* is all he's been doing for the last six months since he started his nightly escapades. He rubs a hand through his hair and then raises his hand.

"Yes, Mr Parker?" Dr Shah looks at him over the rims of his reading glasses, which he'd forgotten to take off his face again.

"Isn't everyone kind of pretending they're something they're not all the time? Like... aren't we all just... I mean—" He isn't sure how to end his question, or if it was a question at all. He considers if this is a sign that he *really* needs to get a better school–vigilante life balance.

"I agree." Another voice speaks up, and Peter almost cracks his neck turning to look back at the person who is speaking.

Mary Jane Watson is resting her chin in the cradle of her hand, head tilted just so to the side. She's using her other hand to lightly tap her pen against the desk. The sun coming in through the window makes her hair look golden red, and Peter is *sure* his pupils have turned into actual hearts. *She is* so *pretty*, he thinks. Then his ears catch up to his brain, and he realises she said she *agreed* with him!

"What do you agree with, Ms Watson?" Dr Shah encourages her to keep going.

"I think, on some level, we're all kind of faking it all the time? And anyway—"

"Not me, baby! I'm one hundred percent Flash all the time," Flash jokes, flexing a bicep.

MJ narrows her eyes at him. "Unless you're stealing the body of an action star so you can pretend to be in *his* movie, Flash." But the corner of her mouth lifts as if to soften her words. *Not that she needs to soften* anything *for Flash*, Peter thinks. "*As I was saying*, I think, on some level, we are all pretending. Like Peter said. And—" But whatever MJ had been about to say is cut off by the ringing of the bell, signalling the end of class.

Peter shoves his notebook into his backpack, not really caring when the cover bends up and over, wrinkling the notepaper underneath. MJ had agreed with him, *and* she'd said his name. Even if the rest of the day sucked, at least he had that going for him.

Dr Shah's voice rises above the ringing.

"Remember! Next week I'm going to assign your groups for the OSMAKER prep project. Start thinking about what you want to tackle."

"Dr Shah, can't we pick our *own* groups?" Liz's voice has a plaintive note. She definitely only wants to work with the popular kids. Which Peter is not. Obviously.

"Sorry, Ms Allan. I have a system, and it works. I'll be assigning your groups; you just think about what you want to work on!"

The whole class groans in response. Assigned groups are horrible. Last year, before it all, Peter got stuck working with Flash Thompson on exactly one science project, and it had been one of the worst academic experiences of his life. Sure, he was only sixteen, but he was pretty sure nothing could top Flash Thompson walking into class the day of the presentation saying, "Oh, that's *today?*" at Peter's tri-fold poster board of mitochondria diagrams.

Peter zips his backpack and hitches it up on his shoulder, letting the class empty out some before walking to the door.

"Mr Parker! Try to work on your focus, please," Dr Shah calls him to as he leaves.

Peter raises a hand in apology. "Yes, sir, sorry about that. Won't happen again."

"You're a bright kid, Peter. Just try a little harder."

Peter shoots him a flat grin that doesn't reach his eyes and nods. He lets the expression fall after turning away. He knows he *has* to get better at this. He steps into the hall, where the sounds of every kid in school commuting to the next class are almost overwhelming.

"Bro, did you see the Wolves' match last night? Brutal."

"And then my mom said I wasn't allowed to go! Can you believe that? All I did was come in, like, five minutes after curfew one night."

"Let's go off campus for lunch. There's a bomb taco place that just opened, like, two blocks away."

"What is Peter's deal? He's been so weird lately."

Peter's ears perk up. That was Liz Allan, and she was walking with MJ. He strains to hear her response, but they're too far away and MJ's answer is lost in the mess of Midtown High's overpopulated hallways. He grips the ends of his backpack straps, pulling them taut and locking his elbows. It's better that he couldn't hear what MJ said. *She probably agreed with Liz anyway.* He throws his head back and groans at the ceiling, standing stock-still on the side of the hallway while students go past.

Universe, could you just let me have one day of being cool? Peter thinks. *Is that too much to ask? Just one day?*

As if in answer, his phone buzzes in his pocket. Probably a text from Aunt May asking if he is coming straight home after school. He pulls the old brick out of his pocket and groans again.

 NEWS ALERT: *SPIDER-MAN: MENACE OR MENACING MENACE?*

Come on, he stews. He stopped two bank robberies and a mugging, *and* helped an old lady take her groceries home last night. In what world was he a menace? *And what is a "menacing menace"? That doesn't even make sense.* He makes a mental note to send J. Jonah Jameson an anonymous letter to the editor asking for more even Spider-Man coverage.

… Again. Maybe this time the Bugle *will print my letter.*

The bell rings, interrupting his thoughts, and Peter's eyes go wide. *I'm late!*

For once, luck is on Peter's side. He manages to slide into a chair in the media centre unnoticed as Ms Vasquez explains they'll be using the lesson to work on researching their History of the Americas essays. He sits at one of the school laptops and brings up the *Bugle*'s homepage in an incognito tab, hoping to read the hit piece Jameson published. He finds it quickly, but he has to scroll to get to it and is momentarily happy that at least it's not the top article on the site. He clicks through. The huge banner on the bottom of the page says this is the first of two free articles he's allowed to read for the month. At the header is a blurry mobile phone shot of Peter in his spider-suit sitting on the grated balcony of one of those three-storey flats in Greenpoint. In it, he's holding a hot dog. He's trying to wipe away a huge glob of ketchup and mustard and onions that has dribbled directly onto the spider in the centre of his chest. His gloves had been sticky for the rest of the night.

Well, more sticky than usual. A gross sticky, not normal sticky. Cinema-floor sticky, not like hey-I-was-bitten-by-a-spider-and-can-stick-to-walls sticky.

In Peter's opinion, any professional photographer would see the picture for what it was – a bad shot that a reputable paper would be ashamed for publishing. He absent-mindedly wipes at his chest, but he knows he shouldn't feel embarrassed for just eating and forgetting to grab a napkin. He ignores the fact that his cheeks are definitely hot and probably red.

Spider-Man was spotted last night hard at work… getting a stain out of his own suit.

Wow, he can't help but think, *such* journalistic integrity.

He skims a little further and finds nothing out of the normal – some light name-calling, some implications about his weak power levels, some *counterintuitive* calls for him to do more but somehow also not do anything. Bugle *gonna* Bugle, he muses.

As he reads, something on the side, in the 'similar stories' section, catches his eyes. He moves the scroll bar back up. There's a small picture of a face he knows *too well.*

FLINT MARKO, A.K.A. SANDMAN,
RELEASED ON GOOD BEHAVIOR

Peter holds the end of his pencil to his mouth and bites at the eraser. He hovers over the link, debating whether to click. He shudders once and then presses down on the mouse.

"HEY, MR SANDMAN, ARE YOU GONNA BRING ME A DREAM?" It wasn't his *best* witty retort, but in

Spider-Man's defence, he was currently buried in sand that was also a part of someone's *body* and it was categorically *gross*. He was a little preoccupied with how gross it was.

"Is this stuff *you*, Marko? Like, is this your foot?" He held up a fist of sand in his hand, the grains sticking to his suit. "Because that is *disgusting*."

"I'LL SMASH YOU TO BITS!"

Flint's voice roared from all around. Spidey would've considered it a neat trick if it wasn't so terrifying. He punched a fist into the air, taking two fingers and pressing them against the button on the inside of his palm. The webs flew out with a soft hiss from the shooter at his wrist, sticking to a rafter in the empty factory they were fighting in. Spider-Man wrapped his fingers around the thin wire and pulled, slinging himself upwards and landing on the bar in a steady crouch. He rested his elbows on his knees and looked down at Marko, who was re-forming into the shape of something humanoid, but all sand. Fun Sandman fact: he's *always* sand.

Spidey needed to get Marko up to the roof. There was a water tower there, and if there was one thing he knew, it was that Sandman cannot handle a little H_2O.

"Can't smash me if you can't catch me!" Spider-Man called out, and then immediately launched up to a hole he'd seen earlier. The light of the moon shone through, giving him a beacon to aim towards. He heard the rush of sand behind him and grinned under his mask. *These jerks never think.*

Marko's voice reverberated along a hundred thousand grains of sand. "I'll get you, you insect!"

"Hey! It's *arachnid*! Haven't you ever read a book, Flint?" he called back, a hint of mocking laughter seeping into his tone. Marko screamed behind him, rushing forwards. Spidey gripped the edges of the hole and pulled himself up, flipping into the air and landing several feet away. The water tower loomed in front of him, standing tall on the heat-reflective paint along the roof of the factory. He shot another web to pull himself up but found himself yanked backwards. A fist of sand grasped his ankle tight.

"AHHH!" he screamed, his ankle twisting painfully in Sandman's grip.

"I don't think so, *bug*. You ain't gettin' rid of me that easy."

Spider-Man pulled hard on the web still in his hands, and Sandman's fist tightened around air as Spidey flew towards the water tower.

"Oh, I think it'll be plenty easy, Marko!" Spidey shouted down. He limped slightly to the tower and ripped off one of the side panels, letting a rush of water out to fall onto the giant form of the Sandman below.

Sandman sputtered and flailed, but it was too late. The water had done its damage, and he clumped together, wet and miserable.

After that, it had just been a matter of time for the authorities to get there. Spidey watched from the safety of one building over as they pulled Marko into a prisoner-transport truck, heading straight for the Raft, the high-security prison floating on the East River.

"HEY, SPIDER-MAN, WE AIN'T DONE YET. YOU BETTER SLEEP WITH ONE EYE OPEN!" Marko shouted before the doors of the truck slammed shut on him. Spidey could see him in the low light of a streetlight – the greens and browns of his shirt looked muddied and yellow, and his face jaundiced.

Spidey hadn't lost a wink of sleep over the threat. Sandman was B-level at best; he was no Doc Ock. That was for *sure*.

That was only three months ago. *How the heck did he get out* so fast?

"Mr Parker, I'm not sure what a scandalous article from the *Bugle* about a criminal being released has to do with the history of the labour movement in America."

Peter closes the window. *Seriously, spider-sense*, come on. *Ugh*.

"Sorry, Ms Vasquez."

PREETI CHHIBBER

Our home gone
> *Gone*
>> *Gone*

Eaten
> *Gone*

We are not sated

Not sated

> *Not sated*

Need more
> *More*
>> *More*

What is
> *Feel it*

> *We feel it*

> *There*
>> *It's there*

>> *We go*

>> *We go*

CHAPTER TWO

The slats running up the face of this two-storey home in Brooklyn are not made for leaning. They are tiered and awkward, but sometimes that's what's available for surveillance. Spidey's boots are uneven by virtue of the broken slats, and he can feel a tightness in his hip from sitting stuck against the house for so long. But he doesn't move. He knows Sandman is in the house across the street. Spidey's been on the side of this building for an hour now, and so far there has been zero movement. But something in his gut tells him to stay put.

The window next to him opens, and he jumps a little at the sound. He knows it's safe, because his spider-sense gave no warning, but he's still a little embarrassed at being taken off guard.

"Hello, Spider-Man." A gravelly tenor cuts through the night air, and an old man leans against the windowsill, lids low and his skin almost blue-black in the dark night. He's wearing a burnt-orange jumper that looks comfortably worn. Spidey can hear a late-night host making jokes on the TV in the man's flat.

"Hey," Spider-Man replies.

"Just hangin' out here tonight?"

Spidey nods. He can never tell if someone's a fan or not, so he's cautious. He wasn't always – his suit smelt like rotten eggs for a week after a run-in with some *Bugle* readers a few months earlier.

"Well, here. At least have some coffee while you're waiting." The man reaches an arm out and hands Spider-Man a steaming mug. Spidey begins thanking the man, moved by the unexpected gesture.

"Oh, uh, thanks, Mr—"

"Ikem. Michael Ikem. Nice to make your acquaintance." The man, Mr Ikem, nods at the building across the street. "You waiting for something to happen?"

Spider-Man shrugs. "I got a hunch," he says slowly, not willing to give too much information to a civilian. He doesn't want to pull anyone into anything, and he's learnt that even off-hand comments can do that.

"A good hunch. Weird stuff happening in that house. Not sure what to make of it. Glad to see you here to handle it. Let me know if you want a refill on that cup; just knock on the window." With that, Mr Ikem waves and makes to pull his window back down.

"Thanks, Mr Ikem. For the coffee and the tip." Mr Ikem smiles and nods once, then latches the window shut and returns to the recesses of his home.

Spidey waits a beat and then pulls up his mask so it rests tight over his nose, leaving his mouth free to sip at the coffee. He lets out an appreciative hum, glad to taste more sweet than bitter, more milk than coffee. Just then, a huddled mass starts moving down the street. Spider-Man takes one more sip of his coffee before leaving the cup on Mr Ikem's sill. He pulls his mask back down over his chin and crawls quietly to a higher vantage point, shadowed by the grated balcony to his left. The mass lifts its head up and eyes Spidey's direction, and Spidey sees that it's him. Sandman. Flint Marko narrows his gaze, searching, but then shrugs and goes back to shuffling towards the door. He makes his way up the stairs with difficulty, like he's carrying something big under that massive coat he's got on.

He looks left once, then right, then left again – *as if he's expecting to be caught out doing something wrong*, Spidey thinks.

But Marko's not doing anything illegal right this

second, even if he is acting extremely shady. Spider-Man watches as Marko fits a key into the lock and carefully makes his way through the door, letting it slam shut behind him. Spidey's eyes narrow in thought, and the lenses of his mask move to reflect his expression. *What are you up to, Marko?*

It's Tuesday morning in the Parker household, and Peter has spent a few days scouring the news for any mention of Sandman or Flint Marko, but he can't find anything. It's as if Sandman has gone totally and completely radio silent. Pete's nightly patrolling hasn't got him anywhere, either. It's like all the major crooks in the city are asleep, which is *great* in his opinion. All he has to do is some minor lifting – just last night he took down a bike-stealing ring!

Turns out, there's a lot of money in bicycles. Who knew?

But even with all that, something in the pit of his stomach isn't sitting right. He had been planning on skipping breakfast, but when he came down the stairs this morning, he realised the world had other plans for him.

"You haven't touched your wheat cakes! I've got enough batter for at least three more."

Aunt May's standing at the hob, her silvery hair pulled up in a messy bun, and an apron keeping her work clothes from getting dirty. There's wheat-cake batter simmering in the pan in front of her, and a slew of bowls and ingredients on the worktop next to her. She's got wheat flour on her nose, and she's pointing at him with her spatula. He shakes his head and sends his aunt an apologetic grin.

"Sorry, Aunt May. Just daydreaming, I guess."

"Peter, are you all right? You've been so quiet lately. Is everything okay at school?"

Peter, again, wishes he could tell her the truth. He hates lying to Aunt May, but... she'd *never* let him do what he needs to keep people safe! He can imagine her lecture now: *you're too young; it's too dangerous.* No, better to keep his secret safe.

"Yeah, everything's fine! Just a lot of homework last night, so I was up really late."

That was true. Granted, he hadn't *started* working until 2:00 a.m., but he was up really late studying ethics in technology and doing his trigonometry homework. May looks at him like she knows he's hiding something, but thankfully, she doesn't push. He cuts into his wheat cake, lifting a gooey, buttery bite to his mouth, watching the syrup leave a long trail connecting his fork to the plate – it makes him think of his web-fluid. He makes a face and puts his fork back down.

"Okay, Peter. You can talk to me if there's anything wrong. I know it's hard to believe, but I had trouble making friends when I was your age."

Peter's head shoots up. He's mildly offended.

"I can make friends!"

But then he thinks about it and realises that, with Spider-Man cutting into his time, he actually *hasn't* been too great about keeping the friends he had *or* making new ones.

"Are you still thinking about getting an after-school job?" she asks him, turning back to the cooker to flip the wheat cake before it burns. Peter takes another bite of the one on his plate, thinking about where he could even apply.

"Mmmyes," he says, mouth full. He pauses and swallows before continuing, "Yeah, I know you could—"

"Peter Benjamin Parker, if the next words out of your mouth are 'use the help', I will ground you from now until eternity so you *can't* get an after-school job. We are fine." Peter thinks that's only kind of true. He's seen the past-due bills and watched Aunt May balance her books, more stressed than he can ever remember her being. So he back-pedals.

"I know you could see me meeting new people at a new job?" he tries. She gives him a knowing look, and Peter holds his breath. But Aunt May shakes her head and smiles a moment later.

"I'll let you have that one, kid." She turns back to the pan and slides the spatula under the cake to clear it for a new one. Peter holds his plate out for another round, knowing that saying no is a lost cause. "Besides," she continues, after pouring the last dredges of the batter into the skillet, "you can join a club if you want. Doesn't have to be a job."

Peter chokes a little bit on the gigantic bite he's just taken.

"Look at the time!" he says too loudly after swallowing. "I'm gonna miss the bus." He pushes back from the table and ignores the slight tear that results when his sleeve gets caught on a splinter in the table.

"Peter!" May looks harried as Peter jumps up, a mite faster than he might have otherwise, and kisses her on the cheek.

"Bye, Aunt May! Love you!" The words hang behind him as he grabs his bag and rushes to the door, somehow managing not to trip on his way out.

Peter pulls his bag onto his shoulder and chuckles a little bit. *That was a close one.* He knows his aunt wants what's best for him, and that she thinks he deserves some kind of carefree life. But that's for kids who can't do what he can do! It's the biggest lesson he's ever learnt, and he can't just ignore it. And helping Aunt May is part of that... *if* someone will hire a sixteen-year-old kid whose only employable skills are sticking to walls and producing semi-good one-liners under pressure.

He laughs at himself as he turns onto the pavement

along his street. *Okay, Parker, let's dial the self-pity back a few beats.*

Mary Jane Watson is running way later than she should be. Her standard is just to grab a few extra minutes of sleep, but today she snoozed three times! There's a pile of clean washing on the end of her bed that she'd been too lazy to fold, so she grabs a pair of jeans and an oversize jumper without having to dig through her wardrobe. After brushing her teeth and rushing through makeup, she makes it downstairs, swipes her phone from where it's lying on the table near their door, and runs outside without stopping to say good morning or goodbye. She takes the stairs down her stoop two at a time and lands at the bottom just in time to see Peter turn off his drive onto the pavement. As usual, he looks like he's a million miles away. *He hasn't bothered to comb his hair again*, she thinks. *Is his sweater on inside out?*

She bites her cheek to keep from smiling too wide. *He's still cute.* He's a few feet ahead of her when she hears him laugh. "What's so funny, Peter Parker?"

Peter twists around to look at her, his eyes going slightly wide in surprise. *He really must be out of it to not have heard me right behind him.*

"Oh, hey, MJ – you're late." He catches himself. "I

mean, we're late. But I'm always late, so this is normal for me. But you're not usually this late. Why am I saying the word *late* so much? Oh my god." MJ can tell that last part was meant to be under his breath, but she's already close enough to hear it.

"I was beholden to the Snooze Gods this morning." She shrugs. "We'll make it to the bus."

Peter narrows his eyes and shakes his head, like she has no idea what she's talking about.

"MJ, you're dealing with Parker Luck now. Or should I say, lack thereof. This is not a normal morning for you anymore."

She puts a hand to her chest, pretending to be shocked.

"Not *Parker* Luck; it can't be. Say it isn't so! What will I do? What can I do? I guess I just have to balance it out with my Watson Luck." Peter lets out a bark of laughter, and MJ smiles, obviously pleased.

"If it's that easy to waylay the ole Parker Luck, then we should walk to school together every day, MJ." They're passing by 71st Avenue now, almost to their bus stop. MJ looks around at the scenery, searching for something else to say – some observation to make – but before she can, her phone lets out a loud chime. Peter looks at her sidelong as she stops walking to dig it out of her pocket.

"Another snooze appointment?" he asks, stopping next to her. She grins while reading through the reminder alert.

Today's actionable item is supporting your local mutual aid fund!

She swipes at the screen, clearing the reminder away before answering.

"Nope, just a reminder I set up so that I wouldn't forget to post an actionable item to my Twitter account!"

"That's so awesome, MJ, seriously." He sounds impressed. *Not that it matters that he's impressed*, she thinks. *But it does feel nice.* "How does it usually work?"

She steps closer to show him her screen so he can read what she's just posted to her timeline. He jumps a little as she steps into his space, and she takes a minor step back to give him some room. But then he steps forwards. She laughs and can't help but notice the red rising in his cheeks. He looks down at her phone and clears his throat before reading: "'Here's a list of five mutual aid funds in New York that you can support today – volunteer or donate, if you can! Hashtag MJsAction.' MJ, this is really cool of you to do."

"Thanks! I mean, it feels good to try and help however I can? I'm going to volunteer at one next week if you ever want to join? But I started doing these actionable-item things a few months ago. I just… feel like people *want* to help; they just don't know how. So I started researching easy ways to get involved in the community, and that's what I share. It's not that big a deal." She tucks a piece of hair behind her ear and looks down. She is a little embarrassed and worried that it sounds like she's bragging. But when she looks up again, Peter is beaming, looking down at her phone screen, where he's scrolled further back.

"It's a big deal! Your last one got, like, two thousand retweets! That's amazing! MJ, this is incredible." Now *her* cheeks heat up. She looks away and watches a city bus roll to a stop in the distance.

"Thanks, Peter, I—"

"Do you think you could teach me how to do this?" he interjects before realising he's interrupted her. "Ah, sorry, sorry, I was just excited. You seem so good at this."

She waves it off and starts walking to the bus stop again. "No worries. Yeah, I'd be happy to help. Why?" she teases. "You want to become Mr Popular Peter Parker? It does have a nice alliterative quality to it…"

"What? No!" Peter replies, a stricken look on his face.

It's her turn to let out a loud laugh. "Kidding, kidding! Of course I'll help, Peter." She knocks his shoulder with hers, and he scrunches his nose before returning her grin. "You know," she says, switching tracks, "I've been thinking that maybe the organising thing would be a good basis for our project in Dr Shah's class? Oh! Maybe we'll be in the same group!"

"Oh man, I hope so – and not just because I haven't

thought about what the project could be and I like your idea," Peter jokes.

MJ opens her mouth to respond when she sees their bus pulling up to the stop. "The bus! Peter, run!"

CHAPTER THREE

MJ moved to town a few years ago, and Peter was *not* ready for her. It was the summer before eighth grade, and Aunt May mentioned meeting their new neighbours. He'd been sitting at the kitchen table doing some of the summer reading and taking notes on a book called *Gabi, a Girl in Pieces*.

"They have a girl about your age, Peter! I told Madeline – Watson, they're the Watsons – that we should set up a playdate for the two of you."

Peter groaned and rubbed at his eyes under his glasses.

"Please tell me you didn't say 'playdate', Aunt May. I'm about to go into eighth grade. We don't have playdates anymore."

Aunt May raised her hands in mock surrender.

"I don't think the girl *heard* me. Don't worry."

"And I don't need you to set up playtime with me and some random new neighbour, *please*. It's the summer; I just want to be lazy."

"Peter! I think you can take one afternoon to show a new girl around the neighbourhood. You're picking her up tomorrow afternoon, and I don't want to hear another word about it." She punctuated her sentence with a stern glare that would have shrivelled even the most stubborn of spines, and Peter nodded. He took his glasses off to rub away the fingerprint smudges he'd just got all over them and sighed again. *Great*, he thought. Now he had to babysit a new kid. All he wanted to do was play the new MMORPG.

Then he met MJ and everything changed.

He'd left his house with a sullen "I'm leaving!" and walked over to the Watsons' next door. He'd rung the doorbell, and who had opened it but the cutest girl he'd ever seen. He noticed she had red, red hair and killer green eyes. She was wearing a black top with a stylised tiger on it and jeans and somehow looked so much more put together than he did – why didn't Aunt May tell him this was… a *cool* girl? But what could she have said to prepare him?

"Peter Parker? I'm MJ." She'd put out a hand to shake his. "I hear we're on for a playdate."

He didn't think his face had ever been so hot in his entire life. In his memories, his face is basically replaced with a tomato.

The date, play or otherwise, was a complete disaster from that point on, and Peter tried his best to never reference it ever again. The smell of an Arnie's pretzel cart still made him nauseous to this day. But *only* Arnie's. So weird.

"Peter! *Earth to Peter!*"

Peter shakes himself out of his memories and looks at the girl he'd been thinking about, sitting next to him on the deeply uncomfortable vinyl bus seat. MJ is gesturing at her mobile phone.

"Sorry! What did you say, MJ?"

"I *said* I set up an account for you on Twitter. I can't believe you don't already have one, by the way."

He shrugs noncommittally. "I think I had a Facebook when I was, like… eleven? But my uncle wouldn't let me use it. I kind of lost interest?"

MJ shakes her head with a smile. "Well, you waited too long, so most accounts with any iteration of 'Peter' and 'Parker' were taken, and you never want to put too many numbers in a screen name, but I got PeterBPark3r with the number three for the last *e*. The password is MJisGr8 with a capital *G* and the number eight instead of *e-a-t*."

He leans over to look at her phone and raises his

eyebrows, pleasantly surprised. "You know my middle name?"

MJ tilts her head and gives him a sympathetic look. "Oh, Peter, you don't think I've heard Aunt May tell you to clean your room before?" MJ moves into a terrifyingly accurate impression of May Parker: "'PETER BENJAMIN PARKER, IS THIS YOUR DIRTY UNDER—'"

"OKAY! *OKAY!*" Peter says loudly, cutting off wherever *that* was going. "Let me see it!" He pulls MJ's phone out of her grasp – it's pretty easy to do considering how hard she's laughing. He takes a second to appreciate the fact that Mary Jane Watson is sitting next to him on the bus and laughing. He sends a thanks up to whoever is in charge for making sure that he'd mostly got through it without embarrassing himself.

He glances at the profile she's set up – not that he needs an account for himself, *but* if he made one for Spidey, this could be a way for him to change the way people see Spider-Man! He knows that with this he could tell his own story instead of letting the *Bugle* do all the talking. And hey, if he gets to hang out with MJ in the process? For once, it seems like a win-win for Peter Parker.

"I—argh—can't believe—HEY!—you—okay, come *on*—are in this situation." Spider-Man balances precariously on a high, thin branch in a tree, trying to get a dachshund out of it. "Heeeere, Mr Meeps, I've got a treat for you..." He holds his palm open, gesturing at the dog to walk down the thin branch back towards the ground. He can't help but wonder, *How did a dog even get stuck in a tree?*

"YOU GOT HIM, SPIDER-MAN? YOU BETTER NOT DROP HIM!" a high-pitched, ancient-sounding voice shouts up at him from the ground.

"I almost got him!" he calls down, only lying a little bit. He looks back at the dog, lenses wide and pleading. "Come on, Mr Meeps. Can you do me a solid? Just come over here, and I'll take you down to your mean owner and then we can never talk about this again."

The dachshund barks once and turns its back. Spider-Man wipes a gloved hand down the front of his mask in frustration.

"You know what? Fine. We *tried* this the nice way, you hot dog."

Mr Meeps's ears perk up like he knows what's about to happen, and his hackles raise. Spider-Man straightens one arm out and shoots a thin line of webbing towards the dog. It's big enough to cover the dog's entire back. Spidey pulls, and the dog is in his arms, yelping at the indignity. He grips Mr Meeps tightly and flips down to the ground, landing on the hard concrete of the city pavement. There's a tiny old white woman waiting for him, covered almost entirely in a head-to-toe puffy jacket despite the mild weather.

"Mr Meeps!" She has her arms outstretched expectantly. Spidey holds the wriggling noodle of a dog out to her. "Did the scary bug man hurt you? Did he? *Aw, you're the bravest puppy in the whole world. Yes, you are.*" Then she kisses the dog on its mouth.

Under his mask, Spidey frowns. *Ew.*

"Uh, anyway, ma'am... try not to let Mr Meeps up any more trees." Spider-Man gives her a salute and braces himself, ready to jump back into the air to continue his patrolling.

"Wait, what the heck is this crap all over his back? Spider-Man! What did you do to him?!"

But Spidey's already careening to the next stop, his web taut.

"Sorry!" he calls back. "It should dissolve in an hour or so!"

"SPIDER-MAN, MY HAND IS STUCK TO MY DOG..." The end of her sentence trails off into nothing as Spidey gets further away. And if his shoulders are shaking with laughter, who's going to see?

He swings down a few streets, keeping an eye out and listening for any signs of trouble. He couldn't keep sitting outside Sandman's flat – *like a creep*, he thinks – so he went back to his normal patrolling. Sandman would do something bad or he wouldn't, but if he *did*, Spidey would be ready. For now, he'll continue to keep the city streets as safe as he can.

He releases the web and flies into a flip, landing on top of a bodega awning, surveying the ground below him. It's quiet. This is his third night in a row of getting dogs (or, more generally, cats) out of trees, or stopping a runaway food cart, or—

"Excuse me!"

Spidey looks down from his perch to find a little kid looking at him, lit up bright by the lights illuminating the produce and various things for sale outside the shop.

"You talkin' to me?"

The kid looks left once, then right. Then he frowns. "Who else would I be talking to? You're Spider-Man, yeah?" the kid asks, not appreciating the pop culture reference, clearly. Spider-Man just jumps off the awning and drops in front of the boy, who can't be more than eight years old.

"Never mind. Yup, I'm Spidey. What's up?"

"I need to get a MetroCard for my abuela. Can you walk with me to the subway? My older cousin was supposed to do it, but he left me here to wait while he went to 'talk to a girl'." The boy rolls his eyes and gags. "Blech. And now he's been gone forever."

"Uh, sure – what's your name?"

"I'm Héctor. My abuela likes you, so I figured I could ask you for help."

"Okay, but uh, don't talk to strangers. I'm the real deal, though, so we're okay." *Although*, he thinks, *even if I wasn't the real deal, I could still* say *that I'm the real deal. Is this even a good lesson? Argh.*

Héctor digs into his pocket and pulls out some crumpled bills and hands them to Spider-Man, who balls them in his fist. Then he holds out his other hand for Héctor to take, and they walk together down to the A/C subway station to buy Héctor's abuela a MetroCard.

After that, it's time to call it a night. The city is quiet, and Peter still has some trigonometry homework to get to. He swings his way to a dark alley, where he has a secret stash of clothes – he only had to fall into the Hudson one time to learn *that* lesson. He changes and shoves his suit into his backpack and heads to the train at 53rd Street.

Peter takes the stairs two at a time down the long staircase. The station always seems much deeper than must be necessary every time he uses it. For once, though, he's actually lucky, and a train whizzes into the station just as he's stepping onto the platform. He runs to the second carriage and flops into an open seat. The train's pretty empty at this time of night, just a couple of students across from him and some older ladies at the other end of the carriage.

He leans his head against the bar on his left and lets his mind drift. He thinks back to his morning with MJ – they separated once they got to school, and since it was an Even Day, they only had English together, but she was called into a Key Club thing and wasn't in class. He has to wait until tomorrow to find out if they are in the same group or not for Dr Shah's class. Peter crosses his fingers; he really hopes they will be.

He feels the change in pressure when the train heads under the river and opens his eyes. The students across from him are having a heated discussion. The girl is holding her phone out to her friend, pointing at the screen.

"I'm telling you, it said that someone's trying to rob the Museum of the Moving Image! Kina tweeted about some huge noise and someone sneaking around inside, even though the museum's *closed* right now."

Her friend just gives her a look. "You can't believe everything you read on Twitter, DeMane – refresh it and see if anyone else is talking about it, first," he says.

DeMane rolls her eyes, pushes her braids behind her ear and turns away before pocketing her phone. "Ugh, whatever. You know we don't have service until we get to the next station, *Nathan*."

It sounds like the beginnings of a fight, but the only thing Peter cares about is the word *rob*! The Museum of the Moving Image is so cool; *why* are crooks so annoying? Don't rob the MOMI! They have a *Muppet* exhibit – which

Peter definitely has not gone to see three times because he is too grown-up for that.

The train is coming up on the second stop into Queens, so it won't drop him off too far from the museum, though he hates trying to swing *through* the borough sometimes – there aren't enough high-rises to get a good velocity going.

Not that I want high-rises in Queens, but it would make my life easier sometimes, that's all.

The muffled voice of the train announcer comes through – 36th Avenue. Ten minutes later, he's suited up and jumping over rooftops in Astoria. He passes over an arepa restaurant, and when his stomach growls, he makes a note to double back if it's not too late – but he doesn't have time for it now. Finally, he turns the corner, and the neon-pink-lined letters of the Museum of the Moving Image come into view. It's a building with a lot of windows but not a lot of ledges. He'll have to be careful not to be seen. But it's late enough that the museum is closed, so the windows are only illuminated by the lowest night-lights and the awning lights are completely off. He swings and lands softly on top of it, crouching near the metallic letter *T* painted onto the glass in front of him. He peers inside. The lobby is nearly completely dark, but he can see a thin silhouette of some kind of apparatus moving slowly across the floor. It's backlit by the floor-to-ceiling windows leading into an open-area back garden, so he can't tell what it is. It's not alive – yet it looks like it's moving on its own. He presses his face up close against the window, eyes narrowed, trying to see better into the dark space.

He needs to get in there. He presses his fingertips against the glass, hoping that no one is paying too much attention to the front of the building – it's usually a popular spot for people to take Insta photos, and he does not want his spider-suited butt photobombing someone by accident. He looks back once, and the space in front of the museum is clear.

Whew.

Spidey makes quick work of the building, crawling up and over and dropping down gracefully into the open space in the back. It's much easier to sneak in those doors, which are barred only by an easy-enough lock. It breaks with a soft crack, and he winces, offering up a silent apology to the museum's maintenance crew. He steps onto the white stone floor inside softly. There's an empty café to his right, and some white plastic chairs and tables to his left. Just ahead, almost to the ticket desk, a big piece of equipment is inching towards the door.

What the—?

There's *definitely* no one pushing the thing, but his spider-sense is going haywire, vibrating up and down the back of his skull. He creeps forwards to get a closer look, stepping quietly – though he doesn't really need to. The sound of the metal scraping along the floor is *loud*. He has a clearer view of the machine now. It's a little taller than he is and there's a wide circle at the bottom, making up its base. It's thick and some kind of dark old metal. A long, thin pole stands at its centre, giving way to a big, metallic-looking box, before the pole continues leading up to a large blocked cylinder that houses what appear to be bulbs. *It looks heavy, whatever the heck the thing is*, Spidey thinks.

And it's still moving, scraping along the floor inch by inch, scoring a mark in the white stone behind it. Spider-Man's ears are ringing, but he's not sure if it's from the scraping or from his spider-sense.

Either way, he can't get a handle on how the thing is moving. He makes a split-second decision and presses two fingers against his palm. A line of web shoots out and attaches to the base of the machine. He pulls back hard, and it moves back way faster than he'd anticipated.

Oops.

Spidey jumps up and out of the way, perching upside down on the ceiling, as the thing crashes onto its side. He waits a beat, just in case, before dropping to the ground to investigate the machine. His spider-sense is still vibrating intensely, but there's nothing he can see!

He moves half a step forwards and leans down to look at the writing on the side of the cylinder:

ARLO FARMS
1899

The letters are recessed, branded into the iron of the pole. He moves his gaze to the black box bisecting the pole; it looks like it's some kind of power hub – there's a few wires connecting it to the cylinder at the top. Spidey is about to lean in to get a closer look at that part when his spider-sense ramps up to a hundred. An unseen force punches him so hard he flies backwards and thuds against the wall! An alarm starts screeching.

"That's not good," he says, looking up at the flashing lights from his spot lying on the ground. He rubs at the back of his head. "And that *hurt*."

But Spidey's on his feet in less than a second, already flipping as far as he can to the other side of the room, heedless of the loud warbling of the alarm. *What in the world was that?!* he thinks.

"You're not even gonna say hi, invisible dude?" he calls out, trying to goad whoever it is into showing themselves. Nothing explicit happens – no noise, no movement. Just stillness. But Spider-Man can feel every hair on his arms raise, like there's a charge in the air. His spider-sense tingles again, and when he dodges to the right, the signboard beside him clatters to the ground, cracking across the centre. He flips again, shooting a web out in case the assailant is really just invisible, but his web flies out and falls to the ground uselessly. Nothing.

But then his instincts scream, and he feels the next blow coming. Hopping up to the ceiling again, he crawls towards the exit as fast as he can. He needs to regroup – *Maybe more light will help*, he thinks. He finds a switch next to the glass doors in the back.

"Okay, so I get the feeling you don't like being interrupted and that's—"

Another shove interrupts *him*, and he falters a little, still hanging from the ceiling. That was *much* weaker than the initial punch. *Interesting*.

"You getting tired, Mr Ghost?" he taunts. But then something grips hard at his mask, and Spidey wrenches his head backwards. "What the—?" he shouts. Something is trying to unmask him!

CHAPTER FOUR

Spider-Man grips his mask tight and pulls away from whatever is grabbing at him. It's disorientating and discomfiting all at once, and he is not a fan. He pushes backwards with his feet and slides towards the broken sign near the ticket desk.

"Maybe you're new here, but *that* is a big no-no, you – I don't know, I want to make fun of you, but you've gotta give me a little more to go on here."

A slight wisp of air hums past his mask, and his spider-sense starts to settle a little. As if whatever was fighting him has just… dissipated.

"Uh… hello?" he asks the empty room, not really expecting – or wanting – an answer. The only response is the still-wailing alarm. He jogs to where the apparatus fell, holding his side where he must have bruised a rib or two. Spidey knows he'll wake up feeling good as new, but it'd be great if that stopped things from hurting completely. He crouches down next to the machine. "It looks okay?" he says out loud to himself. "Not that I know what it's supposed to look like, I guess."

The sounds of sirens interrupt his inspection. He takes a quick shot of the thing with his phone, webs it to the floor just in case whatever was here is still around and trying to thieve, and then crawls back out the way he came. If there's something that's true, it's that Spider-Man should not stick around when the authorities show up. Most of them read the *Bugle*.

Spidey decides to swing home instead of heading back to the subway. His body twinges in pain with every pull of the web, and he makes a conscious decision to not stop for arepas. He just wants to get into bed and ignore his trigonometry homework completely. But when he finally spies his house and crawls up the side to his window, he sneaks in and falls into his bed, only for his brain to stubbornly keep moving.

What was that weird machine, and why would a ghost want to steal it?

Not that ghosts are real, but whatever it was… it was definitely *something* invisible.

He lets out a frustrated whine and rolls out of his

bed to open his ancient laptop. The fan kicks in, and the machine whirs to life. He built the computer from scratch a few years ago, but the parts were old *then*. While he's waiting for the ten minutes it will take to boot up, he changes and shoves his spider-suit deep into the back of his wardrobe, throwing on a T-shirt and pyjama bottoms. Then there's a quiet trip to the bathroom to brush his teeth and wash his face, and he comes back feeling *almost* refreshed. His ribs still ache, but they're already feeling better than they did half an hour ago.

He settles in at his desk and runs his fingers over the initials 'K.M.' cut deep into the wood grain. He has no idea who K.M. is – he and Uncle Ben rescued this desk from a curb four years ago. Whoever had owned it before was throwing it out. "Another man's treasure, and all that" was all Uncle Ben said when Peter asked why someone would get rid of a perfectly good desk.

The computer finally lets out a high-pitched hum that lets him know it's ready. He types in his password – MCMLXII – and once the desktop loads, he opens up a browser. After finding the museum's site, he starts digging into their exhibits. *No, not the Muppets, or classic horror film paraphernalia, definitely not fast-food kids' toys based on famous cartoons—Ah, turn-of-the-century film equipment. That seems like a good bet.*

He's scrolling, and scrolling, and scrolling. His eyes

are just beginning to glaze over when he sees it. The same bizarre thing that was being dragged through the lobby!

"'Alien-powered arc lamp'..." he reads out loud to himself. He starts skimming the description.

ARLO FARMS ARC LAMP. In the late 1800s, most theaters were lit by carbon arc lamps. Designed as a more efficient, stronger lighting for live events, the arc lamps became the standard. Traditionally, the electricity would run between two closely mounted carbon rods, resulting in an arc of light between the two. Hence the name.

But in 1899, ARLO FARMS revealed a prototype of the only known arc lamp long rumored* to use alien matter to power it. Unfortunately, it was only used one single time, in a small shoebox theater in Lower Manhattan, and no one was ever willing to speak of it again on the record. Much of what we know is based on hearsay and the few witnesses standing outside the building. Newsboys selling papers across the street saw bright light pouring out of a theater lobby on Mott Street, describing a light brighter than any other arc lamp known to man in its single use over 130 years

---

* There is no consensus on the material used to power the lamp, as the owners refrained from allowing its study.

ago. Today, we are proud to provide the public its first glance of the Arlo Farms lamp since 1899! It's been donated for an exclusive, limited exhibit thanks to an anonymous donor.

It's GONE

       GONE

TAKEN

       WE NEED

NEED

       NEED IT

FIND IT

       FIND HIM

BREAK HIM

       TAKE IT

BEEP! BEEP! BEEP!

"*Peter!* Are you still here?! Peter!"

Peter blearily opens his eyes and spots his phone next to him, the alarm sounding loudly. *Why is Aunt May yelling? And why is this pillow so hard?* He closes his eyes. *Maybe just five more minutes of sleep...*

Then his eyes shoot open again – he's sleeping at his desk! He pushes up from the chair and hops over to his wardrobe, hastily pulling on some jeans before realising he's trying to put them on over his pyjamas.

"Argh!" He trips and falls backwards trying to pull off the pyjama bottoms and put on his jeans at the same time.

"Peter, you're going to miss the bus!" Aunt May's voice is coming closer. His doorknob starts to turn just as he pulls his Spider-Man suit out of the wardrobe to shove into the bottom of his backpack.

"Coming!" he yells out. He sprints to his door, flinging it open before his aunt can push it from her side. "Sorry, Aunt May!" he calls, already halfway down the stairs.

"There's a Pop-Tart and a banana for you on the table!" she says from the upstairs landing, and he picks up both on his way out the door. He runs down the street, biting into the Pop-Tart as he goes.

"OW!" he yelps when it burns the top of his mouth.

This morning could be going better. He keeps running down the street and turns at the corner just to see his bus moving away from the bus stop.

"Ugh." Peter slows to a stop, Pop-Tart in one hand, banana in the other, and backpack hanging precariously off one shoulder. "Great."

And he begins the long walk to school.

Twenty minutes later – after taking a slight Spidey-supported shortcut – Peter's just a few streets from Midtown High. If he's going to be late anyway, he may as well take it slow and try and do a little more research. He fell asleep last night without finding anything else significant about the Arlo Farms arc lamp – everything was just rumours or message boards, and some science sites that were so advanced they felt like reading another language. But by now someone must be talking about the attempted robbery.

The *Bugle* homepage loads slowly on his phone, and once it's ready, Peter drags his finger up the screen to see if anyone's reported on it. A few swipes and he sees it, a tiny headline:

BREAK-IN AT THE MUSEUM OF THE MOVING IMAGE

He clicks the link and skims through the article. Nothing new – just a quote from the museum director.

UNFORTUNATELY, DUE TO THIS CLEAR INTEREST IN SUCH A HIGHLY VALUED ITEM, WE DON'T FEEL COMFORTABLE MOVING FORWARD WITH THE EXHIBITION. THE MUSEUM WILL BE RETURNING THE ARC LAMP TO THE DONOR AS SOON AS POSSIBLE.

Well, that's a bust. Who would want to steal a dusty old lamp anyway? Peter doesn't remember seeing anything that looked particularly alien-like on the lamp itself. He switches over to his photos and brings up the shot of the lamp. He zooms in as tight as he can on the big cylinder on top – inside he can just make out two glass rods, but they look empty and dark. *The thing can't possibly work after 130 years…?*

Between this unsettling attempted robbery and Sandman's general shadiness, Peter's gut is working overtime. It's never a good sign when random strange things are happening so close to each other. He's about to press the button to close his phone screen when he sees the word *internship* on a banner at the bottom of the page. The *Bugle* is looking for a paid photography intern!

Peter grins. That's something he can do! He thinks back to the terrible photo of Spider-Man they had at the top of their last article. He can definitely get better shots of Spider-Man.

The entrance to Midtown High comes into view while he's considering this, and Peter jogs the last few steps. He puts his hand on the door just as the late bell rings.

Oh well.

MJ's already in her seat in Dr Shah's class when the late bell sounds. She's been there for thirty minutes, after deciding to get to school early to work out what she thinks her group should focus on for the OSMAKER prep project. She's eyeing her phone, which is sitting in a see-through pocket in the rack hanging behind Dr Shah's door. Since she'd got to school so early, her action item of the day had to get posted earlier than usual. Today she asked her followers to call their local government representatives to support a budget reconciliation bill that would provide the city's shelters with more money for toiletries and food they could give to people who were unhoused.

She wishes there was a way to see if her posts are actually making a difference, but for now, she's focusing on what she can do – she might not be old enough to vote, but she still *lives* here. She feels she deserves to be heard. It's in her planner to call her representative's office after school today.

The class is mostly full, with a few latecomers straggling in as the bell rings. Dr Shah sits at his desk.

He's a cool teacher, not usually too stressed if someone shows up a minute or two late. Just as the last chime of the late bell ends, Peter flings himself through the door and collapses into his seat, panting lightly. His brown hair is impressively dishevelled, and there's a light sheen of sweat on his forehead. He pulls his jumper off, and MJ sees a hole in the seam on the shoulder of his T-shirt. She grins. Peter's light was on late last night – he had probably just sneaked back into his house again. One time she saw him creep into his front door at 3:00 a.m. Maybe she'd offer to start calling him in the morning so they could walk to the bus together on time. Yesterday morning was fun.

Everyone around her is still chatting, even though the bell has rung and class has technically started. Liz taps MJ on her shoulder.

"Hope we're in a group together!" she says, leaning forwards and giving MJ a bright look. Liz's hair is in two high buns today, and she's got a choker made of thin black wire. MJ makes a mental note to ask her where she got it, because it's very cute. *Probably some boutique*, she thinks. Liz is from the kind of family where kids get an allowance. MJ is not.

"As long as we're not with Flash. Remember last time? He didn't do *anything*," MJ says with a grin. Liz is about to answer when Dr Shah starts speaking from the front of the room.

"Okay, class! Today's the day, and don't worry, we

won't wait until the end of the class – I'm going to assign your groups now. Wait until I've finished, and then you can all get up and move around to sit with your teams. You might remember that the group with the best grade will go on to represent Midtown High in the Oscorp OSMAKER fair in a few months, so make sure you're thinking hard about what you want to do and how you want to stand out."

Kids are starting to fidget in their seats. MJ just waits patiently. Traditionally, the OSMAKER competition is a huge deal. MJ has never been the best science student, but the winning project can lead to scholarship money, grants and potential internships in a ton of different fields! The last few years have been heavy on the robotics side, but she has a good feeling about her technology-plus-activism idea. *As long as I don't get a crappy group.*

She startles, unsure of where that thought came from. But then Dr Shah starts calling out names, and MJ shakes it off to listen for her group.

"Now, team one: Flash Thompson, Erica Grenier, Juhi Chokshi and Alice Tam."

From behind her, MJ hears Alice lean over to Flash and hiss, "You *better* do your work, Thompson."

Dr Shah clears his throat and glares at the class, and MJ is struck by his glasses reflecting against the fluorescent lights, like he's got laser eyes.

"As I was saying…" Dr Shah goes on to assign students

to each team. As the list gets shorter and shorter, MJ keeps a running tally of who she could end up working with. Peter is still on there, and so is Ellen Park, Liz Allan… "Team five: Mary Jane Watson, Randy Robertson, Maia Levy and Peter Parker."

Peter turns back to smile at MJ, and she gives him a thumbs-up. This will be fun! Randy is always good on a group project, and his dad works at the *Bugle*, so he might be able to get them access to some cool sources. She doesn't really know Maia, who just transferred in a few weeks ago, but she feels like it is going to be a really strong team. She glances back at Randy and Maia, who both sit in the back of the class. Randy is already waving at her, but Maia is on her phone, which should be hanging next to MJ's on the designated phone door at the front of the class. MJ hopes Dr Shah doesn't notice. He *is* cool, but not so much about having phones in his class.

Dr Shah cycles through the remaining names, and en masse, everyone gets up to move to their groups. MJ makes it to Peter's side a few steps ahead of Randy and Maia.

"So, we're on the same team!" she says, and he gives her a small smile.

"I'm glad," Peter says. "I mean, you and Randy will have this in the bag, and I can just sit back and relish the win – kidding!" He laughs, raising two hands in surrender when she opens her mouth in clear indignation.

"When did you change bodies with Flash Thompson?"

Their attempt to move four desks into a square devolves as Peter is laughing too hard to help when Randy and Maia join them.

"You didn't feel like changing later, Randy?" MJ jokes as they push the final desk into place. He is already dressed in his uniform for the football match later that day against Brooklyn Tech, the green of his shirt bright against his dark skin.

"I look good in these colours! Who needs to stress over what to wear twice in one day?" He glances at Maia and adds, "Besides, not all of us can pull off the truly cool threads that Maia rocks." Maia is wearing a very coordinated outfit of high-waisted wide-leg jeans with a light cotton button-down shirt tied at her waist. MJ eyes her clothes with more than a little jealousy. Then she flinches and looks down at her own striped sweatshirt and long black cutoffs, which now seem drab in comparison. "Some of us are more like Pete," Randy continues.

Peter's head shoots up, expression chagrined, from where he'd been pulling a notebook and pencils out of his backpack.

"Hey, leave me out of this; I'm still not awake yet."

"Did you all hear about someone trying to rob the Museum of the Moving Image yesterday?" Randy asks, changing the subject. "My dad was up so late on the ⌐e with people."

Peter glances at Randy with a look on his face that MJ can't quite read. "Oh? I didn't hear that," he says, his tone flat and disinterested like it doesn't matter at all. *He sounds weird*, MJ thinks.

"I saw a headline about a museum being targeted, but I didn't know it was MOMI! I was actually *there* yesterday," MJ says, giving Peter a strange look. She'd seen the story trending but hadn't clicked the link. Maia was on her phone throughout this conversation but finally looks up at MJ's admission.

"What?" Maia exclaims.

At the same time, Peter asks, "Did you see anything suspicious?"

MJ looks between them both.

"Sorry," Peter apologises to Maia. "You first."

Maia just grins and gestures him on. "No, that was going to be my next question."

MJ just shrugs in response. It was a pretty normal visit to the museum. "Not really, honestly, I was just—" But as she's speaking, she notices Dr Shah walking up the aisle towards them, pausing and stopping to chat with groups along the way. "Oh, Dr Shah's going to ask us what we're thinking in, like, a second. I'll tell you about it later."

Peter glances behind him, and MJ notices Maia looks down at her phone before tucking it into her back pocket. *So, she does know it's against the rules.*

"I was thinking we could maybe do something with

tech and activism?" MJ starts. "I'm still kind of organising the idea, but that's where I started."

"I agree!" Peter adds with enthusiasm. "MJ does this really cool thing where she helps people figure out easy ways to help others by sharing daily tips on getting involved with a bunch of causes."

Randy looks like he's into what they're describing, but MJ's surprised to see Maia roll her eyes.

"That could be interesting," Randy says. "Maybe I could ask my dad if he knows anyone we could talk to? I'm pretty sure he was talking about civil rights and social media just the other day..."

"And I can help research. I mean *do* research because it's my grade, too, obviously." Peter laughs awkwardly.

"Maia, does this sound okay to you?" MJ asks.

Maia shrugs. "It's fine – I mean, I don't get the appeal of using social for stuff like that—"

"To each their own!" MJ interrupts. She senses the conversation souring and tries to lighten the mood. "Like today, some random influencer liked one of my posts but didn't share it even though they have, like, fifteen thousand people following them or something."

Maia gives her an affronted look MJ doesn't immediately discern. "That was me," Maia says bluntly.

Crap.

Randy and Peter watch MJ and Maia like it's a game ng-Pong, their heads swivelling back and forth.

"Oh, I mean, that's your prerogative," MJ says in a tentatively diplomatic way. But she can't help but add, "It's *your* platform," in a lofty tone.

Maia offers a frosty smile in response, her lined eyes crinkling and her red lips making her teeth look extra white. MJ braces, waiting for whatever the new girl is about to say. "Thanks. I just don't like using my platform for anything that feels performative. You get it."

Performative?!

Before MJ can answer, Randy's voice cuts through the conversation.

"Hey, Pete, why does your shirt say 'Weinkle's Daycare'?"

Peter looks down at his T-shirt in horror. *Why didn't I take the time to change it this morning?!* Aunt May said it used to be his dad's, but he doesn't remember that at all. He found it in an old box and started using it as a sleeping shirt when he was twelve. He's *never* worn it outside before.

MJ and Maia are looking at him, their fight temporarily stalled. Randy's grin is a little strained, and Peter realises he was trying to break the tension of whatever had been building.

"Oh, uh, I woke up late and maybe came to school in… the shirt… I slept… in…?" He trails off at the end, letting the sentence get quieter and quieter. MJ and Randy erupt into laughter, and Maia looks decidedly unimpressed. He shrugs it off; anything for the team. The atmosphere in the classroom is rowdy now – everyone chatting and coming up with a plan for their potential OSMAKER projects.

In the corner, Alice Tam's voice rings out, "Flash, we are *not* doing a project on cloning your pet hamster!"

Maia peers over her shoulder at their group and turns back. "Well, tech and activism is *definitely* better than that."

MJ gives her a tight smile, and Peter has a bad feeling about how this group dynamic is going to play out. *Uh-oh*.

"Let's see what we can come up with in that space," he says, placating.

"In what space?" Dr Shah has finally made it to their group.

Randy brushes his locks to the side and out of his line of vision before answering Dr Shah. "Tech and activism – it was MJ's idea." He nods in her direction.

"But we're all into it," Peter adds.

Dr Shah is already smiling. He gives them an encouraging nod. "That's a great idea! Lots of areas you can focus on there – mobilisation, implementation, misinformation – there's so much to look at. I love it. Good job. I look forward to seeing what you come up with."

Then Dr Shah turns back to the class. "Okay, kids, lots of interesting ideas coming up today – I'd like you to spend the rest of class drilling down into an actual thesis; then, next time, we'll work out a schedule of presentations. Any questions?" He pauses, sticking his hands into the pockets of his dark slacks, waiting for anyone to speak up. When they don't, he nods once. "All right – if you need anything, I'll be at my desk."

CHAPTER FIVE

They spend the rest of class nailing down exactly what angle they want to approach their project from. Despite their earlier disagreement, MJ and Maia both want to look at it from a mobilisation perspective. How can they use technology – not just social media – to get people together to create change? is how MJ put it. Randy is going to ask his dad if he knows of any reporters or professors they could talk to about this stuff, Maia is going to dig into how they can supplement their ideas with digital messaging and what their focus could be, and MJ and Peter are in charge of brainstorming actual new or repurposed technology that could help mobilise communities.

It all feels a little daunting to Peter.

"All right, sweet, so we can meet at the Forest Hills Queens Public Library over the weekend since you're both in that neighbourhood," Randy says to Peter and MJ just before the bell rings. He had already started packing his things and moving the desk back to its original spot. "And I'll ask my dad about the sources."

Randy's dad! Peter almost throws a palm against his forehead for completely forgetting what he'd meant to ask Randy first thing.

"Hey, Randy," he says. "Do you think your dad could put a word in for me for the *Bugle* photography intern? I saw they're looking for one, and I need to find an after-school job."

Randy doesn't stop what he's doing but answers Pete above the sounds of the classroom. "Totally – honestly, I think they're having trouble keeping people because my dad's boss is, uh, not a nice guy, I guess? Or, as my dad says, 'brilliant but difficult', which sounds like—"

"An excuse to be rude," MJ supplies.

The corner of Randy's mouth quirks up. "Basically." He nods. "But anyway, yeah, Pete, I can ask him for you." He pulls his duffel-bag strap over his head and rests it on his shoulder. "Actually, you know what, I have to go there tomorrow after school because me and my dad are gonna have dinner in the city. Do you want to come?"

Pete pulls on his own backpack and nods his head, reaching out to slap Randy's hand and bump fists.

"That would be killer. Thanks, dude."

"See you guys later," Maia says, already scrolling through something on her phone again. MJ stares at her back, shaking her head.

"That's going to be fun for the next few weeks," she mutters. Peter overhears and notices that MJ looks surprised at herself. She shakes her head once and waves to Randy, giving Pete a small, private smile. Or at least, he reads it as private. But he knows that might be wishful thinking. "Later, Randy. Bye, Peter. Maybe I'll see you later?" She leaves, hurrying to catch up to Liz Allan.

Randy waves at MJ and then follows her track towards the door. "I'll see you tomorrow, Pete," he calls back. "I'll text you where to meet."

"Cool!"

Peter goes to zip up his bag, but the zip catches and he pulls too hard. The bag overturns, and all his books and loose papers spill out onto the scuffed-up linoleum next to his desk. Eyes closed, he takes a deep breath and groans before kneeling down to scoop everything back up and into his backpack. By the time he's repacked and standing, the class has emptied but for Dr Shah, sitting in the front of the room and reading something on the huge old monitor that takes up half his desk.

"Bye, Dr Shah," Peter says as he walks towards the

hallway. He can see his classmates flowing back and forth, and just as he's about to join the fray, Dr Shah calls out to him.

"Peter! A second of your time before your next class, if I may?"

Peter turns and re-enters the classroom, waiting for Dr Shah to speak. His teacher is looking at him over the rims of his frameless lenses, his mouth grinning under the bushy black moustache he sports.

"Good job today. I'm glad to see you engaging again. I was worried for a little while, there. I just wanted to say keep up the good work."

But Peter's not listening, not completely. His attention is caught by what Dr Shah was reading on his computer.

"Sir, is that the thing that was almost stolen from the museum last night?" Peter points a finger at the screen. On it is the same *Daily Bugle* article he'd read that morning. Dr Shah raises his eyebrows and then swivels his chair to look back at the screen.

"What? Oh, yes. The arc lamp. Such an interesting idea!" Dr Shah frowns a little and shakes his head. "I was really looking forward to checking it out. It's quite a wonder, you know."

"Really?" Peter asks, somewhat surprised to think of his teacher as having interests. Dr Shah laughs at whatever expression Peter hastens to wipe off his face.

"Yeah, Peter. I used to work in electromagnetic research

at Empire State University. I've only been teaching here a few years." His eyes take on a wistful look, like he's not really looking at Peter or the classroom anymore. "This thing was a *legend* in the electromagnetic field. A normal arc lamp with, say, carbon or lithium or what have you, the light is a result of a literal electric arc between two elemental rods. But this thing, something that supposedly uses *alien material*? What would that even look like? It's never been confirmed, and there's only a handful of us who *really* believe it was alien in nature, but what else could account for what it's said to have done?" His hands fly fast as he's talking, and Peter can't help but get excited by Dr Shah's enthusiasm. "They say it was the brightest light ever created at the time, which we obviously can outdo these days, but what's more interesting than that is the effect on the people who saw it. That alien piece of it did *something*..." He trails off, and Peter is left standing awkwardly for a moment, fidgeting with the ends of his backpack straps.

"Sir? Dr Shah?" he finally asks, and Dr Shah comes back to himself, his face a little less carefree than it was at the outset of the conversation. *There is something wrong here*, Peter's gut says, but he can't grasp what it is.

"What? Oh, sorry, Peter. Got carried away. I miss my old life sometimes. Thanks for hanging back – oh, let me write you a note because you're going to be late after listening to me ramble." He pulls out a notebook, and his smile has a bit of self-deprecation in it.

"It was interesting! But yeah, Ms Vasquez is going to give me an in-school suspension if I'm late to her class one more time."

Dr Shah scribbles off a quick note and hands it to Peter.

"We won't make a habit of it. Thanks for the conversation, Mr Parker." Dr Shah turns back to his computer, and Peter heads to his next class, unsettled by what he's learnt, but not sure *why*.

After school, Peter goes straight home. He has thought about his conversation with Dr Shah all day and has come to the conclusion that he needs to figure out who owns that alien arc lamp. Something tells him this isn't over yet. The ride home is uneventful – MJ *never* takes the afternoon bus home because she's always got some club or sport. *Not that sitting next to MJ is the only eventful thing that could happen on the bus!*

Peter leans his forehead against the window and sighs, the condensation of his breath gathering on the blurry glass. The streets of Queens go by: mechanics, bodegas, the stray McDonald's and Dunkin' Donuts. He thinks back to the arc lamp – if there's really something alien inside it, like *really*, and it's the only one of its kind, then it could be dangerous and it must be valuable. Someone is still after that lamp, and if Peter can't figure out who has it, the person who donated it is going to get hurt.

The bus finally rolls to Peter's stop, and he bounds off and all but sprints home, ready to try and make some headway in the mystery of the invisible attacker and the alien arc lamp.

By the time the modest brick two-storey comes into view, he's already got his key out of his backpack and in his hand. He jogs up the stairs and fits his key into the lock, twisting once to the left and then back and to the left harder – the lock's been broken for months, and Aunt May hasn't got around to calling a locksmith yet, but they make do anyway. Once the lock clicks open, he pushes the door inside, kicks off his shoes, and starts to head up the stairs.

"Peter, in here!" his aunt calls to him from the living room.

His hands drag back down the bannister from where he was pulling himself up the stairs, and he walks backwards down the steps to follow Aunt May's voice. She's seated in an armchair in the living room and typing away on her laptop when he comes in. She's dressed in a grey trouser-suit, which means she must have just got home from her work at the shelter. Aunt May handles the day-to-day management there, but she's only been back working for a few months and it's been a steep learning curve – she told Peter she had to relearn how to do digital spreadsheets.

Peter pre-emptively crosses his fingers for his meeting with Mr Robertson at the *Bugle* tomorrow.

"Hi, Aunt May." He walks over and kisses her on the cheek. She smiles and takes hold of his hand, squeezing it once before letting it go.

"I just wanted to see how your day was. You ran out of the house so late this morning, we didn't get to chat. Did you make it to school on time?"

He walks around and sits on the old burnt-orange corduroy sofa, sinking into the cushions. He fiddles with the matching covers on the armrests before moving to pick at one of the fraying buttons on the seat next to him.

"I *almost* didn't make it on time," he admits, pausing before adding, "I missed the bus, so I had to walk."

Aunt May looks up from her laptop, the lenses in her reading glasses making her eyes look impossibly large. Peter is reminded of his own spider-lenses.

"Oh no, Peter."

"But!" he continues. "I'm in a group project with MJ, Randy Robertson and this new girl Maia, *and* Randy's taking me to meet his dad at the *Bugle* tomorrow to ask about a photography internship."

Aunt May closes her laptop and claps her hands

together, the light from the window glinting off the bracelet at her wrist.

"That's wonderful news!" She winks at him when she adds, "Sounds like new friends to me."

"Well, *assigned* friends for an *assigned* group project," he retorts drily.

"This calls for meat loaf." She ignores his attempt at self-deprecation, moving her laptop to the table and standing to head upstairs. "I'll get changed and make dinner. How about banana pudding for dessert?"

"That sounds perfect, Aunt May."

Flint Marko is having a terrible day. He's lost his wallet, none of his associates are answering his calls and he couldn't even get into the Café With No Name, where all of New York's most-wanted criminals hang out. He tried, of course, but when he attempted to talk his way through the door, the bouncer said he'd never heard of him. *Me! Sandman! I've been on the Raft. How many of those nobodies can say they been on a high-security prison floatin' in the middle of the Hudson?*

He was tempted to blast sand right through that peephole – straight into the bouncer's eyes. The only thing stopping him was that he wasn't sure who was on the other side of that door. He knew it could have been anyone in that café, and the last thing Marko needed was to tick off someone important. So, he left and got on the subway. *Like some kinda normie*, he thought.

Now Flint is aimlessly walking a few streets away from the flat he hates in Brooklyn, trying to figure out what he's going to do next. *I was just tryin' to find my next paycheck. Since when is that a crime?* The crime part comes after. He stops in the middle of the quiet street, surrounded by empty factories and parked lorries, raises his arms, and yells once into the night sky.

"AAAARRRGHHH!!!!"

To his surprise, someone answers him.

"Heya, Sandy!"

Oh no...

"Not tonight, bug boy." Marko looks into the darkness where he thinks the voice came from. There's something in that childish tenor hitting his ears that sets Marko's teeth on edge. Spider-Man crawls from the shadows into the light of a streetlight, jumping up and crouching on top of it. *Like some kind of, well, not a spider, but somethin' creepy and crawly*, Marko thinks. *That's for sure.*

Marko kicks at a rock and shoves his hands in his pockets. He looks down at his feet and lets out a plaintive sigh.

"Whaddaya want, anyways? I ain't been doin' nothin'."

"Aw, don't be so sad, Flint. You're going to make

me feel *bad* for you. I don't want to feel *bad* for you." Spider-Man hasn't moved from his perch.

"I got bigger problems than you, Spider-Man, so if you're not here to fight me over anything, get lost."

Marko turns away and starts to walk towards his flat. A shadow passes over him, and he looks up to see that Spidey's jumped from one streetlight to another, and now he's crouched on top of the one Marko's walking towards.

"Look, the cops *already* talked to me today about that museum junk! If you're here about that, this is harassment, and I'm gonna complain to the city."

At the word *museum*, Spider-Man launches himself off the light into a flip and lands directly in front of Marko on the pavement. Marko looks down at the rounded, masked head in front of him. Flint notices Spider-Man seems *really* small.

"Did you say 'museum'? What museum stuff?"

"Nothin'! I had nothin' to do with that museum robbery! Those cops came by my place just because I happened to be at the movie museum during the day? What, is it a crime to have *culture* now? Well, excuse me for wanting to broaden my horizons. I don't know nothin' about no freakin' lamp. 'Sides, I wasn't the only 'bad guy' there. Saw Beetle givin' some lady a hard time, too. But did they bother her? Nah. Course not. 'Cause Flint's *gotta* be the one, right?" Sandman's brow furrows, his voice low and rough. *Why do people keep hasslin' me?*

"A lamp?!" Spider-Man grips the edges of Marko's striped shirt now, pulling him down so they're nose-to-nose. "What do you know about the lamp, Flint? Tell me!"

Marko pushes Spider-Man back, but his sticky hands don't let go. Marko pushes again, harder. A rat runs across the pavement behind them and into the pile of rubbish bags on the corner.

"A lamp? What do I care about some dirty old lamp? Would the lamp be able to get me in with a new crew? No? Next question."

Spider-Man finally lets go of him and steps back. His lenses narrow, and Marko wonders, not for the first time, if he's human or if the mask is actually part of his body. *Gross.* Marko shivers.

"If I find out you know *anything* about this, you're going down."

"Try it, bug!" Marko's fist starts to grow into a massive anvil of sand. "I'd like to see you take me down again. Fool me once, it'll never happen a second time!"

Spider-Man crouches, and then he's gone, already crawling up the side of one of the old factories.

"I'll be watching, Marko! Don't forget." His voice settles on Marko's shoulders like an albatross, and Marko just shifts his hand back to normal and sighs again. Then he kicks another rock and keeps walking.

CHAPTER SIX

The sun is *bright* in the city when Randy and Peter step out of Grand Central station and onto the busy street. Peter squints his eyes against the daylight while his pupils adjust, pausing briefly to gather his bearings.

"Excuse me!" A man in a dark blue blazer barrels by Peter to get into the station, his words sounding more like a curse than a request. Peter hops out of the way, before he can be knocked back against his will.

"I *hate* this part of the city," Randy groans. "So many aggressive rich dudes in suits. Come on." He heads east, and they make good time passing by the Grand Hyatt and the Chrysler Building on their way to the *Daily Bugle* headquarters. Peter sometimes feels a little out of sorts when he's in the city without his suit on, like it's unnatural somehow. He realises that he'll have to get used to the feeling if he manages to get this gig.

"If you do start working here, I'll text you a list of restaurants to eat at," Randy says as they turn onto 2nd Avenue.

"I'd appreciate it." Peter grins, thinking that he'll probably bring food from home. They pass a few more restaurants and delis as they walk down to 39th Street, finally coming up to the huge newspaper headquarters. The words DAILY BUGLE stand tall along the roof of the building and cast a huge shadow on the street below. Peter looks down at the pavement and sees that's he right in the centre of the 'G'. Randy has already made it to the front door, which is almost indistinguishable from the leagues of glass around it: huge windows go all the way up to the lettering at the top. Peter shakes his head and follows Randy.

They head into a modern, expensive-looking lobby. The floors are marble and the decor stark, short of a huge DAILY BUGLE sign along the back wall and two gigantic paintings of New York City scenery on the walls on either side of them. One's an impressionist painting of the Brooklyn Bridge connecting Lower Manhattan to the borough it's named for, and the other, of course, is the Statue of Liberty in a long shot of the Hudson River. They're beautiful, but Peter notices they give the lobby a decidedly touristy vibe. In front of the BUGLE signage sits a desk with two security guards. One is heavyset and white, with a bushy blond beard; the other has a medium build, with light brown skin and black hair, slicked into a strong side parting. They're both looking down at something behind the desk, and Peter can't quite make out their faces.

Peter hesitates and pulls Randy back by his sweatshirt, suddenly nervous.

"Did I dress okay? Like, was I supposed to wear a suit?" he asks. He tried to choose something somewhat professional that morning, opting for khakis and a light blue button-down shirt in lieu of his *whatever seemed the cleanest and would fit over his Spider-Man suit* approach to fashion. But now he's worried that he underdressed. He doesn't own dress shoes that fit anymore, so he had to wear trainers. *Is that going to cost me a potential job?* he wonders, staring at his shoes. Randy turns around to look at him and raises his eyebrows. He takes a step back and appraises Peter's look. He taps his finger against his chin and nods, frowning once before he bursts out laughing.

"Yes, Pete, you look great, man. It'll be fine. My dad is chill as heck." He claps Peter on the back before heading straight towards the security guards. "Hey, Tommy, what's up, man?" he says to the larger guard, sitting on the right.

"Mr Robertson Jr! You know how it goes, just chillin' like a couple of villains." He grins, his teeth gleaming behind his huge beard. He reaches out a hand to slap against Randy's in a high five. "Go on through the gates." He presses a button somewhere behind the high wall of the desk, and the security gates to the lifts open up, allowing the boys access.

"Thanks, man. 'Sup, Rodrigo," Randy adds as they go by.

Peter realises the second security man had been looking down at something on his phone when he startles and lets out a distracted "Hrm, oh, hey," before settling back into his seat.

Peter can hear the guard Tommy laughing as they move out of view. "Rods, man, I know this show is good, but it's not *that* good!"

In the lift lobby, Randy moves with purpose, heading to the lifts under the FLR. 22–37 sign.

"This way – my dad's on the thirty-second floor. It's near J. Jonah Jameson's office," he says, and then adds "unfortunately" under his breath.

Peter isn't sure why Randy says it, but he imagines it can't be good. Randy types in the number 32 on the pad, and a woman's voice with a British accent comes over the speaker: "ELEVATOR C FOR THE THIRTY-SECOND FLOOR."

"This place is so fancy," Peter remarks. Randy nods in agreement. The doors to the lift open, and Peter sees a vision of himself and Randy staring back at him from the mirrored walls. He frowns. His shirt is wrinkly and his hair is sticking up on the side. *Ugh.* The lift starts moving upwards, and Peter's stomach starts twisting into tighter and tighter knots. The small screen next to the door is loudly telling them it's going to be another beautiful day in New York City, with temperatures hovering around the mid to high tens. Peter wishes there was a mute button. He swipes at the side of his head trying to get his hair to stay down. He can feel Randy looking at him from the corner of his eye.

"Dude, seriously, it's going to be fine! My dad already likes you because of last year's science fair. He saw your project and said it was, quote, 'surprisingly beyond the scope of a freshman in high school'."

This doesn't do anything but make Peter more nervous, because now there are *expectations*.

"Ha, yeah, okay, yeah. It's all fine. Totally fine," Peter says. "I'm a confident person, and I'm good at taking pictures."

"That's right!" Randy lightly punches Peter in the arm. "You got this."

The lift bell dings, and the doors open, leading into yet another closed-off lift bank. A pair of glass doors are on both sides of the embankment, but Peter follows Randy to the ones on the left. There's a young bearded man with deep brown skin and a bright red turban sitting at a wooden desk just inside. He raises his head when

Randy knocks on the door, smiles, and waves. There's a loud buzz, and the doors unlock with a *click* so Peter and Randy can come through.

"Hey, Rand-man, what's up?"

"Hey, Sushant. My friend Pete and I are just here to see my dad." Peter lifts a hand in hello. Sushant gives him a nod. "What are you doing at this desk?" Randy asks.

Sushant turns back to the phone.

"I'm just covering for Elliott while he went to grab a coffee. I have to... figure out how to use this phone system so I can call your dad. Or" – he looks up from the complex phone on his desk, a faintly pleading look in his eyes – "you can... call your dad's cell phone?"

"Already on it." Randy's not lying, his mobile phone already in his hand and clearly dialling DAD (ROBBIE ROBERTSON).

"Hello?"

Robbie Robertson's deep voice comes through even on the tiny speaker of Randy's phone.

"Hey, Dad, I'm here with Peter Parker. Remember?"

"Oh, yes! Come on back to the office. I'm here."

"'Kay, see you in a few." Randy hangs up and waves at Sushant, who is idly scrolling through the *Bugle*'s Twitter feed with one hand and waving back with the other. Peter trails Randy through a remarkably manic floor – there are multiple people on the phones in their cubicles, a few of them fighting loudly with whoever is on the other side. Someone seems to be yelling at a photocopier, and at least two people are playing videos at top volume in some of the communal areas that Peter can see. There are so many windows that the office gets a good amount of sun, but the ceilings are low and the lighting is fluorescent. By the time they make it to Mr Robertson's office, Peter's feeling some serious sensory overload. *Is this what working at a newspaper is like?* Randy seems unfazed, but Peter realises Randy has been here before. *Probably a million times. It must be old… news… to him.*

Peter bites back a smile at his internal joke.

"Hey, Dad! You remember Peter Parker?" Randy asks, walking into his father's office. A tall, dark-skinned Black man, Mr Robertson gets up from where he'd been sitting. Mr Robertson's close-cropped hair shows just the slightest dash of white amongst the black. He's got a pair of thin, round glasses resting on the end of his nose, like he's been looking over them to see his computer screen instead of just taking them off. He pushes them back up the bridge of his nose now, before reaching a hand out to Peter. Peter puts his own hand out, and Mr Robertson's closes around it in a strong grip, shaking once and then letting go.

"Hello, Peter, it's good to see you again. I don't think we officially met at the science fair last year, but I remember being very impressed when I walked by your project."

"Oh, thank you, that's good of you to say, sir."

Mr Robertson gestures to the seat in front of him.

"Why don't you sit down? Randy, I think there are some sodas and chips in the break room if you want to run and grab them? I'll chat with Peter for a few minutes while you're gone."

Randy gives his dad a thumbs-up and heads out the door.

"Good luck, Pete," he says before he disappears from view, closing the door behind him. Mr Robertson returns to his seat.

"So, Peter, you want to be our photography intern?"

Peter nods. "Yes, sir. I can show you some of my work on my phone? I don't have a printer at home, but I brought a USB drive I borrowed from the school if that's easier. I took photos for the Midtown High yearbook last year and for my middle school yearbook in eighth grade. I have one that we used as a sports highlight in the student newspaper last year."

"Let's see 'em." Mr Robertson is smiling, and Peter starts to relax a little bit. His shoulders drop, and he curves back a little bit against the chair, just the smallest bit less nervous now that he sees how nice Mr Robertson is. Peter reaches into his back pocket, pulls out his phone and brings up the photo he took from last year's homecoming game. As he's reaching across the desk to hand the phone to Mr Robertson, the office door blows open and a rough, deep, *angry* cadence fills the room.

"ROBBIE, WHY ISN'T THE INTERVIEW WITH THE MAYOR ON MY DESK?"

The boss himself, J. Jonah Jameson, storms into Mr Robertson's office. Peter has seen pictures of Jameson before, but he's not sure anything compares to the actual in-real-life experience. Jameson's black flattop and stark white sides sit atop a face with flashing blue eyes and a black toothbrush moustache that's quivering in fury. He's got his sleeves rolled up, and his tie is flying behind him, settling onto his shoulder like he actually ran here. He's got a sheaf of papers rolled in one tight fist, and his other is reaching for—*Oh no...*

"What's that? Who's this?!" he asks, grabbing the phone and gesturing at Peter.

"Uh—" Peter starts as he realises that Jameson is swiping, and he reaches for the phone in a near panic, realising what else he's got sitting in his camera roll. But he's too late.

"Holy cannoli, kid, where did you get these shots of that masked menace?!" He looks up from the phone at Peter, and Peter immediately starts squirming.

"Jonah, this is Peter Parker. He came in about the photography internship."

Jonah holds Peter's phone and points at the picture on the screen – it's a shot Peter set up weeks earlier, during a skirmish with some random petty thief, just as an experiment. He webbed his phone to a pole and had it take a picture every ten seconds. In the photo, he's in mid-air and suited up. He has his knees up against his chest, feet flat and springing out, and both arms are pointing straight ahead, shooting webbing. He's lit almost purple and green in the bright lights of Times Square. It's a really cool shot, he knows, but at that moment, he desperately wishes he'd deleted it. Jonah shakes the phone at Peter's face, which has taken on a light sheen of sweat. "Can you get more of these?" he asks brashly. Then he steps back. "Are you old enough to intern? What are you, eleven?"

"I'm sixteen!" Peter protests, but quietly, unwilling to push too hard against the loud, terrifying newspaper man. "And yeah, more shots, I can do that."

"He's old enough for our junior internship programme, Jonah," Mr Robertson's voice cuts in. Peter gets the sense that he's spent a long time *not* reacting to Jameson's intense energy. Jameson smiles a smile that only just touches his eyes.

"That's great news – kid, you're hired. I'm not going to pay you a lot, but I'll put you on a small – *small!* – retainer to handle our social media. That's a thing children do, right? Post things on the internet? Anyway, you'll get all that and the style guide. You'll also have to handle admin duties around the office one weekend morning a week. How's that sound?"

Peter looks at Mr Robertson, who is smiling at him encouragingly. He looks back to Jameson slowly.

"Yes?" he asks, and it comes out muted and hesitant, like his tongue is made of cotton.

"Was that a question?" Jameson barks.

"I mean yes, sir," he repeats, but this time his voice stays flat and even.

Jameson grabs his hand and shakes it hard, and then is back at the door before Peter can blink.

"Robbie, get me that interview! Kid, Kayla Ramirez will set you up. You'll start immediately. And be thankful you're on this team; Robbie Robertson's the best dang editor in the business, and you're lucky to work for him. And me."

Peter falls back into his seat, puts his hands behind his head, and stares at nothing for a moment, clearly a little overwhelmed by the J. Jonah Jameson experience. He hears Mr Robertson chuckle. Peter looks up, and Mr Robertson's brown eyes are shining with mirth.

"Welcome to news media, son."

MJ is sitting on her favourite old armchair in her mum's office while she waits for Liz to pick up her video call on her family's shared laptop. To pass the time, she's scrolling through Maia's Instagram feed on her phone. The entire feed is a cycle – duck-face selfie, new outfit, fancy dinner, new toy and repeat. MJ scoffs loudly as Liz finally picks up.

"What was *that* sound for?" Liz asks instead of saying hi. She's looking at something off camera, and MJ can see half of a manicure set sitting on the bed beside her.

MJ rolls her eyes in response to Liz's question. "I was just looking at Maia Levy's feed."

Liz raises her eyebrows in an unasked question while shaking a bottle of nail polish.

"We're in the group together for Shah's class. She's being the worst! I sent an email to the group saying we could do tech and climate change, specifically, and she wrote back saying she didn't think it was a good idea! I honestly think she just has it out for me because of that comment about not sharing my post. But it *is* pretty superficial."

Liz looks up from painting her nails a bright blue, a little surprised.

"I think she's pretty nice if you get to know her. You can't really tell what someone is really like based on a few Instagram photos."

"Yes, I can," MJ replies petulantly, and not without a little bitterness in her tone. "I don't even think she cares about the project; it's not her thing at all."

"Okay," Liz says with a shrug.

"What?" MJ bites out, and then hesitates. She's not usually so quick to anger. "I mean, what do you want to say? I don't think I'm off base. I don't know why you won't agree with me." But by the end of the sentence, she sounds even angrier than before.

Liz looks taken aback. "Because you're being *mean*, and this isn't like you. I'm gonna go. Call me when you remember how to be nice to your friends." And she hangs up. *That was so rude!* But then MJ takes a breath. *Wait – I was the one being rude, not Liz!* MJ doesn't typically lash out. She gives her phone a perplexed look, realising that she'd felt better before she picked the thing up to check Instagram. Between that and the quick way she reacted to Maia in Dr Shah's class... *What is going on with my mood lately?*

Turns out when Mr Jameson said "immediately", what he really meant was as soon as Peter got a signed permission slip from Aunt May. Right after Jameson left, a young Black woman had walked into Mr Robertson's office. She was wearing a black wrap dress and had her hair up in a high, sleek Afro puff. Her grin was bright and welcoming. Kayla Ramirez, she introduced herself, and asked him to follow her. Peter thanked Mr Robertson and told Randy he'd see him at school. That was when he called Aunt May. Luckily for Peter, Aunt May was home and able to download and digitally sign the necessary documents right away. Now he's seated on a chair next to Kayla's desk on the seventeenth floor.

Kayla is typing his information into their system, and

a little ID card prints out from a machine on her desk. He'd posed for a quick photo seconds earlier.

She hands him his card, and he looks at the photo – he's mid-blink. Peter bites back a groan, but Kayla notices the mistake just as she hands him the card.

"Oh no," she says. "You know what, I'm out of cards because I don't usually handle this stuff, but we can get you a new one as soon as our actual security guy, Mr Ambrose, is back in the office tomorrow." She gives him an apologetic smile. Peter just shrugs.

"It's fine – I have a feeling it would take a while to get a good shot."

She gives him an indignant look. "Don't talk down about yourself! You'll use this to get through the security gates and into the offices. You're going to sit at the empty desk right over there." She gestures behind her at a desk that is currently covered in paper and folders. "Now, from what I hear from Mr Robertson, you're a good get for us. I usually handle our social stuff, but it's on top of my work as a reporter's assistant, so I'm looking forward to having some help, Peter." She's going a mile a minute, and Peter's wondering if he should take notes. He leans down to open his backpack, but she puts up a hand to stop him. "I'll send you all this in an email to recap; don't worry about notes just yet. So, where was I? Oh, right, to start, I think you should email me when you get a good shot of Spider-Man and some suggested copy – that is, what the caption could say. Mr Jameson wants us to be posting at least once or twice a day to our social media – do you think you could get me one to three shots a week?" Other than the brief aside to stop him from taking a notebook out, she says all this while typing away on another assignment on her computer. Peter is *very* impressed and a little intimidated.

"Um, yeah, I think I can do that," he says, mentally preparing for having to do Spidey-specific photo shoots in the middle of the night. He's excited that he gets to recommend *copy*, though. *That sounds so official! And I can tell them to say* nice *things about Spider-Man for once!*

"Great!" She pauses in her typing, fingers hovering over the keyboard. "Now all we need is—" But she's interrupted by the ring of her desk phone. "Hello?" she answers.

Peter's hackles go up, and he can tell it's Jameson because he's so loud Peter can actually hear him even though the phone is not on speaker.

"Kayla! We just got a report that there's some kind of disturbance happening at the Museum of the Moving Image again! And that's where Spider-Man just nearly committed a crime, stealing that whatchamacallit, the light, lamp, who knows – cops won't believe me, but I know he's the one trying to steal—"

"Ah, Mr Jameson, do you want me to send someone to cover it?" Kayla tactfully interrupts him. Peter's glad to hear it. He knows it's going to take some getting used to, being around that… He turns to the side, eyes bouncing here and there, searching for the perfect word to describe Mr Jameson… Then it comes to him. *Windbag*, he thinks. *I'll have to get used to being around that windbag.* But he hopes that as a junior intern, he won't have to spend much time with the big boss. *Wait – did he say the Museum of the Moving Image?!*

"Yes! Get Leeds on it right away! Find out what's happening!"

Peter has got to get to that museum, too. He reaches for his bag again, only this time to pull it onto his shoulder as he stands.

"Oh, Kayla, I just realised that if I want to get home in time for dinner, I'd better go."

Kayla's distracted, trying to get hold of whoever Leeds is. She waves at him with one hand while dialling with the other.

"That's fine, Peter. We can pick this up over email. I've got your information, and I'll send you a full orientation note later tonight. Ned, pick up your phone!" Peter guessed that last part was directed at the reporter who was not where he was supposed to be.

"Thanks, Kayla. Nice to meet you!" Peter says, turning and trying to remember how to get back to the lift. *I've got to get to the museum!*

CHAPTER SEVEN

Spidey swings onto the roof of the MOMI and peeks over the back end of it to see if anyone is in the back garden. There's only a lone employee, their museum badge barely visible in the twilight. He can't really see much about whoever is down there, maybe light-coloured hair and glasses. That's about it. It looks like whatever disturbance Jameson was talking about is over. Spidey swings down and lands in a neat crouch on the chair opposite of the museum employee. The employee then promptly falls off their chair onto the ground and scoots back several feet on their butt.

"Ahhhh!"

"Sorry! Sorry! It's me, Spider-Man, a good guy!" Spidey points at himself. "Good guy. Me. Yeah."

The worker puts a hand to their heaving chest and takes a deep breath.

"Jeez *Louise*, don't *do* that to a person," they say before standing up, dusting the dirt off the back of their trousers. Spider-Man has a better look at the employee and their badge now and can read the name ALEX in black letters under a picture of the person standing in front of him. There's a big THEY/THEM sticker stuck to the bottom of the plastic holder the badge is in.

"Sorry about that, Alex. Note to self: don't swing down and surprise people sitting by themselves at dusk in the backyard of an empty museum." Spidey puts his hands up in apology and then leans forwards and rests his elbows on his knees.

Alex sits back down and gestures at the chair Spidey's crouched in.

"You can't... sit, like... with your feet touching the floor?"

Spidey looks down and shrugs.

"This is more comfortable."

"So...?" Alex says.

"Right! So, I heard some weird stuff was going down here today. Can you tell me about it?"

Alex taps their employee badge against the table and shakes their head.

"I mean, I can tell you a *little* but only because you're Spider-Man. Just keep it secret, okay? I could get in trouble."

Spider-Man mimes zipping his lips closed and throwing away the key. The corner of Alex's mouth lifts into a half smile. They start tapping their badge again. The low lights of the back garden make it hard to see their expression.

"So, about an hour ago, I was logged in to the computer to check on some of our items – when donors were dropping stuff off, that kind of thing. We have a new exhibit opening up in a few weeks and a lot of new stuff coming in," they add as an aside. Spidey nods but doesn't interrupt. "So, I'm looking at our stock information, and the computer just starts going haywire. The thing is opening files by itself, accessing donor information. Some kind of hack, I'm guessing. But the weirdest thing is…" Alex pauses here, and Spidey realises they're digging their badge into the table, just twisting it and twisting it until the plastic on the corner tears and the card itself starts bending and dimpling the white plastic tabletop underneath. Alex notices what they're doing and stills their hands, laying their badge down, then interlocking their fingers and resting their clasped hands on their lap. They take a deep breath and continue: "The weirdest thing is that I cannot remember what happened after the donor files opened. Like, just a complete brain fart. When the computer started freaking out, it was four seventeen p.m. I remember because I looked at the clock on the screen. Then, all of a sudden, it was four twenty-four, and I have no idea what happened in those seven minutes."

Spidey lets out a sympathetic hum. He's only been at this super-hero gig for a short while, but he already knows more about random memory wipes than he'd like to admit.

"That's horrible, Alex. Can you… go home?" Spidey's not sure how grown-up jobs work, but it does seem like Alex should be able to leave if they're not feeling well.

Alex grins hesitantly and shakes their head.

"Nah, I took an extra-long break. I've only got another hour or so before I can go home. It's just *weird*. I don't feel hurt or anything."

"That's good. Can I ask you just one or two more things?" Spider-Man asks.

"Sure. I've got about five minutes left, though. Then I gotta go."

Spider-Man laughs a little bit.

"Thanks for being willing to spend it with me answering questions. Can you tell me about the actual arc-lamp thing that almost got stolen the other night?"

At this, Alex lights up.

"Heck yeah! I can't believe I am one of the very few

people who actually got to see it in person! It's *legendary* – for a certain sect of nerds, anyway. Didn't get a picture, though. And I *missed* it when Fatima accidentally turned it on for a second – which was a big deal because our boss was very clear that we were *not* supposed to turn it on. The donor wrote it into the temporary loan agreement and everything! But it was only on for, like, ten seconds I heard. Anyway, what's even worse? We have to keep our phones in our lockers while we're on shift – like, if we get caught with them on premises, points are absolutely docked, demerits given, et cetera – so *no one* could show me what that looked like. Ugh. So, the donor must be like… the great-great-great-great-grandson or nephew or something of the guy that invented it. I don't know how else he'd have it. The story is that the original inventor found the alien rock that powered the thing and he only ever got to use it the one time. It's kind of sad…" They trail off, waiting for a signal to keep going.

"I can handle sad, I promise," Spider-Man says.

"If you say so – anyway, so the way I heard it at my college AV club was that the guy does a big event to show people this light powered by alien magic or whatever, and it's the last time anyone ever sees him alive. And every other person who had been in the audience for the exhibition that day couldn't even speak about it. It was like it had never happened, even though family and friends knew they'd gone to the event. They'd just pretend they didn't know what anyone was talking about."

This must be what Dr Shah was referencing, Spidey thought. *The memory loss? The donor? This is a potential lead!*

"Do you think I could take a look at the files that got opened up? Or could you tell me who the donor is?"

Alex hesitates.

"I actually don't know their name. It was *super* hush-hush. Only my boss had access to that file. That's why today was such a big deal."

Spidey frowns, and his lenses crinkle, mimicking Peter's face underneath the mask. Then Alex's wristwatch beeps.

"Oh, that's my break time over. Sorry I can't give you more," Alex says.

"You helped a lot," Spidey protests. "Seriously. Thank you!"

Alex smiles at him and heads inside. Spider-Man watches through the windows as they walk the short distance to the front of the lobby, but then a tall blond man comes up to them and taps Alex on the shoulder. The man holds out a *Daily Bugle* press pass.

Ugh.

Looks like Kayla finally got ahold of Ned Leeds. He's probably going to be here as long as it takes him to get the story for Jameson. Spidey groans. Hopefully Alex won't mention that Spidey was already here. He'd better sneak out while he can. He does *not* want to be a part of this story when it runs tomorrow morning.

After checking the subway status on his phone to see that both his trains are showing massive delays, Spider-Man decides to swing home. As he flies by shopfronts and flats, he thinks about what he knows. *The arc lamp is one of a kind and powered by an alien something. It might belong to a relative of whoever created it. Maybe I can figure this out through the internet instead of having to go back to the museum... What was the name? Arlo Farms... I saw it branded onto the iron bar of the lamp.*

A junction comes into view, and Spidey cuts the corner to the right, soaring over the two- and three-storey buildings below. He's about halfway back to Forest Hills and looking forward to changing out of his suit and maybe even taking a shower. It's been a few days since he washed the spider-suit and he can tell it's starting to get a little ripe. His face twists up. *No one told me how much* laundry *was involved with being a crime-fighting vigilante.*

He's just flipping over the roof of a combination Taco Bell and Pizza Hut when his spider-sense blasts to life in the base of his skull. Before he can react, something hard slams against the side of his head and sends him careening sideways before a wall stops him. He falls to the roof below, rubbing his head and trying to clear his vision. For half a second, Spidey thinks it's the ghost again. But before his vision settles, twin winged beings drop onto the silver-painted slats in front of him, finally settling into one figure as his eyes go back to normal. It's Beetle, her armour reflecting the streetlights and her hands on her hips. She doesn't speak.

"Beetle? What the heck?" Spidey asks, jumping up to a higher ledge on the next building over. Beetle doesn't answer – just launches herself fist-first at Spider-Man's face. Spidey jumps out of the way, slinging a web across the street, trying to find a less populated area so he won't have to worry about civilians. Beetle is clearly angling for a fight, though he's not sure why. *Did she see me at the museum? Was she involved somehow?* The questions run through his head. Then he remembers Sandman mentioning that Beetle had been at the MOMI the day of the robbery, too.

He sees Juniper Valley Park in the distance. It's late enough that it should be pretty empty. Spidey rushes forwards and can hear Beetle flapping her wings behind him, trying to catch up.

Spider-Man swings into the park and takes off running across the large circle of grass in the middle. It's predictably quiet, and he grins under his mask, glad that something worked out in his favour. The hum of Beetle's wings gets louder, and she descends to the grass behind him. The downside to being in the park is that it really is just a huge open space, which means there's nothing to swing from or use to take cover.

"Beetle." Spidey puts his hands up and walks a few steps backwards. "What gives? Did that hard shiny exterior not protect your soft fuzzy insides?" he asks as he shoots two webs towards her helmet. He jumps to flip over her, pulling the helmet off Beetle's head with his webs as he lands on her other side. She still hasn't said anything. Spidey's unnerved, so he keeps talking. "Gotta say, I'm a little hurt that you're not speaking to me. We normally have such a fun routine going back and forth with our banter. Is this because of what happened at the museum?"

Beetle just bends her knees and pushes forwards, charging him full speed, seemingly unconcerned about her lack of headgear. Her dark hair is pushed back by the wind, her teeth are bared in a vicious snarl, but when Spider-Man looks into her eyes, they seem empty. Spider-Man has the briefest second to be shocked before he's bounding out of the way, missing her super-armoured punch by seconds. *What is going on? She's never this quiet, and she's not usually this vicious!* He flips around, firing off a fast round of webbing to jam up Beetle's wings before jumping into the air. She starts to bend her knees again, warming up to run forwards, but Spidey's already shooting webbing at her boots, sticking them to the ground. She struggles, pulling at her feet, grunting and yanking against the strength of the webbing to no avail.

Spidey drops onto the ground a few feet away. "What is your deal?"

Instead of answering, Beetle just lashes out with her fists, and so he webs her hands together and winds a thin line around her so her arms are down and tight against her torso. "Do you know what that thing was at the museum?" he asks. But she still doesn't speak. She looks at him blankly and keeps struggling against the web. Spider-Man's not sure what to do, but he knows *he* can't fix her. Her blank face, void of any recognition, is so disturbing that he just turns tail and leaves her there, webbed to the grass in the middle of the park.

"Freaky stuff really needs to take a vacation," Peter says to himself on his way home. *That fight was bizarre. What a strange day. Shoot!* He realises he forgot to take a photo during the fight for the *Bugle*. He thinks about going back, but it was such an unsettling thing, it makes him feel a little uncomfortable at the thought of it. So instead, a few streets from home, he sets his phone up on a roof's edge and hits the timer. Then he swings by, holding on to his web with both hands like he's slingshotting himself forwards, before doubling back to grab the phone. He stands on a roof, walking up and down the ledge in his spider-suit, holding his phone and thinking about what he should tell them to say about the photo.

He types out: *Just ran across Spider-Man and Beetle fighting it out in Juniper Valley Park – got a sick shot of him leaving the scene! Could the caption be: "Spidey beats Beetle to the punch!"?*

The reply comes almost immediately: *This is great, Peter, thanks! Did you get any pictures of Beetle? Have the authorities picked her up already?* Followed quickly by: *Actually, I'll give them a call – that way they'll owe us a tip later down the line. I'll try to sell that caption on the photo, but it may not get approved. Just as a heads-up. Thanks for your hard work! —K*

Peter smacks a still-gloved hand against his forehead, annoyed that he forgot to call anyone. He shoots a quick note back to Kayla confirming that no, he didn't get a shot of Beetle, as he was too busy hiding, and no, he was going to call when he got home, but he thanks her for handling it. He clicks the home screen and sticks his phone back inside his suit.

Such *a weird day!*

CHAPTER EIGHT

Ms Nguyễn is in the hall speaking with the headteacher, and the class is supposed to be silently reading *Parable of the Sower*, but MJ finished it last night and has already started her essay. So instead, she holds on to her mobile phone, contraband by virtue of not having been placed in the plastic crates at the front of the room. She's scrolling through her Instagram. Peter is in the seat in front of her. She can tell he's distracted because he hasn't turned the page once in the last five minutes. *Maybe he'd be a good person to talk about my… feud… with Maia?* she considers. *Feud* feels like a harsh word in her own head. *A mini fight,* she thinks. *A disagreement.*

In her experience, Peter usually has a good perspective on this kind of stuff – he's always been so even-keeled during their friendship. She remembers the first time they actually hung out – she'd overheard when his aunt had jokingly called it a playdate, but it was more of a setup for a blind date, if anything! He'd shown up at her house in cargo shorts and a plain white T-shirt, hair dishevelled, glasses smudged, and, she admitted to herself, a really, *really* sweet smile. They'd spent the day at Flushing Meadows Park, and while there was some awkwardness – Peter had got sick after eating a bad pretzel – they spent most of the day chatting and people-watching. MJ went home that night excited with how the day had gone. But after that, Peter had never brought it up to her again, so she figured he just wanted to be friends. Now it's two years later and they're friendly, but he's always so distant. Plus, she saw him sneak into his house again last night. She knows there is definitely something going on with him. Just then, he reaches up to scratch the back of his neck, like he can feel her thinking about him. *Oops.*

MJ puts her phone on her desk, Instagram still open, and rests her head in her hands, palms pressing against her forehead while she looks straight down at the screen. She's not surprised to see that the *Bugle* posted a new photo of Spider-Man. She hums appreciatively at the quality of the picture. Usually the images are blurry or a still from a video, but this one is really great. *He is very cool*, she thinks. *Protecting and helping people in the community.* He's definitely saved *her* life before – that time Rhino ended up at their high school and she got stuck in the gym on her own with the Rhino thundering her way. Spider-Man had swung through one of the windows and pulled her out of the way before she could get hurt. It was one of the most terrifying – *but coolest* – things that had ever happened to her. She grins at the thought. But even with that extraordinary anecdote in her back pocket, somehow when she thinks of Spider-Man, what always comes to mind is a video she saw on YouTube of him carrying some old lady's shopping home. In this picture, however, he's clearly on the way back from some kind of fight. His mask has a tear in it along his scalp, though it's too dark to see what colour his hair actually is – probably black or brown. He's mid-flight, pulling himself along above the rooftops. She glances down to read the caption: *BREAKING: Beetle and Spider-Man team up to ruin everyone's day. Spidey leaves partner high & dry.*

Gosh, could the Bugle *be more obvious with their agenda?*

She picks her phone back up, ready to lay into whatever *Bugle* employee is writing these captions – her thumbs are itching to type the words *how dare you you don't know anything omg how terrible can you be you're trash trash trash trash.* She startles herself with the vitriol bubbling inside her brain. *Liz was right. This is* not *like me.* MJ drops her

phone to the desk with a thunk and presses her palms
against her eyes.

Peter hears a *thump* behind him and turns around to look
at MJ. She's got her head in her hands and her phone on
the desk in front of her – which is not strictly allowed.
The phone is on, and he can see the shot he sent to the
Bugle the night before front and centre on MJ's Instagram
feed. The back of his neck heats up. She takes her hands
off her eyes and sees him looking at her phone. She gives
him a look like *Wait till you see this* and flips the screen
around so he can read the caption.

Once the words sitting under the photo register, it's as
if his entire body vibrates with irritation. He nearly laughs
at the absurdity of it.

Typical.

His brow furrows, and he makes a fist against his
thigh, resolving to get photos that can't be editorialised
like this and taken out of context. Maybe he should have
posed victoriously next to Beetle, stuck in her webs. He
grimaces. *No. No. That is not the way, Peter*, he thinks.
MJ takes the phone and types something into it before
flipping it back to him. She's opened her notes app, and
in it are the words:

WE KNOW SPIDEY'S THE COOLEST—NOTHING THE BUGLE CAN DO 2 CHANGE IT (MINUS LIKE ACTUAL FACTS OR WHATEVZ). REMEMBER WHEN RHINO ATTACKED AND HE SAVED A BUNCH OF US? HE'S A HERO.

Peter tries to keep from smiling at how much MJ likes Spider-Man, but he can't lie, it makes him feel good. He takes the phone and types back a quick message.

IKR, THEY GIVE HIM SUCH A BAD RAP + I KNOW THE CAPTIONS BOGUS BC I TOOK THE PIC! (GOT THE BUGLE PHOTOG INTERN THING WILL TELL U BOUT IT LATER!)

He watches MJ as she reads his message, and there's a flash of emotions across her face from something like annoyance to excitement. She looks up at him with a smile so big her nose scrunches and he can barely see her eyes. He's distracted enough that he doesn't wonder why she was annoyed. Then she types furiously into the phone and turns it back to him.

OMGOMGOMG!!!! WANT 2 HEAR EVERYTHING!! MAYBE WE HANG AT MINE AFTER SCHOOL? PORCH TIME? ALSO WANT 2 ASK UR ADVICE ON SOMETHN W MAIA . . .

He doesn't answer out loud but nods, wondering what the thing with Maia is about. Turning back to face the front of the class, he considers the last time they'd met as a group. He thought they'd entered into a truce for the project, but maybe he was wrong?

Ms Nguyễn re-enters the classroom just then and calls everyone to attention.

"Okay, kids, let's dig into chapter four!"

Peter reopens his book and picks up his pen before stealing a glance at the clock. Only a few hours left in the day; he bites back the smile again, thinking about the prospect of his after-school plans with MJ.

SOON

      SOON

It's close

     Close

We're close

Weak

Weak

But close

"Hey, man!"

Peter looks up from the peanut-butter-and-banana sandwich he'd brought from home for lunch. He's sitting at the end of one of the lunch tables in the cafeteria, trying to answer the last four questions in his trigonometry homework before the bell rings for class. Randy Robertson falls into the seat across from him, dropping a boxed salad from the restaurant across the street onto the table.

"How'd your first day go? Dad said everyone loved the photo you sent in of Spidey last night. It's a *really* good one." Randy shakes his salad with two short jerks before opening it and jabbing a fork into pieces of spinach and chicken.

The smell of Randy's vinegar dressing hits Peter's nose and he closes his book, homework forgotten in lieu of the praise. Gratification pulls at his cheeks, and he grins, glad to know that Mr Robertson liked his work.

"Thanks again. I really appreciate you taking me up there. And it was so cool that they used the picture! But they didn't use my caption? And... kind of lied? Spidey was *definitely* fighting Beetle, not teaming up with her." He frowns.

Randy rolls his eyes and adjusts his collar.

"Yeah, Jameson's got an iron fist on *anything* related to Spider-Man. He has to approve all the captions, and he'll never let a good Spidey note get through. Let's be real. Dad says he's a good journalist outside of Spider-Man; just can't be – what'd he say – oh, yeah, *objective*. Basically, with Spidey, it's JJJ or the highway." Randy laughs at his own rhyme.

"Well, that sucks," Peter replies before taking a big bite of his sandwich.

"No joke," Randy replies, spearing another piece of salad. "But my dad also says *other* than that, it's a cool place to work."

"Oh man, yeah, last night as I was leaving, there was some big thing happening at MOMI again and they were gonna send a reporter there. I still don't know what ended up happening," he lies, followed by making a silent apology for lying.

"My dad got home last night and said it was wild – he was on the phone for *hours*. I heard him ask someone about some old mansion near the Cloisters."

Peter stops himself from leaning forwards in eagerness. He takes a sip of his drink first and then asks, in what he hopes is a nonchalant manner, "Oh?"

"But when I asked him about it, he said it was none of my business." Randy shrugs. "Like, dang, Dad, I'm just following in your footsteps!" He laughs again.

Peter laughs with him, but his mind is moving a mile a minute. *A mansion near the Cloisters? That must be where the mysterious donor lives!* He'd done some internet sleuthing when he got home last night but couldn't find anything about Arlo Farms or who had actually worked there at the time, and so he couldn't find any sort of genealogical trail. He'd given up around two a.m. Which is why he was doing trig homework at lunchtime. But this new information might help him figure out who this mysterious donor is, and could get him a step closer to finding out why an invisible ghost thief might want it.

"So," he says, trying not to let his excitement show too much by changing the subject. "You ready for next week's match?" He moves to take another sip from his drink.

"'Bout as ready as you are to ask out MJ?" Randy says slyly.

Peter chokes on his drink.

"Kidding! Kidding! Okay, man. We'll wait till you're ready." Randy's grin is way too big, and Peter narrows his eyes at him. But then Randy launches into a detailed explanation of their strategy for Midtown High's next football match, and Peter takes another bite of his sandwich and chews, nodding along, listening to his friend talk, and trying hard not to be distracted by thoughts of Mary Jane Watson.

DING.

Flint Marko's phone beeps. It's a cheap one he lifted off a rack at an electronics shop in the Village. He picks it up from its place on the floor to look at it. "This better be you, Donnie," he says to himself. He's been waiting for news about a heist and maybe a place for him on a team.

 YOU HAVE UNDER TWENTY MINUTES LEFT ON YOUR PLAN. PLEASE LOG IN TO YOUR ACCOUNT.

He curses. It's just a spam message. He falls back onto his mattress, an old, uncomfortable double that came with this flat. It's on the floor. He looks around. There's not much to even show he lives here – an old photo of him and his mum taken at the beach is taped to the wall. He doesn't remember the day, but he looks happy. There's a turned-over milk crate that acts as a side table, and a small mini fridge he stole a few days ago that he knows has a single leftover bagel in it and half a jug of orange juice.

"This is such crap!" he yells at the ceiling. Marko used to be one of the guys everyone wanted on their crew, and now he has trouble getting a callback for a simple bank job. "It don't make any sense. I'm the perfect guy to have around! I can slip into every tight spot. And maybe I lost my cool a few times, but who hasn't?" He rolls over onto his side and looks out at the brick wall about a foot away. "And maybe I got caught, but it took the *bug* to take me down." He hisses that out between his teeth, like the sentence itself is ticking him off.

He slams a fist against his mattress and then lies back heavily. He picks up the phone again just as a loud knock echoes on the door.

"HEY, YOU, MR ARCHER!"

Flint opens the door. His neighbour stands in front of him, white hair clouding around his head. His brow is furrowed, and he's shaking a bag of rubbish in his hand in Flint's direction. He looks green in the dim light of the hallway, and the ghost of recognition lights across Flint's face as he's reminded of an old comrade-in-arms. Then the man starts talking and the illusion is dispelled.

"Mr Archer, this is the fourth time I am telling you: you can't leave your trash in the lobby! There are trash cans *outside*."

Flint gives him a dirty look.

"Then you can take it outside *for me*, little man," he bites out, teeth clenched. His neighbour's jaw drops open, and he starts sputtering out sounds. Before he can form any words, Flint slams the door shut in his face, walking back to his sad little bed.

The neighbour's voice carries through the door anyway, when he finally finds his words.

"You're outta here, Archer! Just you wait!"

"Try it!" Marko calls back, laughing humourlessly. "Try it," he says in a quieter tone, and it's more tired than angry. His phone beeps again as he falls back onto his bed. He picks it up. *If it's another spam or automated text, I'm going to crush the annoying thing to smithereens.* He looks at it and is surprised to see that there's no number to speak of, just ten digits of empty space at the top. *What the—?*

> HELLO MARKO FLINT HELLO MARKO YOU ARE TO WANT MONEY FOR YOUR BANK TO GIVE TO YOU WE CAN MAKE THIS HAPPEN

> WE CAN FIX YOUR ISSUE

> WE CAN MAKE IT GOOD

> MONEY FOR YOU TO DO ONE INFINITESIMAL THING FOR US WE REQUIRE ONE THING

> ONE JOB

> FLINT MARKO

> SANDMAN WE NEED SANDMAN

> GET ARC ARC LAMP GET ARC GET HOME GET HOME ARC 2275 OCEANIC AVE

> GET

STEAL

ARC

LAMP

FROM

2275 OCEANIC AVE

BRING

US

Marko stops reading and puts the phone down. His eyes are glazed and his grin is unsteady. He feels… furious; he's quivering with anger and anticipation.

One job, he thinks, *I can do one job.*

"MR ARCHER!" his neighbour calls again from the hallway.

One job, Marko thinks, *right after this one. Quick. Thing.*

His fists shift into massive mounds of sand, and he makes for the door.

CHAPTER NINE

"Hey, Aunt May!" Peter toes his shoes off and walks into the living room, but there's no one there. He's a little late, having missed the bus home thanks to what he views as a wildly unfair series of events – he grits his teeth and hopes there's no security cam footage of Spider-Man sneaking out of an under-construction girls' locker room through the school vents. It was just so much faster to swing home than wait for the late bus.

"Up here!"

He follows Aunt May's voice to the stairs, where she's standing at the top on the landing. She's holding up her phone in excitement. "Is that a credit I see to you on the *Bugle* homepage?" she asks excitedly.

"Ahh." Aunt May had been thrilled about his gig at the *Bugle* this morning when Peter had rushed out the door, but he had neglected to tell her about the Spider-Man picture, unsure of how to handle it. "Yeah." He rubs the back of his head as he finally makes it to the last step.

"Peter, this is so exciting! How did you get this picture? It looks like it's from the perfect angle and everything. My nephew, so impressive." She grins.

Peter deflects: "Right place, right time, Aunt May. He swung right by me on my way home yesterday! *Anyway*" – he slides past her on his way to his room, his backpack catching awkwardly along the wall and knocking a picture frame askew as he pushes by – "I have to change! I'm meeting MJ at her house in a half hour to hang out."

"Oh, really?" she asks, and Peter can hear her straightening the photo in his wake. "MJ?" she continues, her tone full of clearly feigned nonchalance.

Peter turns around to protest.

"It's not—"

But he stops at Aunt May's knowing look. She taps against her chin and nods, looking off to the distance like she's just innocently voicing her thoughts.

"MJ's a good girl, Peter. And you're an excellent young man, which I think I can take *some* credit for—"

"We're *just* hanging out for a little while, Aunt May. Please don't start making any big, embarrassing plans," Peter says, imagination running wild with visions of Aunt

May sending out invitations or calling MJ's mum or aunt to "discuss" the two of them. *Oh man, no thanks. I would crawl inside the actual earth and never return.*

"Whatever you say," she says, implying that it's not actually about what he says but what she thinks she knows. Peter gives up, shaking his head. *There could be worse things than having an aunt who just wants you to be happy with the cute girl next door*, he realises. He gives Aunt May a somewhat-pained smile and takes a step into his room. "Have fun!" she says behind him.

"Uh-huh, okay, Aunt May, walking away now!" he replies, and closes the bedroom door. He drops his backpack onto the ground, turns on his laptop and opens his wardrobe. He isn't sure what he should wear. It's not like he and MJ have never hung out before, but something about this feels different. He riffles through his clothes, picking through T-shirts and shirts, trying not to let his brain make any assumptions. No one called it a date. *Argh, Aunt May, why did you get in my head? It's not a date. It's just two friends hanging out. No one said date.*

It'd be cool if it was a date, though, a part of him admits as he continues to try and find something presentable. He briefly forgets to be anxious about what their hangout means as he laments what he's realising is a complete and utter disaster of a wardrobe. *There's* nothing *here*. He throws himself back on his bed and rests an arm over his eyes. *Maybe I just need a minute… I'm not meeting MJ for another half hour.*

His computer makes a loud beeping sound, and Peter gets up to log in. He decides to do a little research first, hoping he'll then be ready to figure out what he's going to wear to this non-date.

"That sounds like a very good plan, Pete." *And now I'm talking to myself.* He opens up a browser and looks up a map of Washington Heights in Upper Manhattan – he scrolls until he finds the Cloisters: an old medieval museum that's part of the Met. He's been to the main museum branch a few times, thanks to school trips and the occasional weekend visit with his aunt and uncle when he was younger, but never to the Cloisters. Unsure where to start, he drags the little stick-figure icon at the bottom of the screen onto a random street to see what the area looks like. The brightness of his screen dulls as it shifts from the stark illustrated map to a satellite view of the concrete and greenery of the city.

Peter bites his lip, moving the cursor this way and that, trying to find anything significant. It's mostly flats, from what he can see, but if he moves around a bit, further northwest and closer to the water, he finds some expensive-looking homes that look like a promising starting point. He marks down the street name on his phone before looking at the screen again. He clicks on a new tab and types the street name into the search bar. A million results tell him that for the low, low price of $10.99 he can find out who lives in these homes.

Yikes.

Another link says, *Protect your information—hire us to scrub-a-dub-dub your online presence!* and he closes his laptop screen. *That's enough of that. The internet is* terrifying, he decides.

Peter looks at his phone again. Fifteen more minutes before he's supposed to meet MJ. *Argh, what am I going to wear?!*

Eventually, Peter settles on something called 'easy casual' that he looked up online. He's got on a clean pair of jeans and a dark hooded sweatshirt with the word MITOCHONDRIAC embroidered across the front. Aunt May doesn't say anything embarrassing when he says goodbye to her, but his relief is short-lived when she reaches a hand up to smooth the side of his hair down before giving him a wave and telling him to be home by ten. When he walks outside, rubbing at his hair so it won't feel so flat, he sees that MJ's already seated on her porch. The sun is on its way down, and MJ's silhouetted against it, so he can't see her face, just the shape of her sitting on the old swing on the edge of her family's porch.

She must see him, though, because the dark shadow of her arm raises up in a wave. He waves back and makes the short walk over, his smile building as he gets closer.

When he gets near enough, he can see that her lips are pulled wide into a grin, and she's patting the seat next to her.

"Hey, Peter."

"Hey, MJ."

He walks up the two short steps and settles gingerly onto the swing next to her. They both sit silent for a moment, and Peter is scrambling to find *something* to say. *Oh no, I've been quiet for too long and now it's awkward and what if*— Then MJ starts speaking and Peter lets out a sigh of relief.

"So, do you know what you're going to write about for English class yet? I'm definitely going to do something about how the book talks about weather and dystopia and connect it to, you know..." MJ waves her hand in the general direction of the world, and Peter can see the braided bracelets she wears at her wrist peek out from the sleeve of the baggy cardigan she's got on over a pair of long shorts and a tank top.

He nods in response. "That makes sense. I don't know what to write about yet – I've still got another seventy pages to read, at least," he says, ducking his head sheepishly.

"Of course you do," she says with a smirk.

His heartbeat speeds up, and he clears his throat. "But, ah, so uh – what's going on with you and Maia?"

MJ leans against the swing and pushes with her legs so there's a light movement back and forth. She sweeps her fringe off of her face and takes a second, gathering her thoughts.

"So, I was talking to Liz the other day..." Then she tells him about finding Maia's Instagram feed and feeling so strangely angry and judgemental. "Liz was right to call me out."

Peter's a little surprised, because that really doesn't sound like the MJ he knows. He drums his fingers against his knees and considers what she told him before he says anything.

"Can I see the email Maia sent? I don't think I read it."

"She replied all, I think? But my phone's upstairs."

"Oh, then I must have it, let me look." Peter takes his phone out of his pocket and taps the screen, wincing at the crack that becomes evident when the phone lights up. He turns it slightly so it's out of MJ's eyeline and opens up his email app. He scrolls for a second, his finger moving up in a slight S instead of a straight line to avoid the jagged edge of the crack. It takes a few seconds, but he finally finds the email in question.

> that's a good idea, mj, but it feels like it might be too big of a topic to pair WITH our organizing idea? open to whatever the group wants tho - maia

"It's a pretty... innocuous note," Peter says tentatively.

"I know! That's what's so weird about it! I went back and reread it after the conversation with Liz, and I couldn't even figure out why I'd been so angry about it? It's such a perfectly pleasant way to disagree? I don't know, maybe it was something I ate?" she jokes weakly.

He doesn't laugh, because it's not that kind of joke. Instead, he cocks his head to the side, taking in her hunched posture and the way she's hiding her face behind her hands.

"I know you, MJ, and I know you're a kind person, so you can figure this out." He pauses and taps a finger against his chin, considering his advice before continuing. "Maybe just be extra thoughtful about the way you're reacting for the next few weeks?"

She looks away, pensive, before he sees her shake her head like she's literally trying to unclutter her brain.

"Anyway!" she says, changing the subject. "Tell me

about this thing at the *Bugle*! I guess if they're using your stuff for their social feeds, you don't need me teaching you anymore, right?"

Peter's not sure he's helped MJ clear anything up, but it doesn't seem like she wants to talk about it anymore, so he doesn't push.

"No, I do!" he says too quickly, and she gives him a wide-eyed look. *Crap, I'm such a nerd, and she's going to figure out she's too cool for me.* He rushes to keep talking. "Uh, so I went there with Randy after school, and I somehow got the job? It was cool, though. I got to see a lot of them in action – it was a lot of J. Jonah Jameson yelling at people on the phone, to be honest." He chuckles. "Right before he left, he freaked out trying to send someone to the MOMI for whatever was going on there—" He stops short, remembering that MJ had been there that day. He turns to face her, leaning in a bit and hoping that his eagerness isn't completely obvious. "Oh, wait, you were at the museum the day of the original burglary, right?"

She nods before explaining, "But I really was only there for a second to use the bathroom and maybe steal their Wi-Fi because I was trying to download an episode of something before getting on the train. Everywhere else in that area makes you buy something to use the Wi-Fi." MJ screws up her face in irritation. "Wi-Fi should be a public right."

"Heck yeah," Peter agrees, but his leg is bouncing,

manifesting his anticipation, and he urges her to keep going. "But, so you didn't see anything?"

"Nothing really – I overheard someone talking about how rude the customers were being that day... Oh! Actually, one of the workers was getting totally reamed out for accidentally turning on some new exhibit that no one was supposed to touch? I think two of the employees got in a fight." She pauses and then shrugs. "I guess that's not all that interesting."

"It is interesting!" Peter protests. *But now I have even more questions. The museum worker Alex had said that someone turned the machine on, but the same day that Sandman and Beetle were there?* Before he can pursue that train of thought, though, MJ starts talking again.

"Thanks, Peter," she says, deadpan. She's looking at him with a slight curve to her lip. "But you know it'd be a way better story if I'd seen, like, a super villain or something. Instead it's just, like, yeah, I used the bathroom and downloaded something and then left. Cool story, bro."

She laughs again, and it's contagious. A rumble of laughter starts in Peter's belly and rolls out of his mouth. Her hand falls, and he can feel her little finger graze his. He doesn't move his hand away, and he notices she doesn't, either.

Hours later, as he swings through the streets of the city, Spidey's face is warm, and he is still holding on to that feeling of Mary Jane Watson's little finger sitting right next to his. They'd hung out until 9:59 p.m., when he knew he had to get back inside or, as much as Aunt May clearly had an idea about what she was expecting out of him, he'd still face her wrath for being in past curfew. Later, swinging through the bright lights of the junction of 58th Street and 9th Avenue at 11:30 at night, the irony is not lost on him.

He *thwips* out a web, anchoring it to a grated balcony far above him, and swings forwards. It's a long, long trek up to the Cloisters. Spider-Man thinks back to what MJ told him about her mood. He can't imagine MJ being so mean. That's one more person he knows who's been acting strangely in the last few days. There is something going on... but... *Argh!*

He can't put his finger on it. There are all these different pieces happening, and his instinct is telling him they're related, but he can't figure out how. There's no way it's a coincidence that Flint Marko and the Beetle were at the museum the exact same day this weird ghost-robbery thing happened. And that Beetle attacked him after he went to check it out again. Spidey doesn't like to believe in coincidences because it usually leads to someone getting the drop on him. His next web catches on the bottom of a neon sign and he sails across 78th Street. His shoulder stretches lightly from the exertion, and he groans softly. He should have taken the subway.

Much, much later, he finally finds himself swinging past Fort Tryon Park, and he can see the entrance to the Cloisters across the way. It's dark and empty, given the late hour. Spidey zips onto the roof of a bodega across the street from the park and perches there, his elbows resting on his knees. His eyes narrow, and he looks around before pulling out his phone. He's still a few streets away from the junction he'd noted, so he puts his phone back and swings the last few roads forwards, landing on a street with several large, imposing homes.

Now what?

He looks up the street and then down. There are massive ironwork gates in front of most of the houses that wrap around to separate them from the pavement and each other. The streetlights illuminate bright spots beneath them, but not much else. Randy had just said his father was asking about a 'mansion', Spidey remembers. *Well, these houses seem like mansions compared to my neighbourhood.*

Maybe if I try to trigger my spider-sense? That's not a thing he's done before, but he figures that theoretically, if he walked by the houses, maybe it could work. *Maybe my spider-sense will go off if I get near the lamp?*

He takes a step towards the closest house, knowing it's a weak idea – but now that he's here, he's at a loss. He groans, realising how naive he'd been in not realising how many rich people there could be living up here. He had thought, *Mansion? How many mansions could there be?*

He shakes his head and shoots a line of webbing up at a streetlight, swinging around and over so he can land on it. He hops to the next one, hoping for the telltale sign of vibrations in the base of his skull, but to his disappointment, it's no dice. He looks down the street again. It looks much longer from this vantage point than it had from the ground. Spidey lets out a deep sigh and braces his knees.

Maybe the next one will do it...

CHAPTER TEN

Sandman slams a fist against the wall right next to Donnie's head.

"You said you were gonna get me on a crew, D. What happened?" he asks in a mockingly sweet voice. The sand crawls from his fist to the space around Donnie's neck. He and Donnie are in a dark alley somewhere in Lower Manhattan. He's got a forearm against Donnie's chest, keeping him tight against the wall. The sounds of the city are loud – cars honking, people chatting as they walk past the alley opening – no one notices Sandman and Donnie.

Donnie squirms against the brick, hands creeping up to scratch at the sand gathering at his throat.

"Marko, I told you, man – the job fell through! But you know I got your back. Whatever you need, man, I'm here. I'm ready."

A feral grin cuts across Sandman's face, and he leans back, pulling his weight off Donnie, who drops to the ground, breathing heavily in relief.

"That's good to hear, D. Because I got a thing that needs doin'. There's a heist, a big job."

Donnie's spine uncurls as he sits back up, his blond hair sticking to his forehead with sweat, and his shirt wrinkled and dirty across his chest.

"What's the score?" he asks, and attempts nonchalance as if the sweat trickling down his forehead and his wavering voice weren't signs of obvious terror. Sandman is satisfied; there's something inside him that respects Donnie for the masquerade.

"You'll know what I think you need to know, okay? I need three guys. A getaway driver, some muscle and a cat."

"Who's the brains?" Donnie asks, perplexed.

Sandman knows this is a fair question. Historically, when there's muscle involved in a job, it's him.

Not this time.

"Me." He leans over Donnie, knowing it will intimidate the little guy, and feeling good about it.

"Okay, okay, whatever you say, Marko. I'll start askin' around, okay?" Donnie slides to the right to get out from under Sandman's gaze, and he waves once before he flees.

Sandman's expression morphs into something resembling a smile once more, but there's something uncanny in it. He throws his shoulders back and moves forwards, every step assured. Every step powerful. He moves like a man in charge.

Since his mysterious benefactor reached out, things have been turning around for Flint Marko. There's an anger that's settled inside of him, fuelling his every move. It makes him stronger, somehow. In exchange, he just had to steal some old lamp. Easy peasy. He wonders if he should be suspicious but reasons that nothing making him feel like this could be wrong. He thinks back to the conversation he had with Jonny Two Rocks, a minor boss in the Maggia crime family, earlier that day. Sandman had done a job or two for him, so he went to Jonny for what people in his business like to call financing.

Sandman had come in strong to Two Rocks's place, sandblasting the two massive security guards out front before they had a chance to blink. He was inside seated next to Two Rocks himself in under ninety seconds. Two Rocks looked at him appraisingly – his white hair combed back off his forehead and his liver-spotted cheeks thin and concave against his jaw.

"Yo, Two Rocks," Sandman said, taking a piece of warm bread out of the basket in the centre of the table. The Maggia boss stayed quiet as Sandman picked up a steak knife and slowly buttered his bread with it, taking care to cover every centimetre, before shoving the entire thing in his mouth and chewing loudly. He swallowed and then pointed at Two Rocks. "You and me, Rocks, we got... an opportunity."

Two Rocks levelled a steady stare at Sandman. He was completely unfazed. Sandman knew the old him would have stammered his way out the door, but now he just waited for Two Rocks to ask the question.

"Do we, Marko?"

"We do. I got a big job, but I need some financing. You help me, I make sure you get taken care of."

The strange texts hadn't promised him exactly that, but Sandman knew if his benefactor could fill his pockets after this job, he could do whatever he wanted to after it.

Even flake out on the Maggia family.

Two Rocks leant back in his seat and steepled his fingers under his chin. He waited a beat, then two.

"I like this side of you, Marko. You've never shown this level of initiative. Thought you were just a goon-for-hire. Okay," he said. "Let's do business."

Two Rocks provided Sandman with *capital*. Now he just needs a crew.

Sandman steps out of the alley and onto the busy streets of New York. He takes in a deep breath of city air. The night is open wide with possibilities, all there for Sandman's taking.

Peter walks into his first weekend shift on the floor of the *Daily Bugle*. He wipes at his eyes and tries to fight through the fatigue. He is too tired to give the moment the excitement it deserves. He's spent the last three nights swinging through the streets surrounding the Cloisters, going up and down, up and down, trying to figure out where the lamp is hiding, but he still doesn't have any leads. *None!* he thinks with frustration.

The internet hasn't been any help, either. He tried looking up everything he could find about Arlo Farms 1899 again, but to no avail. He tiredly holds up his ID card to the guards at the front desk. It's the same two that he and Randy saw a few days earlier.

"Hey, Randy's friend! What's up, kid?"

"Hi, uh, working at the *Bugle*," Peter says. "Nice to see you again..." He trails off, unable to remember the guy's name.

"Tommy," the big guy says, pointing to himself. "And that's Rodrigo." He points to his desk mate, who waves.

"Hey," Rodrigo says without taking his eyes off the security feed in front of him.

"Nice to meet you both. I'm Peter. I'm a junior intern at the *Bugle*." He can't help the note of pride that bleeds into his statement. He rocks back on his heels, before stopping abruptly and straightening, trying to look professional.

"Working for Jameson?" Rodrigo asks, finally looking at Peter and giving him a once-over. "Good luck, kid."

Tommy grimaces, but nods.

"Yeah, good job, kid, but like Rod said, good luck! Just tap your badge on the black sensor bar to open the gate. Then it's up to the seventeenth floor." He points at the gates between Peter and the lifts. Peter feels slightly less prepared for his first day after that exchange, but he squares his shoulders and nods.

"Thanks, guys. I'll see you on the way out, I guess."

He taps his card against the flat black sensor and heads further into the building. Fifteen minutes later, he's seated at his desk behind Kayla, who is typing away on her computer. She's given him some old photographs to file into actual file folders that he would have to take down to their records room later.

"Oh, Peter." Kayla swivels back round in her chair and hands him a stapled packet of paper. It's not very big. "I printed our social guidelines out for you – you're doing great! But just so you know the kind of copy Jonah's looking for."

Her expression contorts slightly as she says it, and Peter sighs. He can tell what's coming. He takes the pages from her and flips to one in the middle. There's a photo of Spider-Man sitting on the side of a building. Peter wonders when this is from – he doesn't remember this shot being in the paper. Underneath the picture there's a series of bullet points, and the top one says: *MAINTAIN TONE ON SPIDER-MAN*.

"Showing the new guy the ropes?" A man's voice carries over the side of the cubicle behind Peter, and he looks up to see the same reporter he'd seen at MOMI. Tall, with coiffed blond hair, and standing on the other side of Kayla's cube. Peter can see the hint of a chequered shirt with a starched collar and a red tie. "I'm Ned Leeds, intrepid reporter, at your service." He's a little over the top, but Peter waves all the same.

"This is Peter," Kayla says. "He's our new junior photography intern. He's helping out with the social media stuff. You know, since Jameson refuses to hire a full-time person to do it." She pauses and glances at Peter apologetically. "No offence."

"S'fine," he says, waving it off. He looks back at the paper in his hands. "But..." Peter hesitates, unsure if he should ask what he's thinking. *What the heck does "maintain tone" even mean?*

"Yeah?" She waits for him to continue. He looks up at Ned and then back to Kayla and steels himself. *I'm a professional*, he remembers. *I can ask questions.*

"What does 'maintain tone on Spider-Man' mean? I was surprised to read the caption the other day because, well, that's not what happened."

Kayla and Ned share a look. She sucks in her teeth and shrugs before gesturing to Ned. Peter's not sure what's just happened, but it's Ned who answers him.

"So," Ned starts, "the head of the paper is J. Jonah Jameson, who... has a very strong idea on what kind of person Spider-Man is—"

"But it's the wrong idea! I... like Spider-Man? Isn't there any room for the truth?" Peter interrupts, his brow knit in confusion. He's leaning back in his office chair and looking up at Ned, who has sympathy etched across his features.

"I like him, too!" Kayla says.

"But..." Ned interjects, giving Kayla another look that Peter can't decipher, which she frowns at. "This is JJJ's paper. He gets to decide what our coverage looks like. And I don't know about you guys, but it is not worth losing my job over a dude in a spandex suit."

Peter glowers and decides he and Ned Leeds are probably not going to be friends. Kayla is already taking the papers back from Peter, but she gives Ned the side-eye as she's doing so.

"You're right, Peter. Spidey is *awesome*, and it is really kind of wild that one man's vendetta can shape a whole newspaper's perspective. I thought the press was supposed to be free and independent, Ned." Her tone is light, but there's tension in the air, and Peter gets the feeling that maybe Kayla and Ned have had this conversation before.

"LEEDS!" J. Jonah Jameson storms into the area. Peter wonders if he knows how to enter a room quietly. "Oh, you're here." J. Jonah Jameson seems to be the kind of person with two settings: Mad and Madder. Peter's never met a guy like this before in his life. *Which does beg the question, why does he hate Spider-Man so much?*

Jameson turns his blue-eyed gaze on Peter, like he can hear what he is thinking. Peter pushes his desk chair further back into his small cube.

"Patrick!"

"Peter," Kayla says, straight-faced.

"Peter! Right." Jameson doesn't stumble, despite the correction. "Great job on the photos of that spider-freak. Really got our readers excited. Doesn't mean I'm giving you a raise, though, so do *not* ask me for one. Do not even look at me. In fact, get back to work. Leeds!" he yells again. "Follow me!"

"Yes, boss." Ned throws an easy smile back at Kayla and Peter and walks off behind Jameson, who's stalking towards the lifts like a bull on a mission.

"Maybe I can use memes? I feel like Mr Jameson might not understand memes," Peter says to Kayla, and she just laughs.

"Now you're getting it."

"*Please* don't be mad, please don't be mad, please don't be mad." Peter is repeating the words to himself over and over, hoping that they will magically enter into his teammates' brains when he finally makes it to the Forest Hills library. He left the *Bugle* on time, but the train he was on stalled under the river. For once, it wasn't a Spider emergency ruining his day. There were no villains to blame, just faulty infrastructure.

Sprinting around the corner, he bounds up the stairs when he gets to the library entrance. He uses a little too much force on the door, and it bangs loudly against the wall. The librarian putting books onto a cart next to the front desk sends him an affronted glare.

Sorry, he mouths at her before walking as quickly as he can towards the area the team had agreed to meet in. He sees the back of MJ's head and Randy's in profile. Maia's facing him, and she looks bored as usual. Randy must see him in the periphery, though, because he shoots a hand up in greeting before Peter can say anything.

"Pete, hey, man!" Randy sounds strangely relieved.

MJ turns around and shoots him a tight smile; Maia gives him a nod.

"Sorry I'm late! Train trouble—" Peter says as he drops into the open seat at the square table across from Randy and pulls his notebook out of his backpack. Maia has her tablet out on the table, and the screen is dark.

"Yeah, we figured you got stuck." Randy waves him off. "Not a big deal."

"We've barely started, really," MJ adds, but she's looking at her phone. The energy is strained, and it's clear that something happened before Peter got there. "So anyway," MJ continues. "Like I was *saying*—"

"*Lecturing*," Maia mumbles under her breath. Peter cringes and tries to catch MJ's eye, but it's like she's deliberately avoiding his gaze. Instead of looking at him, she's narrowing her gaze at Maia.

"We're doing climate change and tech," MJ says, a mite too loudly. Someone coughs at a table near them, but she either doesn't notice or doesn't care. "Because it *makes the most sense.*" Peter looks at her sharply, surprised by the animosity in her tone. He thinks back to their conversation and wonders if she even realises how she sounds.

"It's a good idea!" Randy says. "So, let's come up with a thesis."

Maia shrugs, tracing figure eights into the wood of the table with her nail.

"Maybe renewable energy?" she asks.

MJ rolls her eyes at that and scoffs. Peter runs his hand through his hair, frustrated by a scene he doesn't understand.

"It's not a bad call, MJ," he tries to say. But Maia has already started speaking.

"You know, MJ," she says with a frown, "people said you were really kind and welcoming, but you really seem more like a bully to me." She's looking at MJ with something like pity, and Peter is dismayed to realise that if he didn't *know* MJ, he'd agree with Maia based on today.

MJ's face turns red, and her chin comes down so her gaze is shadowed. She grabs her notebook and her bag and stands. "Fine," she says. "Renewable energy, whatever. It's basic, but obviously we can do whatever you want to do. Since clearly my opinion doesn't matter, I'll just go home. And, Peter" – she turns to him – "if you want to have an opinion, maybe you should care enough to show up *on time*." She spits the rest of her sentence out before turning on her heel and leaving the three of them to look at each other, shocked expressions on their faces.

Peter feels like he should say something, but he isn't sure what. His jaw goes slack, and he scrambles for the words.

"MJ's not... usually..." He hesitates, the end of his sentence hanging open in the air.

"Like that," Randy finishes, still looking towards the front of the library, as if MJ would be turning round and coming back.

Maia shrugs.

"I don't know, she hasn't been all that great to me."

She opens up her notebook and puts a pen to the page. "We may as well work on this. I don't want to waste my whole Sunday because she's in a bad mood."

Randy agrees. "She's right – I know MJ, and she'll be back here in a few minutes apologising, is my guess."

"Whatever," Maia says, bringing up a browser on her tablet. "Let's get started."

Peter looks at the library entrance again, torn between staying to help with the project and going after MJ. From his perspective, it didn't really seem like she wanted to be around anyone. *If I was in that kind of mood, I'd definitely rather be alone.* He hears Maia's nails *click-clack*ing against the screen of her tablet and he decides. He'll send a text, that's what he'll do. He pulls out his phone and types out a message and hits send, then returns his attention to the group.

"Okay, so… what part of renewable energy? Geothermal, hydro, cellulosic ethanol?"

Maia and Randy look at him, slack-jawed. "What?" he asks, grinning. "I read!"

CHAPTER ELEVEN

MJ bursts through the library doors, and the cool air outside feels good against her face. She's so angry. *Renewable energy is so basic; we should be doing something forward-thinking.* She stomps down the stairs and throws herself onto a bench just outside and sits, seething. She knows that most people barely understand how renewable energy works – that people *barely* understand climate change. MJ sighs. Her heart has stopped racing, and she can think more clearly. *Maybe renewable energy isn't that bad of an idea.* She looks down at her hands, fisted in her lap, and deliberately relaxes them.

Then she scowls, confused and frustrated with her own reaction.

She's not afraid to get mad, or even furious. She's learnt that anger can be useful. But she knows that being angry and using that anger isn't the same as being mean to someone for no reason. Maia disagreed with her, and MJ remembers sitting in the library getting more and more heated. MJ's phone vibrates in her pocket, and she pulls it out, seeing a text from Peter.

> **ARE U OK? DO U WANNA TALK?**

> **OR BE ALONE?**

> **EITHER WAY OK! JUST LEMME KNOW**

She drops her phone to the side and slumps down on the bench, sliding forwards, letting her head fall against the backrest. She counts the clouds in the sky for a few moments. She shouldn't have spoken to Maia like that… or to Peter. She just couldn't stop herself. It felt so right in the moment. There's a thread poking out from the hem of her jumper, and she pulls at it, watching the line unravel slowly. She feels unbalanced, and she does not like it.

Her phone buzzes again, and she glances at it, perplexed. Two hours ago, she was in a great mood. She was looking forward to project planning because it meant she'd be working on things she cared about. And her heart was racing just the smallest bit at getting to spend an hour or so with Peter, who – she is willing to admit – she may have a little bit of a crush on. She spent an inordinate amount of time this morning planning her outfit and curling her hair. Last night, she'd read through pages and pages on how activists were using the internet to find each other and work together to support their causes. She was ready for it to be a good day. Then, during breakfast, she spent most of it looking at her phone. First, she took some fun selfies to text to Liz. Then she posted her action item of the day – linking out to organisations fighting for equal pay and some volunteer opportunities. One of her volunteer tweets for a local food bank went viral earlier that week, and *every* single volunteer spot had been taken for the next several months. It really felt like she was helping to make a difference beyond her own time, helping other people to use *their* time. She'd sat at her breakfast table, finishing up her cereal but not feeling the usual sense of accomplishment she did after putting something positive out into the world. In fact, the more she idly scrolled through her feeds, the more anger started seeping into her brain. *Didn't these people have better things to do?* By the time she left for the library, she was in a terrible mood.

It was exactly like she described it to Peter a few evenings ago.

She picks her phone up and unlocks it. It's strangely hot in her hand, but she imagines that's just the battery of an old model. The little squares stack up on her screen, and she holds her finger down on the glass until the boxes start shaking. Then she begins deleting the social apps one by one.

"I hope this works," she says out loud, manifesting it to be true. Part of her suspects that this is just a stopgap measure. But it's an experiment that affects her mood; she'll *know* for a fact that something bad is going on.

Spidey crouches on top of a billboard near the Cloisters on the West Side of Manhattan. He's been scoping out the scene for several nights in a row, hoping to find any kind of sign of whatever old rich person is hiding this alien artefact. Unfortunately, that afternoon's fight still has him feeling off. MJ had replied to his text with a thumbs-up and a message that said *I'm sorry for being a jerk, let's talk later?* He'd immediately responded with *Yes!* but he hadn't otherwise heard from her all day. He thought about stopping by her house when he got home from the library but cringed at the thought as soon as it crossed his mind. That felt too weird. *Who just shows up at someone's house?* He remembers they're getting together so MJ can give him some social-media tips later this week and breathes easier. Since she hasn't cancelled yet, he figures they're still on. The other day while he was waiting for the train, he set up a SpiderManEnWhySee account, just a little miffed that he couldn't include a hyphen in the screen name.

So far, he hasn't posted anything except a selfie in his suit on top of the Empire State Building. He's giving a peace sign. *I can make it to the top of the Empire State Building. It's a humblebrag, but I gotta post it* was the totality of his thought process.

To his chagrin, no one is paying attention. His post got three likes and a single retweet. And the person retweeting just said, *Wow, this green screen looks fake as heck.* His only follower is XXXXXXXXXX. He remembers MJ's notes about numbers and assumes it's a bot. *How am I going to take control of my own image if I can't even get people to notice me? Ugh.* The *Bugle* has fifty million people following them. He makes a mental note to ask MJ how to get followers. *As long as she doesn't cancel.*

Before he can continue that line of thinking, he hears the sounds of an alarm blaring loudly from somewhere a few streets south of him. He jumps off the billboard, shooting out a web and propelling himself down the avenue. There are a few people out, pointing at him as he swings by, and he tries to wave and nearly loses his grip.

"AH!" He scrambles, grabbing the line of web. "I meant to do that!" he yells down at the crowd, hoping they didn't notice it and that no one had their mobile phone out. The alarms are getting closer and louder, and finally he flies by a side street and sees the source.

There's a small, darkened shopfront with a smashed window recessed a few stairs down into the ground. Sirens sound somewhere in the distance, but they're still so far away that Spidey feels fine jumping down to the ground to investigate. It looks like a smash-and-grab gone wrong, except that it's a hardware shop, not a jewellery shop. The sign above the broken window says WILLIAMS & KIDS, HARDWARE in white paint with a red border. *Who's smashing up a window for some spare nails?* he wonders. Just then, a bald white head pokes out the door, and Spidey sees a pair of eyes go wide when they notice him standing out front. The figure lets out a quick yelp and scurries back into the shop.

"What the—?"

Spidey jumps down over the stairs, sticks his head through the door, and calls out, "Hello? You know I saw you, right?"

The shop is a mass of shelves filled with tools and various sundry items. Something big and metallic rattles and then drops heavily to the floor with a loud *clank*. It's dark, and the alarm is reverberating along the walls and inside Spidey's head. All of a sudden, his spider-sense goes wild, and he tucks and rolls into the shop as two nails embed themselves into the wall where his head had been a second earlier.

"WHOA, WHOA, *WHOA*!" Spidey yells. "We can figure this out, man! Let's talk!" He crouches next to the wall and slowly crawls up it, careful not to disturb any of the items on the shelf next to him. He can hear something skittering in the back of the shop. He presses his fingers and toes lightly along the wall, moving up until he gets to the ceiling. He hesitates for a moment, and then a second crash spurs him to move onto the ceiling, inching along, keeping track of the floor below him for any movement. He makes it one foot, then two, three, four, five, but the green-and-white tiles below him remain clear.

Finally, about twelve feet from the entrance, he sees a figure crouched behind a group of long-handled paint rollers. He's peeking around the corner, holding a nail gun. Spider-Man puts a hand out and points his web-shooter downwards, pressing against his palm. His web hits the nail gun, and he yanks it, flinging it away to the other side of the shop.

"NAILED IT!" Spidey yells gleefully before dropping to the floor directly in front of the thief. He's surprised to see it's someone he knows.

"Corey?!" Spidey asks, lenses wide, as the man in question throws a fist his way. He dodges, easily. Corey's a low-level criminal that Spidey's dealt with before – he's usually just a grab 'n' go from a corner bodega, and generally Spidey lets him off with a warning. This sort of thing is very out of character for the minor thief. Spidey bends his head to the left as Corey throws a box of lightbulbs at him. "I thought we were friends. Last time we saw each other, you told me you liked my suit and *everything*."

Spidey ducks as Corey tries another punch. "Okay, that's enough of that." He crouches and sticks a leg out to trip him, and Corey goes down hard, face-first.

"Man, what are you *doing*?" Spidey asks, still crouched and resting on his toes next to the man's head. There's a glare on the back of his shiny bald head.

Corey just groans in response. The sirens are closer now, so Spidey webs Corey's feet to the ground and tries again.

"What are you doing here? This isn't usually your MO..." He trails off and tilts his head, taking in the scene. There's something boxy sticking out of the top of Corey's back pocket. Spider-Man reaches down and pulls it out. "Now what's this?" He stands to see it better in the low light of the shop.

The box reads *LOCK PICK-ER 9000—locked out? We're here to help!* The price tag on the sticker says *900* next to a monetary symbol he doesn't recognise. Spidey nearly drops it.

"Nine hundred what? Dollars? This must be the best lock-picker on the *planet*." He squats down next to Corey's head again. "Now what would *you*, a pretty petty criminal, want with something heavy-duty like this?"

Corey is mumbling something in response, but Spidey can't quite make it out. He ducks closer but shoots back up to a standing position when he finally hears what Corey is repeating to himself.

"Gotta get this and get the lamp. Gotta get this and get the lamp."

He's whispering over and over. He sounds completely terrified. Spider-Man looks at the lock-picking box again and then back down at Corey on the ground, thinking again how he feels about coincidences. He's about to ask Corey more when the sirens turn the corner. That means he's overstayed his welcome. He drops the lock-picker on a high shelf, and then he zips out of the front of the shop just as the police cars slow to a halt.

"Hey!" he hears as he webs a crane and starts swinging, "Come back here!"

Not a chance, he thinks. He swings several streets south-eastward before finally finding a quiet rooftop to rest. He pulls his mask off to wipe at his face. There is something building here; he needs to find whoever that lamp belongs to and fast. Whatever is going on with Corey isn't quite the same as it was with Beetle. Beetle seemed *empty* and vicious. Corey was *scared*.

No more snooping around hoping to find it. He has to be way more proactive. But all his leads are exhausted. He thinks about sneaking back into the MOMI. Or, he realises, he has Dr Shah's class tomorrow. He thinks back to their earlier conversation. Peter hadn't actually asked him who *owned* the lamp. There's a chance Dr Shah might know. If not, then as a second option, he could try his luck at the museum again.

Spidey wipes his face one more time before pulling his mask back on. But first he needs to sleep. He shoots a web into the city streets and takes off swinging.

CHAPTER TWELVE

Peter runs into Dr Shah's class, dropping his phone into the plastic rack hanging on the back of the door. He sees MJ sitting in her seat a few rows behind him and sends her an awkward wave. Her wave back to him is just as awkward. He sighs. They haven't spoken since yesterday at the library. *Someday*, he thinks, *I will wake up early enough to take the bus again and have a nice, quiet moment with MJ.*

The late bell rings and Peter notes the empty desk at the front of the room. It's strange that Dr Shah's not there yet, but it means that Peter has time to make it to his desk and fold into it despite being so late. He hopes there isn't a substitute today. He ignores the rumble of conversation around him, tapping his pen in a fast staccato against the fibreboard of his desk anxiously. He needs to ask Dr Shah more about the arc lamp. The experience with Corey the night before left him unsettled – usually Corey is a gregarious guy. Really friendly, if a chronic maker of bad decisions. Peter barely recognised the man he fought last night. His thoughts are cut short when Flash Thompson's loud voice breaks through.

"If he's not here in five minutes, we legally get to leave," he says from the back of the class.

"That's not a thing, Flash," Liz says.

"Yeah, that is definitely not true," someone else pipes up, laughing.

"Well, it should be," Flash retorts, a small element of whininess in his tone.

And for once, Peter's inclined to agree with Flash. *Not that I'll ever tell* him *that.*

Just as the classroom starts to get more excited than might be expected at 8:30 in the morning, the door flies open and Dr Shah enters, looking just a little worse for wear. Usually fastidious in his appearance, today Dr Shah's white button-down shirt is untucked, his blazer is wrinkled and there are deep bruises under his eyes, making his brown skin look almost purple. He puts his briefcase down and looks at the class. Then he takes a deep breath.

"Sorry I'm late; it's been a rough morning. We'll start

with reading through chapter seventeen – the practical application of ionization. In the second half of the class, we'll do some worksheets." He doesn't wait for questions and sits at his desk, turning on his computer. Peter opens his book to the chapter, but his eyes glaze over and he continues to pull at all the disparate pieces in his brain.

Sandman. The strange invisible foe. Beetle. The lamp. The mood shifts. The lock. The mysterious donor.

They're all just puzzle pieces floating around, refusing to connect. He puts his head down on his desk as if he can ingest the reading through osmosis. Nothing happens. He sighs and straightens, looking back up at Dr Shah in the front of the class.

His teacher is not even pretending to pay attention to his students. Peter can hear Liz and MJ speaking softly in the back, and the sounds of other people not doing the reading. Since he's not focusing on the chapter, he decides to deal with the other problem in his head instead. Pushing up out of his chair, he walks to Dr Shah's desk and gets a glimpse at the computer screen. It looks like a research paper on electromagnetic waves. "Hey, Dr Shah, what are you reading?" Peter asks. Dr Shah starts, and Peter apologises. "Sorry, sorry, didn't meant to scare you, sir!"

Dr Shah shakes his head.

"No, no, Peter, it's okay. I was just reading up on what my old team at Empire State University is doing.

It's quite exciting." Despite what he's saying, Dr Shah sounds sad. Peter winces, thinking how strange the idea of a teacher having feelings is. Dr Shah laughs a little at Peter's expression. "I know, it's hard to think of us as real people," he says, giving Peter a sly look. Peter's happy to see a little of his normal disposition returning to the surface. But then Dr Shah's gaze goes distant as he turns back to the computer. "I *used* to be a bit of a big deal in the world of electromagnetic research."

"Would you say your work was… *magnetic*, sir?" Peter asks with a half-hearted laugh, attempting to break the melancholic mood. Dr Shah breaks himself out of his reverie and lets out a quick snort of laughter.

"They actually did," he tells Peter. "But I had to… give it all up a few years ago." He shakes his head, and his eyes clear up, as if he's suddenly realised he's said too much. "Anyway! You came here to ask a question, I assume. What can I do for you, Mr Parker?"

"Oh, uh, well, it actually has to do with that arc-lamp thing we were talking about last week. I just can't get it out of my head, honestly," he says. "I was wondering if you know who owns it?"

Dr Shah shakes his head.

"No one comes to mind, no. *But* an old colleague of mine did a research paper on it years ago, and I think they might have actually found a name, if I'm remembering correctly. It's a secret that's not much of a secret in the right crowd, if you know what I mean." He winks. "And what I mean is electromagnetic-research doctorates." Dr Shah pauses like he's waiting for a reaction, and Peter realises he's supposed to laugh. He lets out one short bark, and Dr Shah grimaces. "Not as funny as I thought, huh?"

"Sorry, sir." Peter grins sheepishly.

"So, to answer your question more succinctly – no, but I think I have an old paper that I can send you that might have it in there somewhere."

"That would be awesome! Thank you, Dr Shah!"

Finally, he thinks, making his way back to his seat, *maybe a step in the direction of figuring this all out!*

Sandman is fuming. But not in what he thinks of as the good way, not in a way that makes him feel powerful. Donnie recommended a colleague, Corey, for an important part of this job, and Corey ruined everything. Flint remembers his sand morphing down into a fine point, inches from Corey's face, trying to drive the fear of a perfect robbery into him. To remind him that all he had to do was get in and get out of the hardware shop with the piece they need. It hadn't worked.

That shop was the only place in the city that had the tool they were looking for. It is so powerful, the United States has put it on a watch list, not allowing anyone to bring one into the country – which means only people like Sandman, who like to live on the other side of the law, can get it. And there's a lot of interest in this device, lots of powerful people gunning for it. Sandman needs to be first. He's standing on a corner now, not far from where the attempted robbery had gone wrong.

The directions from whoever is pulling the strings are clear in his mind – get inside a giant house on Oceanic Avenue and steal back an old lamp. He turns onto the dark street, and his fury reaches higher levels at the sight of police tape in the distance. He knows he put the fear of everything into Corey when he sent him on his way. *I should be able to delegate! Do I have to do everything myself?!*

He sidles up to Williams & Kids, Hardware. The street is deserted, and the police tape across the window shakes back and forth slightly in the light air coming up from the grates below. Sandman knows that there's a chance the device he wants isn't even here, that the owner moved it or took it home, but he's got to try. He melts into a puddle of sand and slides down the stairs, slips in the door underneath the police tape and spreads himself thin, flooding the space, covering every nook and cranny to find what he is looking for.

Sandman loves flowing out like this. His perception grows exponentially when he's so massive. He feels every bit of the shop, from its hammers to its mousetraps. Like all good small NYC businesses, this place even has an assortment of random chemist-like items – over-the-counter pain medication, nail polish remover, ChapStick – but not what he's searching for. He keeps going and moves into the back office past the counter and till. The grains he controls seep over tile and floorboards. They cover the worn office chair and slide into the locked desk – *there*. The bottom drawer of the desk, behind a false backing. He can feel it.

He re-forms into his normal body in the office and wrenches open the drawer, breaking the lock in the process. It's metal, but it's no match for Sandman's strength. He holds the small box in his hands, and half his mouth comes up in a satisfied smirk. But the smile isn't really a smile, and he's on the verge of baring his teeth. He shakes his head and turns the box over in his hand. *All this fuss over this little thing?*

But he knows it's important. The rumours on the street are that this contraption can neutralise *any* home security. It's why the government isn't too keen on it showing up here. Every attempt to smuggle one in was thwarted except for this single unit.

Thank goodness for New York and its fine, fine crime enthusiasts. Sandman shoves the box into his pocket and walks out the door, trusting in whatever is giving him this good luck to keep it going. He feels untouchable, like there's no way he'll be caught tonight. He steps up the stairs and out onto the street, whistling a tune as he goes.

Peter's seated in front of his laptop at home. He logs in to his school email and finds something from Dr Shah – it's a link to the paper he mentioned.

> **Hey Peter,**
> **I didn't reread this, so I'm not sure the information you want is in there, but I think it might be. If not, look up additional work by Dr. Monica Diaz. Good luck!**
> **Dr. S**

Peter clicks through to the link, and a massive wall of text opens up in a new tab. He reads across the top of the screen.

AMPLIFICATION AND PENETRATION OF ELECTROMAGNETIC WAVES IN HUMAN BEINGS

Well, this is going to be fun. He starts reading and is surprised to find that he's actually *very* interested in what Dr Diaz is discussing. She theorises that a high enough level of electromagnetic radiation could alter a human being's brain. But so far, there's nothing about the lamp other than a brief mention of its existence.

A lot of the science goes over his head, but Peter can understand the basic gist. An hour goes by, and he finally gets to the end of the paper with no name associated to the arc lamp. Gripping the edge of his laptop screen, he nearly slams his computer shut, but he takes a deep breath, moves his hands back down to the keys, and opens up a new tab instead. He types 'Dr Monica Diaz, arc lamp, alien' into the search bar. The first few results are all about recent awards won by the researcher. According to some of the headlines, Empire State University just got her back from Oxford and she has her own division at ESU.

He keeps scrolling. He gets through one page of search results, and then two, and three, and four. Then, on the fifth page, he sees a link to an old message board posting. It's on an Empire State University server and looks like a mostly defunct board from about a decade and a half ago. He clicks on it and pushes away from the desk, his vision assaulted by what he can only describe as an awful web design. *Is this what the internet used to look like?!* The messages are in a typewriter font and are all in a harshly bordered table, with underlined blue usernames and broken linked images as icons on the left and their messages on the right. There's only one message on the table – it's clearly a board that was rarely used. The username is DocDiazDidItAgain, dated fourteen years ago. The message says:

I DID IT ☺ ☺ ☺ ☺ ☺

I DEF FOUND WHO OWNS THE LAMP

SOME GUY NAMED ALREDGE

There's a single reply, also from DocDiazDidItAgain, a month later. It just says:

AND I GUESS NO ONE CARES! ;(

Alredge, Peter thinks. *I can work with that.* He hits the back button to get to the results page and put in a new search for 'Alredge, New York City' when he sees Dr Shah's name in one of the results on Dr Diaz.

EMPIRE STATE UNIVERSITY STAR RESEARCH
DIRECTOR TAKES LEAVE OF ABSENCE

Peter hesitates, his finger hovering over the track pad, unsure if he should click on it. Is this a violation of Dr Shah's privacy? It's on a public site, after all. Peter can't help himself, and he presses his finger down on the pad. The article opens. He skims the first few sentences and puts his hand to his mouth. *Oh no.*

Dr. Samir Shah left Empire State University today after a tumultuous few months. The professor, who recently suffered a tremendous loss—his wife and daughter were lost during an attempted bank robbery by Max Dillon, a.k.a. Electro—is leaving the university life to be a high school teacher, it seems. His colleagues cite a lack of focus as the deciding factor. "It's a huge loss for us," says Dr. Monica Diaz. "Dr. Shah is a friend and a partner in our work. He'll be sorely missed around the lab, but we all wish him well."

That's where Peter stops reading – this had happened a few years before he put on his spider-suit. He put Electro away a few months ago, and he feels even better for having done it. Grief recognises grief. He looks at a picture of himself, Uncle Ben and Aunt May, standing on the corner of his desk. Dr Shah lost everyone. *I'm going to be better*, he thinks. *I'll be more thoughtful in Dr Shah's class. I swear. I'll stop being late.*

Peter knows it won't fix what happened, but if it will make Dr Shah's day just the smallest bit easier, then it's worth it. Decision made, he hits the back button again. *Now I need to figure out who this Alredge person is.*

The search engine brings up two results of Alredge in New York – the first one is a young marketing professional named Brian Alredge from Brooklyn, according to his social profiles, so that's wrong. But the other one shows promise.

PREETI CHHIBBER

ADDISON ALREDGE

He updates his search terms with the first name, and a slew of newspaper articles come up about Addison Alredge, a reclusive millionaire. *Bingo.* He clicks through and sees a blurry picture of a hunched figure walking towards a house, and Peter recognises it! He's been by it at least seven times on his search for the lamp. It's on one of the quiet side streets he tried, with a tall barrier of wall and hedge.

As he starts to read the caption, Peter sees his phone light up out of the corner of his eye. It's a news alert from the *Bugle*:

 NEWS ALERT: *CITY HARDWARE STORE WILLIAMS & KIDS BREAK-IN ALERT: TWO TIMES TOO MANY*

Peter looks at the screen in disbelief. The alert blurb continues: the only thing missing is a prototype device, the only one of its kind, the owner says. And that he's very desperate to get it back.

Peter groans. He can guess what *that* is.

CHAPTER
THIRTEEN

Spider-Man drops to a crouch in front of the still-broken shopfront for Williams & Kids. It's pretty early in the evening, so the sun hasn't completely set, and he can see someone moving around inside the building. He jogs down the stairs and ducks under the police tape.

"Hello?" he asks, waiting for whoever is in the back to come to the front.

"Who's there?!" calls a voice with a heavy New York accent.

"Uh, Spider-Man," Spidey answers.

"I told you, I'm tired of the pranks – oh, it *is* you." A short white man has walked through the shelves and stops short at seeing Spider-Man standing in the doorway. He's got on a pair of brown trousers and a maroon jumper. His thinning hair is dark brown and flows into a neat beard on a rounded chin. Spidey raises a hand in a wave. The man glowers, decidedly unimpressed.

"It's me." Spider-Man pauses. "Uh, are you… Mr Williams?"

"Should hope so. It's my store," the owner, Mr Williams, answers. "What are you doin' back here? Decide to let another person rob me? Wanna leave that gross web stuff all over my floor again?"

Spidey's taken aback.

"I— What?"

"You couldn't catch the *second* guy?" Williams asks as he starts sweeping up some of the dust along the aisle. "Ugh," he says, looking down at the ground and scuffing at it with his boot. "I know I told Park to sweep up last night and *still*, still! There's sand everywhere."

It's official, Spider-Man thinks. He does not like this guy. But he's zeroed in on one word in Mr Williams's complaining.

"Did you say *sand*?" Spider-Man asks, walking over and kneeling to get a look at what Williams is sweeping up. He picks up a few grains and pinches them between two of his fingers. He rubs them together, and it's exactly as Williams says: actual sand. Which reminds Spidey of exactly one person. He looks up at Williams. "Is there any reason there would be sand on the ground? Like… do you sell… sand?"

"Do I sell *sand*? I sell *soil*. But no, Spider-Man, I do not sell *sand*."

Spider-Man looks down at the sand again. *Another coincidence, or something more?* he wonders. If what they took was the lock-picker that Spidey saw the night Corey broke in, then whoever did this is almost certainly going after Addison Alredge's mansion, assuming that's where the arc lamp is. He thinks back to Corey's refrain:

Gotta get this and get the lamp. Gotta get this and get the lamp.

If that's the case, it means that tonight is going to be all about surveillance.

"So this thing that was taken…" Mr Williams's mouth tightens into a small, thin line under his moustache, but Spidey keeps going. "It's a device to pick locks?"

"It was just a… prototype for something I was thinkin' about figuring out how to make over here in the States. That's all," he says, his words clipped.

"A prototype," Spidey says, disbelief lacing through his tone. He'd seen the packaging. That was no prototype. "How powerful is it?"

"Yeah, a *prototype*," Mr Williams mimics. "And as for how powerful, who knows. I barely got to look at it – got it from my cousin visiting from overseas just three days ago

– before some jerk took it from me." From his non-answer, Spidey gets the feeling Mr Williams isn't going to tell him the truth. This "prototype" was a real-deal lock-picker, probably only used by a select group of *criminals*, and this guy would not incriminate himself by admitting it. "Any other things you wanna ask me, remembering that you didn't stop someone from ROBBING ME?" Mr Williams says again, putting the broom down and fixing his hands on his hips, staring down his nose at Spidey.

"Maybe you could invest in a security system that doesn't involve me randomly swinging by your store when it's being robbed?" Spider-Man asks, with a little bit of a bite in response to Mr Williams's rudeness.

"Excuse me?" Mr Williams glares at him. "Are you bein' smart with me?"

Spidey shrugs.

"I *am* smart. I have a 4.2 to prove it."

At that, Mr Williams's jaw drops. "A four point… what? How old are you?"

Uh-oh. Mr Williams narrows his eyes at him.

"Are you old enough to be doing this? You *are* pretty short…"

Spidey rubs a hand on the back of his head.

"I, uhhhh…"

He takes a step back before turning to sprint out of the shop, leaving his goodbye hanging in the air behind him. "Gotta go! Thanks for your help!"

Peter skips over the last two stairs leading up to MJ's porch – he's late *again*. In his defence, he had to stop some guy from robbing a woman at an ATM and then literally trying to take candy from her baby. Peter can't be totally positive, but it does seem like thieves have been getting cockier lately. He'd got home, changed into something kind of resembling a normal outfit, and rushed over to MJ's.

He rings the doorbell, huffing slightly and hoping he doesn't smell like a sweaty Spider-Man suit. Mrs Watson opens the door, red hair just like her daughter's piled up in a high bun and a pair of thick-framed glasses magnifying her eyes.

"Peter, so good to see you!" She widens the door, welcoming him in.

"Hi, Mrs Watson," he says, but she starts speaking before he can ask where MJ is.

"So, you and MJ are... hanging out?" she asks, a look on her face so exaggeratedly innocent it can't be real. He's sure she stopped just short of wagging her eyebrows at him.

"Um, yeah," he says, feeling supremely awkward.

"Seems like you've been spending a lot of time together?" she observes nonchalantly, and he might be mistaken, but he thinks she's biting the inside of her cheek, based on the strange indentation that's appeared on the side of her face.

"I guess so?" he says. "I mean maybe?" They're standing together in the entrance. The Watsons' home is similar to the Parker residence. There's a staircase several feet into the hallway, an open door to a kitchen on his left and an opening to the living room closer to the base of the stairs. But where the Parkers have a generic wooden floor along the first level of their home, here the floor is covered in patterned laminate tile. There's a pile of shoes near the entrance, so Peter kicks his own off while he's talking to Mrs Watson.

"I'm glad to see MJ being friends with such a nice young—"

"MOM!" MJ's voice breaks in from somewhere upstairs. "Please let Peter come upstairs so I can show my FRIEND how to be funny and relatable online!"

Mrs Watson lets out a loud laugh, and Peter finds himself grinning, liking her all the more for it.

"You better head on up, Peter. I'll bring you guys some snacks in a few minutes."

"Thank you!" he says, meaning it, before heading up the stairs. He makes it to the top, passing by a series of framed photos, and it's funny seeing little MJ become the MJ he knows by the time he gets to the landing. "MJ?" he asks, a little quietly, unsure if there's anyone else upstairs.

"In here!" she calls from a room down the hall. He

walks forwards on the dark blue carpeting and stops outside a door that's slightly ajar. He pushes on it lightly, but just as it starts to open, it gets pulled from inside. MJ stands, hand still on the doorknob, looking more relaxed than the last few times he's seen her. Her hair's up in some kind of a messy braid and she's got on a loose T-shirt with grey joggers that have tiny little stars all over them. Peter takes a deep breath. *She looks perfect.*

"Hey, Peter," she says.

He smiles apologetically. "Sorry I'm late, MJ. I was—"

"It's fine! I was just taking it easy," she interjects, the corners of her mouth turned up. He steps inside. It's not like he hasn't been in MJ's room before, but it's been a *while*, and today feels different. MJ follows him back in and settles on the end of her bed. He stands in the same spot, a foot or two into the bedroom, the door open behind him, unsure of where to sit. She points at an old beanbag in the corner.

"You can sit down." She laughs. Her room's not very big, so they're only a short space apart.

"It seems like you're doing… better than you were the other day?" His sentence turns into a question halfway through, and she grimaces.

"Yeah, I owe you a *serious* apology. I'm *really* sorry about the way I acted. That was *not* me," she says vehemently. "I don't even know who that was. Maia and I are getting pizza tomorrow to talk. Well, I'm buying her pizza to talk. She was understandably not super psyched to hang out with me." She laughs shortly, without any real humour in it. "And Randy, well, it's *Randy*." She shrugs. "I said I was sorry and offered to buy him lunch, and he clapped me on the back, said 'We all have our days, MJ', and walked off with some of the kids from French club. I wish I could be as cool as he is." She's kind of rambling, and Peter's struck by a strong sense of affection for his friend.

"It's okay, MJ," he says.

"It's not." She frowns. "But thank you for saying it anyway."

"So," he asks, "what happened? I mean, we don't have to talk about it—"

"No!" she says. "No, I mean…" She pauses, as if considering what she wants to say. "So, I know we're supposed to talk about being on the internet and how to be better at it and all that stuff today, but I started just… limiting my phone use, and it has done a *total* one-eighty on my mood. I just feel totally different. Kinda seems like I was just spending too much time on it and letting the little things get to me."

He nods in understanding. That's something he can relate to.

"We don't have to do this screen stuff tonight," he offers.

"No, no, it's fine! Really. I feel great."

"Okay," he says as he grins, leaning back into the beanbag to get more comfortable. "Well, tell me about today's MJ's action first."

"Today" – she adopts a television host's pose – "we're asking people to help fund a community garden in Forest Hills – or wherever they live, if they don't live in Queens."

"I didn't even know we had a space for a community garden."

"You have *got* to get out more." Then she claps her hands together. "Okay, okay. My mood is lifted, Peter." She gives him a bright smile. "*And* I got permission to have the laptop tonight, so we are good to go! Let's start breaking down some internet 101, Parker." She opens the laptop sitting on her bed, but then she gets up to sit on the floor next to him and he slides off the beanbag so he can join her as they hunch over the laptop screen. Peter's eyes dart to the side when their shoulders touch, and he hopes she can't hear how fast his heart is beating. "So," she says, turning to him, "you've *really* never had any accounts of your own?"

He shrugs.

"I just got my own phone, like, a few months ago? And my laptop is a hundred years old. Like I said, the last thing I had was Facebook, and I wasn't even really allowed to use it. I mostly just use my computer to watch video game clips, to be honest." He doesn't say it, but it wasn't until Aunt May got her job that they could afford the phone. Still, it's a pretty limited plan, so Peter tries to be careful with how much data he uses. Even *with* all this stuff MJ's showing him, he knows he'll mostly limit it to when there's Wi-Fi around. "Honestly, by the time I looked into it, there were a billion sites to make profiles on, so I've never really felt like I needed to be on there, I guess. The coding part is way more interesting – building computer programs? Plus, basically everyone I care about talking to is, uh, close by." He coughs a little, trying to obscure what he just said. The truth is, he's been so busy with being Spider-Man that by the time the people he knows started caring about this stuff, he didn't have the time or interest. He always felt like there were more important things to be doing.

"That's fair, but if you want to learn, welcome to the wide world of social media, Peter Parker." She grins, hitting enter on the URL she'd just input.

"Oh, then I just have just one question." MJ looks at him expectantly. "Do I need a passport for this?"

Peter's cheeks warm, and he's gratified to hear a loud bark of genuine laughter from the girl next to him, even when she follows it up with "That was a *terrible* joke."

Hours later, he's still feeling the high of his evening with MJ as he swings through the city heading towards Addison Alredge's house. It's going to be a good night.

It's deeply dark outside when Sandman and his crew roll up to the big brick house in the middle of Oceanic Avenue. The streetlight closest to the mansion was conveniently broken earlier that day, so the wrought-iron and stone fencing around it is just a silhouette, and the garden inside is completely indistinguishable.

"That's it, boss," Donnie says from behind him. The black van they're in has the name of a phony, generic electrician on its side. They're stopped across the street. In it sit Sandman, Donnie and two guys named Mike and Matt. Sandman glances between the two – both large, with short-cropped hair and equally mean expressions – he's already forgotten which is which. One is there to drive the van; the other one is going to follow Sandman and play lookout while he sneaks inside the house.

Sandman spent last night reading through all the material in the lock-picker box. All he needs to do is attach it to the door, and it should neutralise every single security measure the house had feeding out to anyone. That way, even if an alarm is tripped, no one will know. The lock-picker name itself was a misnomer in the end. It's really there to cut out any hope of help coming. Sandman turns the device over and over in his hands in anticipation. He doesn't need to pick a lock. As long as there's a space the size of a grain of sand, he can get inside. He just needs to not get caught.

"All right, tough guys," Sandman says, grinning.

"Let's get to work. Donnie, you make sure this guy keeps the engine running, and keep watch up and down the street. You" – he gestures to the other man, a giant nearly his own size – "follow me."

"Okay, Marko, but I got a bad feeling about this," Donnie says with a tremor in his voice. "First sign of trouble and I'm out."

"There ain't gonna be any trouble, buddy. Just stay where I tell you to stay and move when I tell you to move. Easy as pie. Now, let's go, big man."

He slides the van door open and steps heavily onto the street outside. Matt – *or Mike*, he thinks, uncaring – trails after him in silence. They walk to the gate, and Sandman hands the device to the man with him and bites out a quick "Wait here." He puddles into sand and flows through the cracks underneath the gate before re-forming. "Toss it over," he hisses, and he sees the dark shape of it fly over the tall gate a second later. He catches it in his hand and moves slowly to the door, thankful for the cover of darkness. Just as he goes to press the box against the door, something yanks his hand backwards, and the box goes flying somewhere into the shadows of the garden around him. A loud voice cuts through the quiet.

"WHAT'S UP, SAND-DORK?!"

CHAPTER
FOURTEEN

Spider-Man flips onto the scene, crouching low to the ground with one arm and leg tightly against him and the others outstretched so he can bound forwards and fire a web at Sandman's face. Sandman's standing at the door, dumbstruck.

"Good to see you, Flint! We're spending so much time together; do you want to get a coffee or something?" Spidey says, his casual greeting belied by the tension in his stance.

Sandman roars in fury and starts growing in size, his hands becoming sledgehammers and his body slamming forwards in a rush of rough grains. Spidey presses his feet into the ground and launches himself upwards, flipping and *thwip*ping a pair of webs out to a branch above Sandman's head, pulling hard and letting it fall onto the mass below. But he can't stop to see how it connects, already moving so Sandman can't catch him. That would be the worst thing, he knows, because the minute he's caught, he's done for, and there's no giant water tower around to save him this time.

"Flint, Flint, Flint," he singsongs as he jumps up to the roof. "I thought we agreed you wouldn't get involved! What are you doing here, man?"

Sandman just yells a series of infuriated sounds, none of which make any sense to Spidey.

Weird.

"What was that, SandBAG? I can't hear you over the sound of you being a HUGE LOSER!" Spidey yells down, jumping forwards and off the roof just as a huge fist of sand barrels towards him. He manages to barely dodge the first one but isn't quite so lucky when a second punch lands against his chest. The sound of his sternum creaking is loud in his ears as he flies to the left and lands heavily on the manicured lawn. Huge security lights have turned on, flooding the formerly beautiful garden in the front – now it's a mass of broken bushes and smashed flowers. Spidey makes a pained expression under his mask. He tries to stand and groans as the ache in his sternum announces itself loud and clear. "Marko!" he yells regardless, crouching into a fighting stance again. "Why are you *here*? Is there a playground somewhere missing its sandbox?"

An impressively loud alarm starts blaring out from speakers all over the garden. Sandman doesn't answer, instead trying to throw another massive fist towards Spidey's face. Spider-Man backflips out of the way, landing to the side, right leg outstretched and his left tucked underneath him, his fingers already pressed against his right palm to shoot a web in Sandman's direction. But he stalls, seeing there's something strange going on with Marko – the alarm's in surround sound, and the vibrations are breaking Marko's hold on his own sand. He solidifies down into his normal size and runs towards the gate, pieces of sand breaking off him and falling to the ground.

"You'll be sorry for this, Spider-Man! I'll get that freakin' thing if it's the last thing I do," he screams as he breaks the gate's lock.

Spider-Man, as if not to be outdone, yells back, as loud as he can, "There's the Flint Marko I know and don't like at all!" He slings a web at the streetlight just outside the gate and flies towards it, hoping to follow Marko wherever he's headed. But Sandman drops down into a puddle of sand, flowing too fast down the street for Spidey to follow in the dark. Spider-Man jumps down and lands on the concrete, letting out a quiet "No!" as he realises what's happened. He looks back at the house

Sandman was attempting to rob with his hands behind his head, considering it. If this is where Sandman brought the lock-picker he stole from the hardware shop, which he was using to get a lamp, *and* he was at the museum the day of the arc-lamp robbery… Spider-Man assumes the building is Addison Alredge's mansion.

The house alarm is still blasting. Strangely enough, but to Spidey's relief, no one has come outside to see what's going on. A few of the other homes on the street are waking up, though – he can see lights pouring out of windows, and a few doors have opened down the street. A man a few houses over shouts, "Hey, you! The cops are on their way, so you better stay put!" His voice is getting louder, like he's coming to make sure that's the case.

Spidey takes one last look at the house and sighs. *Argh.* He's not going to get any closer if the police show up and hassle him. He shoots a web at another light further down the street, and slings forwards, with one hand rubbing at his bruised sternum.

The fight with Sandman leads to a full twenty-four hours of disappointment for Peter Benjamin Parker. After the fight, he sneaked back into his room through his window and collapsed against the wall. He pulled his mask off and rubbed at his temples. He couldn't help but be absolutely livid with himself at having lost Sandman. Once he picked himself up off the floor, he spent a few minutes on his computer trying to find any kind of phone number for Addison Alredge, to no avail. So, he wrapped his chest with a bandage and got a few fitful hours of sleep.

After an unremarkable day at school, he was back at it, sitting on a rooftop near Addison's home, watching the mansion. The lawn had already been fixed, and the gate replaced, but it didn't seem like anyone was actually home. He waited four hours in the evening only for nothing to happen. He even tried hopping down into the front garden and walking up to the door and knocking on it. No answer, no movement behind the curtains, just nothing.

Now he's on his way home from a waste of a night, unsure of what he's going to do. He knows that's Addison's home and that the arc lamp is probably in there, just sitting and waiting for Sandman to turn around and try to steal it again, and he's not sure Alredge will be so lucky a second time. *Why was Sandman so desperate to get that thing?* It's not like him to come in hot in the front of a heist – he's more of a soldier, working for someone else. But, Spidey remembers, Sandman had said, "I'll get that thing," not "*We'll* get that thing."

It's late by the time he makes it back to Queens, and the street is quiet, so there's a comfortable ease in his step as he crawls up the side of his house and sneaks into his bedroom window – until, that is, he notices the light on the porch next door. He freezes.

MJ is sitting outside her house, a blanket wrapped around her shoulders and a mug in her hand. Her head is turned away from him, and he breathes out a sigh of intense relief. That's not the kind of luck he usually has. He quietly pushes the window open and slips inside, pulling off his gloves and reaching for an old pyjama shirt before pausing and looking back through the window. *What is MJ doing up?*

MJ can't sleep – it's late, she knows, *and* a school night, but for some reason, her brain just won't stop working. So after tossing and turning, she goes downstairs, grabs a cup of hot chocolate, and heads outside to sit on her swing. It's no wonder she can't stop thinking with everything she learnt today!

She spent the afternoon at the library after an awkward lunch with Maia – that had gone about as well as expected, but MJ deserved a little awkwardness, she supposed. They probably wouldn't be friends anytime soon, but they ended their lunch with tentative smiles and it seemed there was a truce, at least, for the remainder of the project.

When MJ got to the library, she walked in and asked

for any articles about subliminal messaging and digital marketing the librarian could help her find. It had been an interesting few days, not turning to her phone every thirty seconds to look something up or scroll mindlessly through thousands of updates or check her email for the hundredth time. Her head felt clearer, and she felt happier – or maybe just calmer. She could go about her day without everything feeling so dire. So, she wanted to learn more – and for better or for worse, she did.

What she read about in the library was that headlines, promotions, *advertising*, all of it is written specifically to make people feel a certain way – which she knows makes sense! The point of advertising and marketing is to get people to buy products. But now that everything is online and so accessible, people have learnt how to change a person's *mood*. So, she started doing some preliminary searches – there were a few reports of rage and hot tempers running all over the five boroughs. People who described the exact thing she was feeling – like she couldn't help it, but it felt good somehow until just after the fact. Just that morning, she yelled at her mum for putting one of her old jumpers in the tumble dryer and shrinking it. "But how come I'm still getting mad *after* I deleted all those apps? I don't even *like* that sweater," she murmurs to herself. Something in her gut is telling her to put some distance between her and her phone, so tonight it is sitting powered-off on a table in the study.

She grips her mug tighter and lets the warmth seep in. She sighs. There is *something* happening, but what? *Is it just some secret evil company figuring out how to do this to people?* She sees a light go on next door in her peripheral vision. She turns to look, and Peter Parker is standing in his window, waving at her. Her mouth turns up in a soft smile. He points to himself and then points back at her, a question on his face.

She nods, and then he walks over a few minutes later and waves before taking a seat on the swing next to her.

"Hey, MJ," he says. He looks like he was getting ready for bed, in loose trousers and the same old Weinkle's Daycare T-shirt he was wearing the other day. She feels a surge of warmth that he'd come hang out with her even though it's so late.

"Hey, Pete," she answers.

"What're you doing up?" he asks. She tells him about her day and what she's been working on. Peter sits quietly and takes it in, in a way she really appreciates, genuinely listening.

"So, I think there's something weird going on with people and their phones – and I don't know if it's *just* New York, or maybe it's a particular service? I haven't figured out what it is – did we all read the same website? Maybe we all got sent the same spam email? Maybe it's all the same model phone? But there is *something* going on! I'm an *extremely* online person, and I've never felt like this before.

I saw, like, five or six people who had the exact same thing happen to them – like, they can't *help* but lash out."

Peter levels a long look at her.

"That's interesting… and really messed up," he says slowly. "Who would do something like that?"

"I don't know. I wish I did. But companies all over the world use this stuff to…" She pauses, searching for the right word. "Manipulate us," she finally says. He looks away, but she can tell he's thinking about what she said. His eyes drift around like he's watching her words float inside his brain and connecting them together.

"Isn't… everything kind of about manipulation, though?" he asks her. And she takes one hand off her mug and fists it into the blanket. "Like, say, someone writes a book – they're hoping it'll make the reader feel something, right? Or makes a movie or writes a song?"

MJ nods her head. He's not wrong. But – this is different. "There's something gross about this, though – okay, so, something I found out today is that, like, companies pay for our data and then can target us so specifically to get us to give them our money. Say I like a picture of a dog in a costume on Instagram."

"What kind of dog?" he asks, with a crooked grin. She shoves him lightly.

"A small, cute one. Obviously."

"Okay, okay, I'm picturing it. Go on."

"And then I like someone's post about how great

Halloween is." She sees him furrow his brow in confusion. "I swear this will make sense. So they know I like dogs and I like Halloween, and they tell some random ad agency, and then *I* start seeing ads for doggie Halloween costumes."

"But why is that wrong?" he asks. "I'm not saying it isn't, but… I'm not totally sure I get it?"

"It's hard to describe… It's not *wrong*, but it feels a little *blech* when I just want to be excited about a cute dog without worrying there's some guy in a suit who is writing down the fact that I" – she points to herself – "Mary Jane Watson in Forest Hills, Queens, likes dogs and Halloween and maybe I'll spend money on this company he's working for. *And*, if they can do that, think about what else they can do if the tools get more sophisticated! If you pay enough money to put ads in the right places, you can convince us to do things that are bad for us. It's like someone else is deciding *for* me. Although now," she continues, "I deleted all those apps off my phone after that library debacle, and I'm *still* having these super-weird mood swings, so I'm starting to think there's some secret evil company using my actual physical phone to make me mad! On top of all this internet stuff!" She lets out a little huff with all her frustration.

Peter's face is scrunched up like he's eaten something sour.

"Well," he finally says, "I *hate* that." And he's so

earnest and hilariously *Peter* that she nearly spills her hot chocolate in his lap because she's laughing so hard.

Later, when he's back home and under the covers in his bed, Peter thinks about what MJ told him. He traces the whitewashed boards of his walls up to the ceiling with his eyes, and to the darkened light fixture in the centre. He turns onto his side and hugs the pillow to his head.

He is starting to think that he shouldn't sign into *any* website ever. The things MJ talked about were horrible. And the idea that someone could actually *do* that – control people's moods – there is something nauseating about it. He didn't like the sound of what MJ said – the lashing out, and the anger. It made him think briefly of Beetle, but then he shook his head – Beetle wasn't lashing out, she was fighting with purpose. And she didn't seem particularly sorry after the fact.

Peter is glad that, aside from his strange interaction with the ghost thief, his biggest problem right now is Sandman. He scoffs quietly, turning back onto his other side. *I can* handle *Flint Marko. I've handled him before, and I'll handle him again.* He closes his eyes, content and very happy to have a normal bad guy to deal with. But then MJ's words come back to him and his eyes shoot open again as his mind races, thinking of some invisible person using the internet to change people's entire moods and actions. That would be a really powerful person to go up against. He shivers and hopes that that's not something he'll have to deal with anytime soon.

His plate is full as it stands. Tomorrow, Peter decides, he's going to find a way to get Addison Alredge's phone number – whatever it takes.

CHAPTER FIFTEEN

It's later than Spider-Man is used to, which means that it is capital-L *Late*. The Astoria streets are totally deserted. He's stationed on a building across the street from the Museum of the Moving Image. He sees the late-night security officer doing his fourth round of the night, so Spidey knows he's got the timing down perfectly. If he sneaks in now, he'll have about twenty-five minutes to get in and out before the man makes it back to the lobby.

He shoots a web across the street and zips to the roof. Spidey looks around for a second and finds the entrance he's looking for. Earlier, he made a rush stop at one of the local municipality offices after school and found out that blueprints to every building in the city are a matter of public record – which meant he could easily access MOMI's! The receptionist, a kind older woman, was happy to help with his essay on 'local modern architecture' and pulled them out.

Blueprints are not easy to read, but from what he could tell, there is a ventilation system that runs through the building that should be wide enough for him to climb through. So that's where Spidey is now, looking down at the square metal grate at the top of the building. He pries his fingers underneath the edge and gives it one quick pull. With his strength, it comes away easily, and Spidey looks down into the dark hole. He asked Aunt May the easiest way to find someone's phone number at breakfast in the morning, and she laughed and told him how they used to send *full books* to people for free with thousands of phone numbers.

That would have been so much more convenient.

"I really hope there aren't any rats in there." He shivers once. He shines his phone's torch down the shaft. *It's not too far of a drop, eight feet? Maybe ten? Easy enough.* Spidey takes one last look around. "Well, here goes nothing," he says to no one. Then he hops feet-first into the hole and lands with a loud *thump*.

It was the fastest way down, but he really hopes no one heard that.

He pictures the map of the building in his head; if he's correct, he just needs to go left, then down, then right, then down, and repeat until he makes it to the first floor.

Spider-Man turns left and starts crawling. His mouth twists up, and his nose wrinkles under his mask. *Why does it smell so weird in here? Ugh.* Then he runs head-first into a dead end. "What the heck?"

He thinks about his map again, picturing the blue lines on the thin paper, and he realises that he'd turned himself around. Time to backtrack. He twists his way back to the shaft he'd entered through and keeps going. He's creeping along, pressing his fingers lightly against the metal of the vent until finally finding another hole and dropping down a floor. Most of the journey is uneventful, except for once where he has to bite his lip to keep from yelping when the biggest rat he's ever seen runs right over his hand. Its gigantic hairy form just pushes by him and rounds the corner like Spidey isn't even there.

In the rat's defence, Spidey supposes *he* is the interloper on the rat's turf. *Doesn't make it any less gross*, he thinks, his whole body shuddering. Shortly thereafter, he finally makes it to the bottom floor of the building. He finds a vent and can see the lobby through its slats. He quietly pulls the vent up and into the duct so that he can easily replace it on his way out. He wraps his fingers around the edge of the opening, the red of his gloves showing easily against the silver.

Spider-Man pulls himself out and crawls onto the ceiling. From his last visit to the museum, he knows there is one camera he has to worry about; it faces the door and can see the entire front-desk area. He spots it in the corner, about ten feet ahead of him. He starts moving towards it, angling away so he's never in its direct sight. When he gets close enough, he shoots a small amount of webbing to smear across the surface of the lens. It'll dissolve in an hour, leaving nothing but a smudge behind.

There, that should handle that.

He drops down off the ceiling and lands in a crouch. A few feet later and he's standing in front of the computer. The monitor is dark, but he can hear a telltale whir. He hits the space bar and the monitor comes to life. There's a log-in window; the username is STAFF.

Okay, now what?

He starts rummaging through the drawers in the desk, hoping for anything to tell him what the password might be. There are plenty of office supplies and a book or two that some employees must be reading, but no conveniently placed Post-it to tell him how to sign in. He stands in front of the computer, and his fingers are poised over the keys. Pressing the first button down, he types out an educated guess:

Muppet!11106

Not sure what he was expecting, but he's not surprised to see an error pop up telling him he has four more tries to type the password in correctly.

Shoot.

By sheer lack of options, he lifts the keyboard up and looks at the desk under it, but it's clear of any hidden passwords.

Then a bright piece of something catches his eye as he goes to put the board back down. He turns it over. There's a Post-it note stuck to the bottom of the keyboard that just says:

Astor!aMov!ng!mag3

Spidey lets out the bellyful of air he was holding and grins. The keys click softly as he types the password in, and then the desktop comes to life. He quickly locates a donor Excel file and sees Addison's name listed *and* his phone number. It's a 212 area code; Spidey wonders if that means it's a landline. Programming the number into his phone, he resolves to call it first thing in the morning. Much as he'd like to, he knows he shouldn't call an old millionaire in the middle of the night. Though, he considers as he presses the power button on the monitor, did he *really* care about a millionaire's sleep patterns?

No, no. It would be wrong... But would it?

Spidey grins ruefully under his mask and pockets his

phone before springing up to the ceiling. He's got about five minutes to get out of here before the security guard gets back. *Plenty of time.*

"Hello? Hello? Who is this? Hello?" A fragile-sounding voice answers the phone. Peter is sitting cross-legged on his bed, laptop in front of him. The voice is coming through thinly in his headphones, though he's not sure if it's his connection or the voice itself.

"Hello? Is this Addison Alredge?" he asks, hoping his laptop's mic is good enough to pick his sound up. This morning has been spent scouring the internet for a free phone service online, since he knows enough not to dial from his personal phone. That means he only has a short time to tell Addison Alredge everything he wants to.

"Hello? Yes, who is calling? What do you want? How did you get this number?" The voice is less fragile-sounding now and more angry.

"Sir, this is—this is Spider-Man."

"*What*-man?" he asks, and Peter groans. There isn't enough time for this.

"It's *Spider*-Man," he says again. "I only have a few minutes, but you're going to be robbed."

The voice laughs an old, gnarled-sounding thing into the phone.

"Is this one of those, what do you call it, those crank calls?"

"No!" Peter bites out. Closing his eyes, he sucks in a deep breath and tries to even out his voice. "This is serious. A man named Flint Marko tried to rob you the other night, and he's going to try again. He wants your Arlo Farms arc-lamp thing."

There's a sharp intake of breath on the other side of the phone.

"I don't know how you found out about that, but you better forget you know anything about it. Just listen, young man, that item is very safe, and you don't need to worry your little head about it. I've managed to hold on to it for this long. I don't need a little *arachno boy* to solve problems they've invented for me. It's secret and safe, good day." And then he *hangs up the phone*. Peter stares at his laptop, gobsmacked at how poorly the interaction had gone.

He throws himself backwards onto his bed with a grunt of frustration.

Great! Now what?

GET ARC ARC LAMP GET ARC GET HOME GET HOME ARC 2275 OCEANIC AVE.

The words are running over and over and over and over

in Sandman's head. He's sitting on an old mattress in the middle of a large, empty space. It's one of the abandoned warehouses in north Brooklyn, and the safest place he could think of with the cops and the Maggia family on his tail. Two Rocks isn't too pleased that Sandman didn't deliver. Out of habit, Sandman is stretching and compressing a long stream of sand from one palm to the other, a nervous tic from his early days as a super-powered villain.

Freakin' Spider-Man!!!

Sandman resists the urge to scream. Everything he knows he is entitled to is just one short heist away. He's done a hundred of these in his life, but this is the important one – this is the job that can lead to everything he's ever wanted: power, money and an easy life. And there is just one thing standing in his way.

The sand flowing between his hands explodes out as he slams them together, picturing a tiny spider sitting between his palms.

GET ARC ARC LAMP GET ARC GET HOME GET HOME ARC 2275 OCEANIC AVE.

Sandman rests his face against his fisted hands and screams. Lifting his head, he looks around at the decrepit floor around him, furious at his circumstance. "How am I s'posed to fix this?" he grits out. "My crew's in the wind, and nobody's gonna touch me with a ten-foot pole with the cops on my butt."

He starts to pace, steps heavy, before falling back down to his bed, like he can't decide what to do with his body, let alone his life.

"Maybe it's time for me to go. Maybe I gotta run?"

On the floor, the screen of his phone lights up, and it vibrates against the hard floor. The buzzing sound echoes in the expanse of the empty warehouse. Sandman slowly stands again and curls up to his full height, walking over to where he'd thrown the phone in a fit of rage earlier. He picks it up. The screen is cracked, and the corner chipped. It's still working, though, and he sees a new text from the mysterious blank-numbered person.

> GET THE LAMP GO TO THE HOME
>   GET THE LAMP GO TO THE HOME
>   GET THE LAMP GO TO THE HOME
>   FIND IT
> FIND IT
> FIND IT
> OR ELSE OR ELSE OR ELSE OR ELSE OR ELSE

A few days later, Peter walks into another shift at the *Bugle*. He's had several pictures go up on their social feeds – one that he thinks is *very* cool from the night of the

MOMI soft break-in. In it, he is all the way down in Coney Island in his spider-suit to pre-emptively alleviate any suspicion in case someone figures anything out. Peter waves at Tommy and Rodrigo on his way in, and they wave back with distracted hellos. As he goes by, he sees they're both intently watching a football match on Rodrigo's phone.

When he gets to his desk on the seventeenth floor, he sees Ned and Kayla there. It sounds like they're arguing, but their tones are hushed, and he can only just make out what they're saying. Ned's standing over Kayla's desk again, leaning with his chin resting on his crossed arms over the top of her cube wall.

"I'm telling you, Ned. Jonah's gonna sink this paper if he keeps going, and I don't know about you, but I would like to not ruin my entire professional reputation before I've even had a chance to build it." Her brow is furrowed, and she's gesturing emphatically with her hands.

"Hey," Peter says loudly, just to make sure they know he's there. Kayla waves but doesn't turn to look at him, obviously distracted.

"Listen, Jonah's not a bad journalist, it's just his one thing. Like... his *one* thing. Any other situation, he might be a loud-mouthed jerk, but he'll be open to discussion. Not a lot of publishers would," Ned replies, without responding to Peter's greeting beyond a short nod of acknowledgement.

"I *know*," Kayla replies. "But we have to do something. The captions he approved for the Spider-Man photos we got this week were absurd. Seriously. Sushant and I are thinking about writing him a letter and getting it signed by everyone for more fair coverage, so we don't *all* look bad."

Ned's eyes get wide, and he pushes back from the cube wall like Kayla's words had actual, physical force behind them.

"You're gonna put *your* name on a letter to J. Jonah Jameson telling him his coverage of *Spider-Man* is unfair?" he asks, incredulous.

"Yes," Kayla replies primly. "But we're going to make it about the damage he's doing to the *paper*, not to Spider-Man, obviously."

The back of Peter's neck burns, and he *really* hopes he didn't start this. He turns around to face his desk, pretending not to listen, but quietly freaking out all the same. *I need this job!*

He starts riffling through the papers on his desk just to have something to do with his hands. If Kayla asked, he knows he'd sign his name to the letter because it's the right thing to do – Jameson's captions this week have been out of control. On the shot in Coney Island, Peter had suggested *Quick break for a pretzel before getting back to it!* – Jameson changed it to *Spidey, stealing pretzels and wasting our time at Coney Island!*

In reality, the pretzel guy had offered Spider-Man the pretzel for stopping someone from stealing his tips!

So, if they wrote a letter and asked him? He'd sign. He sighs, looking at the stack of folders on his desk to be filed.

Maybe I can start some kind of crowd fund for being Spider-Man? No... that would be a logistical nightmare.

When the time comes for their next OSMAKER group meeting, Peter's already sitting at the table, waving at Randy as he walks into the library.

"Hey, Pete! Nice punctuality," Randy jokes as he sits in the seat next to Peter. Peter just shrugs in response, but his smile is wide. MJ and Maia both join them a few minutes later in quick succession. MJ gives them both a wave and mouths a *hi* at Peter.

As soon as they're settled, Maia pulls a pile of papers out of her backpack. "So, I did some research, and actually, renewable energy has been trending up on Google searches consistently for the last few years." Her tone's polite, if not particularly warm, and the tension Peter was holding in his shoulders eases just the slightest bit. It seems as though everyone's being very cordial, and if that's what it takes to get this project done, he'll take it.

"That's great!" MJ says brightly, but Peter can hear a note of nervousness in her voice.

"And my dad set us up with a few email addresses of people he said would be willing to answer some questions," Randy adds. "Two of them are kind of about activism, and the third person is a climate scientist. We can split 'em up maybe?" Randy types on his phone and looks at the rest of the group after hitting one last button. "There. I sent everyone the list. It's only three people, so one of us won't have to do it."

Randy and MJ both look at Peter.

"What?"

"You *never* check your email. So maybe not you."

"I do, too!" he says, affronted. But then thinks about the last time he checked his actual email, and it was to get the note from Dr Shah a few days ago. "Okay, fair. I can do something else."

Maia was quiet while Randy was sharing the emails, but now she passes out the papers she brought. Peter sees that she's printed individual packets for them.

"Oh, these are awesome, Maia. Thanks," MJ says as she takes one.

"You're welcome – I basically just broke down, like, the best parts of all the messaging things that are out there right now, and the worst things, so we can start figuring out how we want this thing to work."

"And I was thinking," MJ says hesitantly while looking down at her packet, "that while we can definitely still use renewable energy as our basis, the actual project would be creating a program that makes it easy for people to create language around activism – so, you put in your cause and what you want people to do, and the program can help you build a campaign."

"Ooh." Randy leans forwards in his seat. "We could definitely do this as a proposal for class, and if we get picked, we could build an actual program for the OSMAKER competition!"

"Yeah! And maybe it can also pull information from online so that if someone else is doing the same thing you want to do, it'll tell you? So for kids who want to do something, it's an easy place to start," she continues.

Peter's nodding along, hard enough that he has to push his hair back from his eyes.

"It sounds like Maia's info and your idea will work great together," he says, maybe a little more joyfully than he needs to.

Maia gives him a short smile but nods nonetheless. Peter pulls his sleeves up, humorously overexaggerated in his movements.

"Well," he says, cheeks rounded by a wide smile on his face, "let's get to work!"

They spend another hour in amiable work mode, but when it's over, Maia gets her things together and leaves before the rest of them have even started packing up. MJ sighs.

"Ugh, I'm the *worst*."

Randy shrugs.

"It happens, MJ. Everyone has weird days. Maia's cool; she'll come around." He gives her a cheesy grin and a thumbs-up. "Besides, we all know we're gonna get As, and that's the most important thing here."

"Is it, though?" Peter asks, narrowing his eyes in mock concern.

MJ steps alongside Randy and nods.

"He's not wrong. Or wait, no." She taps a finger against her chin. "Or is it that grades are fake and don't matter…? Which I think is what I *think* you said in pre-calc yesterday, Randy."

Randy puts a hand to his heart. "MJ, way to give away all my secrets!" He harnesses his bag over his shoulder and looks at his phone. "All right, I gotta get outta here. We're taking my sister out for her birthday dinner tonight, and if I don't have time to change into something nice, my mother's going to ground me for a hundred years."

He throws a hand up to them both and turns to leave. MJ leans down to put her things into her backpack, so it's only Peter who sees Randy point at MJ and mouth, *Ask her out.*

Peter's eyes widen, and he shoos Randy away, vehemently waving his hand in the direction of the exit. Randy walks away, and Peter can see his shoulders shaking from laughter as he goes.

A few minutes later, Peter and MJ follow Randy's path and walk out the door together. As soon as they hit the pavement, MJ starts talking.

"Ugh, I *know* it's my fault that our group feels so awkward, but it still sucks!"

"All you can do is keep being nice from your end, MJ. I think she'll come around, seriously. You're awesome," he says, trying not to blush. She looks at him and smiles that smile that makes him think she can read his mind. "Oh," he says hurriedly, trying to change the subject. "I wanted to thank you for all your social tips – my boss at the *Bugle* loves them. She says I have a 'knack for tone'." He air-quotes the line Kayla said to him.

"That's great, Peter! I hope it's helping make their Spidey stuff a little nicer."

Peter stumbles a bit.

"I mean, if it does, great, but if not, that's not really up to me," he rushes out. MJ just gives him an appraising look that he doesn't like, so he keeps going as fast as he can. "But it has been *really* cool seeing my pictures get noticed by so many people! There were, like, a hundred comments on the last one."

"Okay, okay, fair," she says, then startles, looking around them. "Oh, we're already almost home."

They're quiet for a few minutes as they head up the

street to their houses. At the front path of MJ's house, she stops. Peter waits; clearly MJ wants to tell him something. She faces him, nods once, and balls her hands into fists at her side.

"Peter," she asks, "do you want to go on a date with me this weekend?"

What? Peter's brain shuts down. "Uh, ah, I mean—"

"You don't have to! I'm sorry if I—"

"No!" he says, too loudly. "No, I mean, yes. Yes. I do. Yeah. I mean. Yes. Thank you for asking," he adds. *Too formal*, his brain screams.

MJ's face breaks out into a huge grin, and her green eyes sparkle in the setting sun. "Great! We'll figure it out later, but I'm glad!" And with that, she turns to walk inside like she hadn't just upended his world. "I'll see you tomorrow, Peter."

He can't find the words, so he just puts up a hand and waves, sure that his cheeks are glowing radioactive red in the low light of the evening. Once she's inside, he interlocks his hands behind his head, looks up at the sky, and groans before turning to head back to his own house.

Thank you for asking? he thinks. *Ugh, be less weird, Peter!*

CHAPTER SIXTEEN

Whew, Sandman thinks. *The subway tunnels of New York City stink to high heaven.* A rush of sand is what he is right now, moving silently through the underground transportation labyrinth, careful to avoid the electric third rail. He doesn't like being so close to it; electricity is one of the few things that can hurt him, calcifying his sand so he can't move if it's a powerful enough charge. The third rail sparks once on his right as if to remind him that this is definitely powerful enough. He moves as far to the left as he can without losing momentum. This is the safest path for him to move about now that there's a police alert on him. The tunnels should take him right to the same street he was at a few nights ago.

He'd nearly walked away, but something deep inside his brain was telling him that this was the right move – this would be his final winning ticket. He slides his sand along the sides of the tunnel until he feels the rumble of an approaching train. Then he spreads himself thin along the wall as it rushes by. Once it passes, he continues his trek. This late at night the trains don't run that frequently, so he manages to make it uptown without another incident. He pours out of the underground and onto the pavement, inching along until he makes it to a familiar gate.

On his way, he passes by a storm drain that leads down into the sewers, and though he doesn't like the idea of being around so much water, he thinks maybe it'll make for a quick getaway. He's learnt a few lessons in the past few days. Last time showed him that even *with* an alarm blaring, he can count on a fairly easy getaway. Spider-Man himself couldn't stop Sandman in the moment. So this time, he just has to get *in* without being noticed. He slides right under the gate – it doesn't look like they've changed anything at all since he was here last. The garden's been cleaned and the gate fixed, but other than that he spies the same floodlights and alarm speakers that went off during the last wayward attempt.

A bad call, he thinks. *Underestimating me. They'll be sorry.*

He's on the garden pathway now, leading up to the

door. He's moving grain by grain, barely upsetting the air around him, let alone any motion detectors or lasers or whatever. *When I get a house like this, the first thing I'm gonna do is install some lasers.*

Just getting from the gate to the front door takes over an hour. But Sandman is here to be meticulous. He can be whatever he needs to be. He's *malleable*.

He finally inches up the stairs and starts crawling into the smallest crack between the door and the door frame. When Sandman touches his last grain of sand inside the door, he's in a darkened foyer. All around him the air is still and quiet. He spreads his sand out thin and finds absolutely nothing to worry about. No hint of any sort of alarm system inside.

Fools!

After all that setup, he's almost disappointed in how easy this has been so far. His sand quivers as he pauses, deciding where to go. But then something tickles at the back of his consciousness. He doesn't need to decide. He can feel the remnants of *something* calling to him. Sandman slides forwards, across the black-and-white-tiled marble flooring, past the doors to dining rooms, sitting rooms and rooms dedicated to however else rich people use their unnecessary amounts of space. At the end of the hall is a large metal door. It doesn't fit in with the classic architecture of the rest of the building. This is a door that's there to keep something safe. *Ha*, Sandman thinks.

It might be tightly sealed, but not tight enough. There's *always* a tiny fracture. A tiny crack. And he'll find it.

A few minutes go by, then a few more, and he's getting frustrated. His sand is streaming up and down the door looking for that imperfection he *knows* must be there – and then! In the top right-hand corner, the smallest of fissures underneath a bolt. Sandman streams towards it and flows through. Grain by grain. On the other side there's a set of stairs going deep into the ground, and he follows the trail. Still, there's something tickling at the edge of his perception, egging him on. It's small, like a single blade of grass softly grazing the bottom of a bare foot. He clutches at it, following the sensation as it takes him through stairways and hallways and doors until finally he pours through an old keyhole and finds what he's been looking for – the arc lamp. The itch doesn't quite settle, but he's distracted now.

"It don't look like much," he says after he's re-formed into his usual body. He walks around the arc lamp. It's flimsy-looking to his eye, a long thin iron bar with a black box in the middle and a huge cylinder on top. *How am I gonna get this thing outta here? I thought it was gonna be a little desk thing I could carry with my hands!*

The lamp in front of him is pretty big, and it's a long way to go up and through the house. He puddles back into sand and pours into the hallway from the keyhole in the door, sliding along until he finds a solid wall made of stone squares, stacked together with some kind of concrete or clay. Whatever it is, it's *porous*. If he can get his sand behind this rock, he can probably tunnel out with the force of his sand pretty quickly. He slides into the edges between the square grey rock and flattens his sand behind it, in between the stone and the earth, and then he pushes with all his might. It moves slowly at first and then all at once, sliding out with a loud *scccratch* across the floor. Behind it, Sandman can feel dirt, and that's something he knows how to handle. He makes quick work of six more of the stones and then there's a hole big enough for him and the lamp. He drills into the earth until he pops up somewhere acres away from the mansion on Oceanic Avenue. The exit is far enough away that it will take a regular person ages to crawl through a hole that Sandman just flew through in no time. Even when they figure out how he got out, they won't be able to catch him in time.

He flows back down through the tunnel he's made and into the hallway and returns to the room with the lamp. From his perspective, there's no more need to be quiet. He picks the lamp up, breaks the door down from the inside. Alarms immediately start blaring, but Sandman ignores them, rushing through the hall to his makeshift exit. His sand is already in fast motion, the lamp locked somewhere inside his streamlined form, carried along with him, up through the tunnel and out.

Peter has been racking his brain about where to take MJ. He tried asking her to see if there was anywhere she wanted to go, and she just gave him a mischievous grin and said, "Hey, I handled asking you out; now you can take care of the planning."

It was sweet and funny, and he appreciated it in the moment, but now he was in full panic mode. He meant to do some of that planning last night, but then he got waylaid by a bank robbery in progress and that took almost *all* night. So now here he was, morning of and at a loss. *Where do you take a girl? Where do you take a smart, cute girl? Where do you take Mary Jane Watson? She's so... MJ and I'm so...* He looks in the mirror – at least he's settled on something decent to wear. At least, he thinks so. He's got on a pair of jeans and a jumper with the NASA logo on it. *Space is cool, right?*

Not that he thinks clothes will save him if he takes her somewhere terrible. He starts pacing in his room, counting down ideas on his hands.

Coney Island? No, that's so far. It would take us so long to get there, we'd probably have to turn around and come right back to make curfew.

The Museum of Modern Art? Definitely not. What if we go to an exhibit I don't understand? And, oh man, if the exhibit was experiential? Talk about aaaawkward. That's a no.

Maybe Central Park? He pauses his movement and looks outside. The weather *is* gorgeous, but that just means everyone and their mother will be at the park today. He rolls his eyes and gets back to pacing. *Basic as heck.*

Maybe just movie and pizza or something? Ugghhhhhhh.

He needs another perspective. He wrenches his door open and runs down the stairs, taking them two at a time.

"Aunt May?" he calls out, but finds her before she answers. She's sitting at the kitchen table reviewing some paperwork. Looking up from whatever she is reading, she smiles warmly before doing a double take.

"Hey, Peter – you look nice. Did you… comb your hair?"

He rubs the back of his head in apprehension, avoiding her gaze.

"I always comb my hair," he protests weakly, knowing it's not true.

"Did you need help with something?" she asks, gracefully moving the conversation along as only his aunt can.

"I'm… going out with MJ today, and I can't think of where to take her." He collapses into the chair opposite hers. She puts her papers down and takes off her glasses.

"Well," she says, giving him a sly grin. "Take her somewhere special – where you'll have something to do, but also, and more important, space to talk." And then in a surprising burst of inspiration, it comes to him. He knows the perfect place.

MJ's sitting on the two-seater subway seat next to Peter and they're headed into the city.

"So where are we going?" she asks, turning to face him as she does. He's looking away from her, and she can take a second to appreciate how cute he is with his smiling brown eyes, hair a chaos of curls that tell of a likely haircut in his near future, and his adorably dorky jumper.

He picked her up and immediately got tongue-tied when she opened the door, but what he doesn't know is that so did she! She is trying very hard to seem like she isn't nervous and she hopes it's working. In response to her question, Peter swivels his head back to her and grins.

"There's this part of the Met that's up in Washington Heights called the Cloisters – honestly, Aunt May recommended it, kind of. It's a lot of open-air stuff, but it's *not* Central Park."

"Oh, that sounds really cool – I haven't been there before."

"I've swu—walked by it a few times," Peter says, before hurrying on, "I thought we could pick up some bodega sandwiches for lunch when we get hungry. I think there's a deli across the street from the park."

She leans a little closer, ostensibly to speak over the sound of the subway moving under the river, but happy for the excuse.

"That sounds *excellent*."

They spend the rest of the trip in relaxed conversation – and this is one of MJ's favourite things about hanging out with Peter. That he is so easy to talk to. They make the transfer to the A train, and once they settle into their seats, Peter pushes his fringe back from his face and looks up to count how many stops they have until Dyckman Street. There's a cowlick sticking up from the back of his hair, and MJ itches to press it down. *Too weird!* she thinks.

He reaches a hand up to point at the stops, and something in his movement reminds MJ about how she saw him sneaking into his house, and she wonders if she should ask about that. It's happened a few more times in the last several weeks. But she isn't sure what Peter, of all people, could be hiding. He's the kind of person who wears every emotion on his face.

Though there were those times she noticed him taking a second too long to answer or moving on from a topic at hand like he didn't want anyone thinking about *it* and *him* in the same thought for too long.

"Just ten more stops," Peter says, with some light sarcasm, breaking her out of her thoughts. They fall back into their discussion about who would win in a race – Sonic the Hedgehog or the Road Runner. They go back and forth on this important clash of titans, until finally—

"The Road Runner, easy!" MJ says. "Because they would fight *dirty*."

"But we're just talking about a race – not, like, a tactical battle." He flings his hands out to punctuate his point.

"It has to be tactical! And a battle!" she exclaims just as the conductor comes on the loudspeaker to announce Dyckman Street. They exit into the mid-morning sun and walk south a few streets to the entrance of the park leading into the Cloisters. It's beautiful. As they walk, Peter points out a deli they can pick sandwiches up at later.

They stroll into the entrance of Fort Tryon Park, the area surrounding the museum itself, and then it's like they're not even in the city anymore. The wide path is surrounded on either side by foliage and trees, and the sun cuts a path through the branches onto the ground below. MJ can see the old stone of the Cloisters themselves in the distance. She turns to Peter as they're walking.

"So, what made you want to come here?" she asks.

He pauses a moment and then shrugs noncommittally. "I don't know, it just seems interesting? This random medieval-looking building in the middle of New York? And it's far enough up that it probably wouldn't be *super* crowded with, like, tourists or whatever."

"Well, whatever the reason, I'm glad." She dances forwards a few steps, too excited for a boring old walk, and leans over the edge of a stone wall overlooking an open space. There are groups of people picnicking and a few sunbathing or reading quietly with headphones in. "I feel like usually people might be like, let's go eat pizza and watch a movie – which are fun!" She laughs at Peter's stricken face. "That would have also been fun," she repeats, "but this feels…" Now it's MJ's turn to pause awkwardly. She shoves a strand of hair behind her ear and turns away before finishing, looking back at the people on the lawn. "It feels special."

When she glances back at Peter, he's grinning widely and motioning for her to follow him.

"Come on, let's get to the museum part," he says.

They spend the next few hours walking through what she assumes is an accurate version of an actual medieval cloister – she's never been out of the country before, or really out of the tristate area, but it *feels* very European to her. There are arches and cobblestones and beautiful square gardens surrounded by stone walls. Then, when she and Peter are scooching by a group of very loud tourists in one of the tighter hallways, they're close enough that their hands brush together and she links her fingers through his. She doesn't stop her stride, like holding hands with him is the most natural thing in the world, but she hopes that her hand doesn't feel like it's shaking – or like it's sweaty. She can feel a momentary surprise from him when he stops abruptly for the briefest of seconds, but he settles quickly and holds her hand back.

Later, after exploring the museum, they re-trace their

steps to the park itself. She's about to ask a question when Peter gestures to something with their joined hands.

"What's that?"

There's a crowd gathered about twenty feet away. It's not huge, but there's someone speaking in front and a bunch of people listening.

"Let's check it out," she tells him. They walk towards the crowd, and as they get closer, MJ's mildly shocked to see she recognises someone. "Is that… *Maia*?"

Peter squints like it will help him see better, but when he opens his eyes wide again, he nods. "I think you're right."

They're close enough now to hear what the person speaking is saying.

"Everyone deserves the right to a place to live and feel safe!" There's an East Asian woman with crutches standing in the front, speaking loudly to the group. A few people in the crowd yell back affirmations, agreeing with her. Maia's near the back, with friends that MJ doesn't recognise. They've got signs and clear backpacks with bottles of water and a few other things in them.

"Hey, Maia!" Peter says as they walk up to her. She turns, and for a split second, she looks completely shocked but then schools her features. She looks as put together as usual, MJ notes, with her long hair tied back into a fishtail braid, a yellow bandanna around her neck, a black tank top and a pair of stylishly distressed shorts.

"Oh, hey – what are you guys doing here?" she asks, before looking down at their hands and mouthing a silent *oh*.

"What are you doing here?" Peter asks.

"Oh, it's a protest for affordable housing—"

MJ interrupts, seemingly unable to help herself. "I didn't know you were into this stuff!" she blurts out, and then puts a hand to her mouth. "Sorry! Sorry. I mean—"

Maia gives her a sardonic look. "You thought I was *just* what you saw online? And you didn't think that maybe there was more to me than some pictures on Instagram?"

MJ blushes, knowing that Maia's right. Peter squeezes her hand, and she looks up at him. His brown eyes are huge, and he's not-so-subtly nodding towards Maia with encouragement. MJ squares her shoulders and looks at Maia straight on.

"You're right," MJ says. "I was a jerk for multiple reasons, and I am sorry. I never should have judged you for what you're into. But," she continues, "I am super excited to see you here – and not because what I think matters! But because we have something in common!" She steps around to look at Maia's clear backpack. "So, I see water bottles and bandannas, but what's your favourite kind of energy bar to bring to a protest?"

Maia gives MJ a long look, like she's deciding something – and then she smiles, wide and welcoming.

"Obviously it's—" and then MJ joins Maia for the

end of the sentence because she knows what's coming: "PRO-TRAIN," they both say together and laugh.

Peter is a little out of his depth in the conversation that MJ and Maia are having – they've been chatting for twenty minutes about different protests they've gone to, first with family and then with friends.

"Do you fight with your mom every time you want to go to one of these?" MJ asks. "Because I definitely do. And then I'm like—"

"But you're the one who taught me?" Maia asks, mimicking what Peter assumes is her mum's voice.

"Yes!" MJ screeches in laughter.

It's not really something he knows anything about, but he's happy to be listening and learning and also *MJ held my hand. And we're still holding hands.* Like she can hear his thoughts, she squeezes his hand and gives him a look out of the corner of her eye.

Maia notices.

"Sooo," she says, "what *are* you guys doing here?" Only now she's got a teasing note in her voice, and MJ scrunches her nose.

"What we are *doing* is going to go pick up some sandwiches," she says with a grin. "But I'm really glad we ran into you."

"Me too," Maia says, and Peter can hear the honesty in her voice. "I'll see you guys at school. Have fun!"

They're walking back towards the exit to find the bodega they'd passed earlier, and Peter is euphoric. This morning, when it had hit him – he's been spending *so* much time near the Cloisters during the night, what a great way to see it during the day like a normal person with someone he likes – he had no idea what a good idea it would end up being. The sun didn't stop shining, he didn't think he'd stopped smiling, and he only *slightly* embarrassed himself at the ticket counter, but he didn't even think MJ was paying attention.

That said, until MJ made the hand move, he had his hands in his pockets almost the whole time because he didn't know what to do with them while he was walking, and the back of his neck is burning slightly, which means he is probably sunburned, but he doesn't care. Nothing can compete with the fact that MJ held his hand. *Sunburn is a small price to pay*, he thinks.

Peter holds the door open for MJ when they get to the bodega – they order their sandwiches, grab some drinks and crisps, and head back outside to find an empty bench to eat their lunch. He's got the black plastic bag looped around his wrist, and they're standing on the pavement across the street scoping out the border of the park when MJ turns to him.

"This is really fun, Peter. I'm glad you said yes."

She grins, and he can't help but smile back, supremely thankful at how un-awkward – *Un-awkward? Is that a word? At ease?* – he feels. He notices she's stepped closer, and that they're only a hair's breadth apart. *It's happening.* Her eyes are closed, and her eyelashes look gold in the afternoon sun. He leans forwards, and just as he's about to kiss the girl he's liked since *eighth grade*, he hears someone across the street scream, "HELP ME!"

CHAPTER SEVENTEEN

Peter's spider-sense is going wild, buzzing intensely in the back of his head. He can hear more people screaming from inside the park. MJ's gripping his hand tightly, and he's sure her nails are going to leave impressions on the back of his hand, but he doesn't blame her. There's something bad happening.

"Something's wrong. MJ, get to the bodega, I'm going to try and find Maia!"

MJ looks across the street and she looks steady, but when she talks, Peter can hear a note of fear.

"No, I'm coming with you" is what she says, and he's not surprised. His brow furrows and his mind races, trying to come up with an easy way to get her to stay behind. He doesn't want her to come with him, and not just because he can't change into his spider-suit while she's here, but because he doesn't want her to be in danger!

His mind blanks, though, and he doesn't have time to argue, so he grips her hand and they run across the street into Fort Tryon Park. It's pandemonium. There are dozens and dozens of people trying to exit, and Peter and MJ are forced to go against the crowd. He nearly loses her to the flow of backwards traffic once or twice but manages to hold on tight without *looking* like he's holding on tight, and they're able to stick together. There are sirens going off somewhere, but he can't tell from what direction with all the chaos.

Finally, they find the clearing where they'd seen Maia last, but there are people *everywhere*. A woman's voice to Peter's left screams out, "You'll never catch me, you jerks!" and he sees a figure in what looks like a panda suit. He'd laugh, but she's holding a massive boulder, deciding which direction to throw it in.

"Peter? MJ?!" All of a sudden, Maia's standing in front of them, panting. "Where did you come from?"

"We came to make sure you were okay!" MJ says, taking Maia's hand. "Now we found you, let's go!"

Peter needs to deal with the panda lady, but he can't do it in front of MJ and Maia. He deliberately loosens his hold on MJ's other hand.

"Let's go!" he says, turning to run. "But if we get separated, we'll meet at Edward's, the bodega, on Broadway and Thayer!"

MJ and Maia nod their heads in agreement, and once they've stepped into the massive crowd moving away from the violence, he lets his grip slip loose of MJ's hand.

"Peter!" she cries as the crowd pulls them apart.

"GO!" he yells. "I'll find you!" He pretends to stumble, and then once they're out of sight, he doubles back.

It's time to deal with the panda.

Spider-Man runs onto the scene – *annoying park with its annoying lack of buildings!* The woman dressed like a panda is still on the green. She's pulled up a tree and is now swinging it at a group of what looks like park security guards.

"Hey!" Spidey yells, shooting his webs at the tree and pulling it out of her arms. She spins around, and he can see that under her panda hood she's a white woman with deep black makeup messily rubbed around her blue eyes.

"NO!" she bellows. "Not *you*!"

Spidey puts a hand against his chest, lenses wide and innocent.

"What'd *I* do? Have we met? I feel like I'd remember meeting an evil bear."

She growls and uproots another tree, ready to throw it at him. He jumps high into the air, flipping and shooting two webs down at the trunk in her hands before yanking it backwards so it falls heavily to the ground. Then he lands gracefully on it, crouching on the trunk, with the branches behind him.

"What gives, lady?!"

"Shut up, spider-freak! I just scored big, and I am *getting out of here*!" Instead of a tree, this time she picks up a fleeing tourist and *throws the tourist*. Spidey jumps up and shoots out webs in repeating bursts, webbing the guy up so he's safely hanging from a tree branch. His bumbag's a little worse for wear, though, covered in webbing and torn on the sides.

"Uh, sorry about that," Spidey calls as he zips back to the panda. She already has another random park-goer in hand. "PLEASE STOP!" He cups his hands around his mouth so the sound will carry.

"No can do, man! I gotta get out of here so I can buy an island, and you're in my way!"

Then she throws *that* person, and Spidey has to play catch with human beings for the next several minutes.

"This is not an effective battle strategy!" he huffs after putting down the fourth human projectile. They rasp out a *thank-you* before rushing off to get the heck out of the park.

The park security officers have all but abandoned the fight, which Spider-Man appreciates. At least he doesn't have to worry about them getting hurt! But he could still use their help. They're standing on the periphery, yelling things into the walkie-talkies on their shoulders.

"Get everyone out of here!" he yells back at them before jumping to get into closer quarters with the panda. He hopes he doesn't regret this. He sticks a web to a tree on one side of him and then another web to a tree on the other side. Pulling back hard, he slings himself forwards feet-first and connects squarely with the panda's gut. She lets out a loud *"OOF!"* and goes flying backwards.

Spidey wastes no time in following. Unfortunately, even lying on her back, she's ready when he lands in front of her. She does a kip-up onto her feet and follows that with a swift punch to his face. It's hard enough that he sees double for a second, and when he tucks and rolls out of the way, she comes back with another punch. It's more luck that she misses than any of his skill. From his spot on the ground, he jumps high up and onto the side of a tree.

"Who even *are* you?" he yells down, *thwip*ping a web at her hands at the same time.

"I'm *Panda-Mania!*" she yells back, arms up in a victory pose. Spidey's lenses narrow, and he looks at her with distrust.

"I can't tell if you're messing with me or not."

"It's a good name!" She starts running towards another tree. Spidey realises she's about to pull it up by its roots, so he pushes off and jumps high over her, flipping upside down and landing on his feet behind her so he can end this. Just as she gets to the trunk, he shoots out webs in quick succession until she is stuck tight to the tree, face-first, arms around it. He stands up straight, breathing heavily, and limps over to, *ugh*, Panda-Mania.

"Why are you like this?" he asks plaintively. She looks back at him, petulantly, her cheek smushed by the tree bark.

"I want an island."

Spidey sighs. "You ruined my date."

Just then he notices a woman from the protest, hiding behind a tree. He's glad to see she's still got her forearm crutches and her backpack.

"Hey!" he calls. "Hey, you!"

She peeks out from behind the tree. "Me?"

Spidey nods. "Yeah! Are you good? Like… do you have anywhere you need to be?"

"Yes, I'm good, and no, I don't have anywhere to be, I guess?" she says quizzically.

"Cool, cool, cool. Do you have a phone? Can you call, uh, whoever is supposed to deal with this? Park security, maybe? I really have something I need to get back to."

"Um, sure," she says, probably wondering what Spider-Man needs to be doing that isn't dealing with a lady in a panda suit who just wrecked half the park. He doesn't stay to explain. Running back to where he left his clothes, he's horrified to see that they're not there anymore.

The bush he shoved them under wasn't a bush so much as a small shrub, and someone must have found them.

Ughhh, I loved that sweatshirt! And so much for getting back to MJ! If ever he knew there was someone somewhere deciding how his life was going, he knew it today, and he knew they hated him.

He sits down on the ground, cross-legged, and takes his phone out.

> **HEY MJ! BAD NEWS: FELL IN A LAKE AND AM SOAKING WET. GONNA HEAD HOME TO CHANGE**

> **WILL SEE U LATER!! (??)**

> **OH AND I HAD A RLY GOOD TIME TODAY!!**

The little speech bubble pops up on the left side of the screen. The ellipsis animation just going…

And going…

And going.

He stands again and starts pacing back and forth. Should he say something else? *No. No, it's probably fine.* Or maybe he should—

Just as he's about to type something else, anything else, her message comes through.

> **GO GET CHANGED**

But, instead of a full stop, she used a laughing cat emoji to end her text. He can feel his face heat up under the mask, and he's smiling so hard his cheeks hurt. He's more thankful than usual for his mask right now because he is sure his expression is ridiculous. He looks down at himself again and moves to leave. He may as well try to find one of his clothes stashes. There's one down on 49th Street somewhere. But this time, he's definitely taking the train.

This is so typical. Can't even get through a date without some C-list villain showing up and ruining it.

The worst part was MJ WAS ABOUT TO KISS ME.

The arc lamp stands tall on the floor of Sandman's abandoned warehouse. He feels delirious, and he hasn't stopped grinning. Though if the reaction of the old lady while he was bringing the lamp in was any indication, it wasn't a particularly *friendly* smile on his face. There's still that itch though, softly going all along his spine. He looks at the lamp again.

Who gives a crap?! I have it. Soon, I'm gonna get paid. Forget the cops; forget Two Rocks and his Maggia goons. Forget Spider-Man.

There's a roll of copper wire sitting on his mattress, and he grabs it now, along with a pair of wire cutters. Unwinding a few long strands, he cuts them cleanly. Once they're free, he weaves them together in a thick braid. There's a generator in the corner that he stole from a flat a few streets over, and he uses it now, wrapping one end of the braid around the exposed battery. He takes the other end and wraps it around the dilapidated power cord ends of the lamp itself.

He takes a deep breath. *The moment of truth.*

When he flips it on, the generator comes to life with a loud hum that fills the space – but he's not worried. This dank, wet place is as deserted as they come. The only roommates he has here are the rats, and they don't bother him. Not after he taught them a lesson on their first night together.

The generator hums, and Sandman waits, staring at the lamp. Waiting for it to do something. Anything. A few minutes go by.

"Why ain't it workin'?" he mutters, perplexed. His brows come down low over his eyes as he looks at the thing like it just insulted his mother. He puts a finger against the wiring, and his whole body vibrates from the shock. He snatches his hand back, hissing in pain. But now he knows it's definitely not a power issue.

He walks closer to the lamp itself, looking it up and down. That itch gets a tiny bit louder, more insistent. He sees the coils of the lamp, and the iron pole holding it all up. He sees the black box that holds all the wiring, but... he looks closer and lets his sand flow into the space between. The glass tubes are *empty*. Somehow, he knows that whatever is missing, whatever thing is meant to go inside those rods and between those two coils, is important. Then he notices a small chunk of *something* left behind. He can feel it sitting there. It's radiating some kind of waves, and it's small and dark. He sits heavily onto the floor, dropping his head into his hands.

He'd been so close.

How could I miss this?!

All of a sudden, something pushes him flat onto his back. He tries to push up against the floor, but he can't. The thing is all around him, keeping him solid, not letting him puddle into sand. He's being pressed from all sides, tighter and tighter and *tighter*. He lets out a high whine because it's all his vocal cords can do in the moment. He's never been so uncomfortable in his life. The sand grains that make him are grating against each other and every part of him wants to expand and be free, but he can't. He wants to scream; he tries to re-form into anything, but there's too much of him and the force around him is winding him closer and closer together.

He can't—
    he can't—
        he can't—
            he *can't*.

Just as he's about to give up, to fall into that tiny grain of sand that holds every part of who he is – the pressure lets up and he's free. He immediately grows as big as he can in the space of the warehouse and morphs his fists into sledgehammers. Out of the corner of his eye, he sees the bright screen of his phone light up on his bed. He turns towards it and picks it up in one giant sand hand.

> NOW YOU KNOW. YOU CANNOT FAIL. AGAIN.

> FIND THE ELEMENT. BRING OUR HOME.

CHAPTER EIGHTEEN

It's an Odd Day at school, which means it's a day that starts with Dr Shah's class. When Peter runs into the room thirty seconds after the late bell, the first person he sees is MJ. She brightens at his entrance and waves; he sends her a small one back and can feel a blush working its way up his neck and into his cheeks. He hasn't seen her since their painfully interrupted date. They've made do with texts, but it's not the same as seeing her in person and he is not prepared. What if she actually had a horrible time on their date and was just being nice?

He rushes to his seat as Dr Shah says, "Hello, Mr Parker, thank you for joining us." There's a note of sarcasm in his greeting. There's some light laughter, but Dr Shah is smiling when he says it, so Peter doesn't feel too bad, though he does sink just a tad lower into his seat. This is the first time in a while he's been late, trying to fulfil his promise to make Dr Shah's life a tiny bit easier in whatever way he can.

"As I was saying, we'll use today to do some group work. I hope your projects are all coming along nicely. Don't forget you need to turn in a summary of the project and some of your findings by next class, so maybe spend some time working on that paper today."

Peter's eyes go wide realising he's going to have to talk to MJ *right now*. He'd really hoped to use the class time to amp himself up into not being a complete weirdo when they finally spoke. He feels like *such* a dork for having to run off because she thinks he fell in a lake. *Sorry, MJ, I had to leave because I'm basically a cartoon character.*

He crosses his arms on his desk and rests his head on them.

"Okay." Dr Shah claps his hands together. "Go ahead and get to work. Feel free to come up to my desk and ask questions if you need help."

Peter looks back in panic when he hears desks start to scrape along the floor as students get into their groups. He stands up to help organise the desks closest to him, and maybe just to have something to do when MJ – "Hey,

Peter" – gets there. He turns to face her and immediately trips over his own feet, managing to sit down hard in his seat instead of on the floor. She bites her lip, and he's guessing she's trying not to laugh. Her hair is in a ponytail today, and she looks *very* pretty in a dress with bright splotches of flowers printed all over it.

"Hey, MJ," he says dejectedly.

"Hey, Peter," she says again, tone decidedly lighter. She slides into the desk right next to his, and he gives her a small smile.

"You look nice," he says quietly, and he's gratified to see her duck her head, bashful. *Maybe the date wasn't bad.*

"Thank you," she replies, and looks like she's about to say more when Maia and Randy join them. She closes her mouth abruptly, but Peter's distracted by Maia's expression. She looks back and forth between Peter and MJ, her grin getting wider and wider. Everyone pulls out their project materials, but before anyone can start talking about activism, Maia speaks up.

"So, how did the rest of the date go?" she asks, resting her chin on her steepled fingers.

Randy, who had just taken a sip of water, nearly chokes and sets the bottle down so he can cough and laugh at the same time. He finally clears out his throat and then shoots them both a thumbs-up.

"I definitely need to hear *all* about how this went

down," he says. But, unfortunately, Randy's not the only one who heard Maia's question.

"Date?" Flash Thompson walks up the group, looking at Peter and MJ incredulously. "You?" He points at Peter. "And *you*?" He points at MJ. MJ's face flushes, and her chin juts out. She glares at Flash, who is now standing over her, leaning on her desk. Peter's about to speak up when MJ stands up, forcing Flash to step back.

"What is *that* supposed to mean?" she asks icily.

Flash sneers and barks out a mean-sounding laugh. Then he gestures to all of his six-foot, blond-haired, letterman-jacket-wearing self.

"I mean, I'm right here, MJ. Come on."

Peter curses his spider-powers – *Why can't spiders disappear when they want?!* But then MJ *scoffs*, and Peter has never liked her more. Maia's standing now, too, and looking at Flash like he's gum on the bottom of her shoe.

"Flash, can you please shut up?" MJ says, and Maia joins her for the end of her sentence.

The two of them telling Flash to shut up in tandem is music to Peter's ears. Randy starts actually guffawing at the dumbfounded look on Flash's face. Peter knows that if he wanted to, he could make Flash Thompson stop talking but he *really* appreciates MJ and Maia speaking up. Maia turns on her heel and walks up to Dr Shah's desk.

"Excuse me, sir?" she asks.

Dr Shah looks up from his computer. "Yes, Maia?"

"Do you think my group could go work in the library? The classroom is" – she pauses, glancing back at Flash with absolute disdain before turning forwards again to Dr Shah – "distracting."

"Of course." He scribbles out a few passes for their group. "Just don't forget – summary is due next class!"

Peter, Randy, MJ and Maia pack up their things and walk out of the classroom. Peter hears Alice Tam shout back to Flash as they're leaving, "DANG, FLASH, YOU WANT SOME ALOE? BECAUSE YOU LOOK *BURNT*."

Peter wonders if he can pull a muscle smiling. They chat as they're walking down the hall, Randy and Maia leading the way with MJ and Peter trailing behind. They're laughing about Flash and how ridiculous he is. Peter knocks MJ's shoulder with his and then reaches down to take her hand. She doesn't stop talking, but she grips his hand tight.

That evening, Peter's at home, getting ready to go out patrolling. He already said goodnight to Aunt May before putting his suit on, and the neighbourhood is dark. He opens his window and puts one boot up on the sill. Then he hesitates, looking back at the computer sitting on his desk.

Every night, he's checked the free phone number he signed up for, to see if there's any messages – just in case Addison Alredge decides to call back. And every night it's blank, with no messages. Tonight, tired of being disappointed, he chose not to. There hasn't been a peep from Sandman, though he heard chatter from some Maggia goons he caught the other day that the family was not too happy with Flint Marko for messing up that last job. Peter's not sure what to make of *that* team-up, but it sounds like it was over before it started.

He scoped out the mansion for a few nights, barring the one before his date with MJ, when he got distracted on the way by that bank robbery. The one that took all night to stop. But other than that, he'd been outside Addison's house every night for the last few weeks.

Sighing heavily, Peter steps back into his room and pulls off his mask, sitting at the desk and opening his laptop. He waits the ten minutes for it to boot up and then pulls up the free phone site, using a VPN to keep his IP address private. He's not even sure why he's doing it. *Why would anything be different tonight?*

He types in his name and password and waits for the page to load – it's all blue and white and graphic, advertising *free calls abroad*. But there, in the top corner of the screen, there's a little red dot on top of the bell symbolising notifications. His breath catches in his throat, and he clicks.

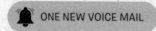 **ONE NEW VOICE MAIL**

"Spider-whatever, Spider-person, this is Addison Alredge. I—yes, *Brewster*, I am on the phone—apologies, but we need to meet. I need to tell you a story." Alredge rattles off an address, which Peter recognises as the same home he's been surveilling. "Please come as soon as possible; we'll be here, waiting."

The time and date on the message are from about forty-five minutes earlier. Peter's not sure what changed in the time since his last interaction with Addison. And who is Brewster? And a *story*? He has to admit, it sounds more intriguing than worrying.

This whole thing gets weirder by the minute.

Spidey swings uptown – he was *going* to take the train as far as he could go, but the A train stalled and everyone got kicked out at Port Authority, so now he's swinging. He wonders idly if there's any sort of charitable cause he can sign up for to get the subway some help because from what he can tell, it really needs it. He'll have to ask MJ next time they hang out. He grins, thinking about how it could be fuel for conversation.

He turns onto Broadway at Columbus Circle. When he passes by Lincoln Center, he wonders if that might be another good date spot. *Maybe I can save my money for tickets to… something. The ballet? Is it the ballet at Lincoln Center? Does MJ like the ballet?*

Something to file away as *another* thing to talk about, he thinks, trying not to smile too big while he's swinging because it seriously dries his mouth out. Another twenty minutes flying his way uptown, a quick hitch-hike on the roof of a city bus, and he's finally back on the corner of Addison's street, turning onto Oceanic Avenue. He swings to a stop in front of the mansion, dropping directly onto the pavement leading to the front door as he did all those nights ago and stares up at the big house. It feels strange not watching it from afar, especially knowing this time he might actually get some answers! Shaking himself out of his reverie, Spidey walks up to the door and rings the doorbell. It opens immediately, like the person on the other side had been waiting for the bell to be rung as a nicety before pulling it open.

"Hello?" Spider-Man asks. The man in front of him grimaces. He's tall and *old*, with a large white moustache covering his mouth entirely, and a beard that goes to his ears and then peters out somewhere near the top of his head, never quite making it to the middle. He's clearly dressed for bed in a pair of burgundy-and-white-striped pyjamas and a deep-black robe that makes his skin look paper-white.

"Mr Spider—"

"Man," Spidey supplies before he can say whatever he *thinks* Spidey's name is. The man just gives him an impenetrable look.

"Whatever you say. My name is Brewster Alredge. I believe you're here to speak to my husband." His words aren't particularly rude, but somehow Spidey gets the feeling that Brewster is not a fan of this meeting.

But he just nods once, and Brewster steps aside to let him in.

"Sooo," Spidey starts, but then completely loses track of what he's about to say as he steps into the home. It is absurdly opulent in way that he imagines most rich people's homes must be. Not that he's seen a lot of rich-people houses. The floor is black-and-white marble, and there's an honest-to-God spiral staircase with an ornately carved bannister going up to a second floor. The doors all have gold doorknobs and some sort of illustrative reliefs pressed into the wood. He's so distracted by the luxury around him, he almost doesn't even notice the ancient man sitting in a cushy dark wooden chair lined with green velvet and a plushy pillow. The man is dressed in a pair of pyjamas that match Brewster's and a warm-looking robe, only his is a light grey instead of black. On the label are the initials AAA. This must be Addison. Brewster has taken the seat next to him and is speaking to him in low tones. Addison catches Spidey's eye, and he grins sharply.

"Hello, Spider-Man. Brewster doesn't think we should be having this meeting."

Brewster glares at his husband.

"*I* think we should be going to the proper authorities, Addie."

Addison Alredge is a thin man and has clearly been on this earth a long, long time with his wispy white hair and his sharp angles, but his eyes are clear and searching.

"Spider-Man, I owe you an apology," he starts, which is the *last* thing Spider-Man expected to hear. He's not sure anyone's ever apologised to him before.

"Oh, uh," he says, uncomfortable. "It's fine?"

Brewster rolls his eyes.

"I need to apologise for my hubris the last time we spoke. You see… the lamp has been taken, just like you said it would be."

"What?!" Spider-Man starts. How could he not have known? He's been here *every* night except – it must have been the night of the bank robbery. *No!*

CHAPTER NINETEEN

"Listen," Addison continues, "it's no one's fault but mine." Spidey isn't sure he agrees, but he nods for Addison to continue. "My family has long been isolated from the trouble of the arc lamp. It's been generations since it was last used! We all heard the stories growing up, but… surely if there had been no trouble in all this time, then what's the harm? But—"

"But we *never* should have offered it to the museum!" Brewster interjects, and Spidey realises this is a fight that has *been* ongoing and he's just coming in midway.

Addison glares at Brewster and then continues speaking. "I should have donated my old film prints, but

I offered the lamp on a whim. Unthinking. I honestly didn't even think it worked."

"Unthinking is right," Spidey hears Brewster mutter. But Addison either doesn't hear or is choosing not to respond. *Rich people are weird.*

"But no one should have to pay the price should the conducting rod fall into the wrong hands."

"The conducting rod?" Spider-Man asks, unsure what Addison is talking about.

"It's what powers the fury, Spider-Man. Keep up. Or perhaps I better start at the beginning with my great-great-great-uncle, Arlo Alredge."

It's 1899, and Arlo Alredge is napping on the far end of his family's fields in northern New York. He's just at the border of the Arlo farms – named for *his* great-grandfather, which leads to a painful number of mix-ups where he has to admit that he's not the owner, just a third son who likely won't inherit much. Anyway, Arlo is sleeping, head propped up on a tree root and eyes covered by a bandanna. His legs are crossed, and his hands are settled on his stomach. A high-pitched sound enters his consciousness bit by bit, and he's slow to wake up. Slow, that is, until a burst of sound shocks him all the way awake and a large black stone hurtles out of the sky and lands about two feet away from his head, blasting his right ear clean off!

"Or, this is what family lore says," Addison acquiesces. "We know of course that if a meteor had landed that close to his head, he wouldn't have one anymore."

"Ew."

"But that's the nature of legend. He maintained it was a meteor, and so in this story, it's a meteor."

Arlo comes to, and there's a big block of *something* cratered in the ground next to him, and it's *glowing*. So, he pokes at it and he prods, and it's unlike any kind of metal or rock he's ever seen, especially since it's emanating some kind of light as far as he can tell. Its presence gives him an idea. Now, Arlo had just come from a big exhibition in the city. It was a live showing of a new technology that would be hitting the theatres soon, a new version of electrical lighting and sound systems. They'd be safer and longer lasting, with musical amplification, and, best of all from Arlo's perspective, *huge* moneymakers. He was something of a budding inventor himself – granted, his 'inventions' were usually more disasters that, if he were a tad less lazy, could have been turned into something great, but it could not be denied that Arlo enjoyed fiddling with things.

So, Arlo finds this rock, and Arlo has just been to see the newest wave in technology. What he does next is carry the rock to his workspace in the barn, where he has an old carbon arc lamp he'd purchased from a friend years earlier. He'd been tinkering with the lamp for ages, hoping to stumble into something new to patent but had thus far been unsuccessful. His family was decidedly unimpressed. But now, with this... *space rock*, he has something new to try!

With this meteor, Arlo is more driven than he's ever been. He eats, sleeps and breathes tinkering with this rock in his barn. Not long after it shows up, he figures out he can conduct *power* through the rock. It's after that his family notices that he's quiet and withdrawn, more fidgety, less apt to be the kind and funny man they thought they knew. One day, Arlo snaps at his mother, furious that she's burned his toast. Another, he kicks the dog out of the way as he storms out of the house and into the barn where he's begun to spend his days and nights.

But his rough edges pay off. Arlo comes out of the barn after a successful experiment to find his brothers working in the field. He's covered in dust and soot, and his grin is awful wolfish.

"I've done it!" he says, and his brothers look at him blankly.

"Done what?" the eldest Alredge, Jack, asks.

"I've created the *brightest light known to man*. Brighter than the sun!" But his brothers don't react how he wants. They just pause and then burst out laughing at him.

"With that rock you found? Same ole Arlo," they say. "Tall tales and no good deeds."

"That rock from the *sky*," Arlo seethes before retreating, the sound of their laughter following him back into his barn.

What he does manage to do, despite his family's disregard, is build a lamp the likes of which has never been seen. He's shaped the long oblong meteor into two rods, which he fit into the old mould of the carbon lamp, where the carbon would typically go. It's a strange material, he knows it now. Definitely not metal and definitely not rock. But he fits them into the arc lamp, and he turns it on, and it nearly knocks his eyes out of his head. The next time, he puts on a pair of shaded glasses, and it's a mite easier to see. He only ever turns it on for a few seconds at a time, worried that he'll run out of power and material before he can make a demonstration and sell the patent. Something, not quite luck, is on Arlo's side. He takes some trips into the city and finds a few seedy investors and loan sharks willing to give him money at high rates, project unseen. He'd hoped his tale of the space rock and his prowess as an inventor would be enough, but in the end, he has to resort to using the Alredge name. It leaves a bitter taste in his mouth, but he's able to rent a theatre for a limited engagement.

It's a small theatre, mind you. No more than thirty people can fit into the space, but it's what Arlo can get for the money he's been able to raise. And he knows the thirty seats will be full, with people wondering what Arlo Alredge's grandson will have to show them. The night before opening day, Arlo walks into the hall. The curtain is a little moth-eaten but has been recently washed and mended. The floorboards are creaky but clean. Arlo stands in the centre of the seating and looks at the stage and nods once. He imagines the show can go for a few weeks at least. In all his preparation, in all the months leading up to this day, the rods have shown absolutely no deterioration whatsoever. He's been very careful with their use. This will be a way to make *his* name. He goes up the stairs to the stage where the lamp is already situated, stage right. He runs his fingers along the iron pipe making up its stand, one he's repurposed from an old farm tool, so the branding on the side still bears his grandfather's name. Though after this, the Arlo people remember will be *him*.

SPIDER-MAN'S SOCIAL DILEMMA

"So what happened, Mr Alredge?!"
"I'm getting there! Don't interrupt!"

The day of the exhibition dawns bright and clear. Arlo is feeding off the energy of the crowd, and he peeks out from behind the curtain. The vast majority of the thirty seats are filled with a wealthy elite – the latest fashions, jewellery and pocket watches glint in the sun coming through the windows. But there is a small contingency of people who won a ticket lottery. Arlo felt strongly that the crowd should be a mix of people. Ushers are giving out cheap sunglasses at the door, heightening the buzz in the room. Then the lights go low, and it's time.

"Ladies and gentlemen, welcome to the brightest day of your life," Arlo calls as he struts out onstage.

"How do you know what he said? I heard no one ever talked about it again."
"Spider-Man, I am a storyteller. Have you never heard of a thing called creative licence?"

The audience claps and whoops in excitement. Arlo picks a woman out of the crowd. She's got on a plaid dress, high-necked, with buttons all down her front. "You, there! Young lady."

In response, the woman points to herself in question.

"Yes, you! Have you ever looked directly into the sun?"

She laughs in response. "Of course not, Mr Alredge."

He goes on this way, singling people out in the audience, asking them ridiculous questions, building up the suspense. Then, when the crowd is in a fervour, he finally does it. "Ladies and gentlemen," he says again, "please place the tinted goggles on your faces." He waits until every last person has done so.

"AND NOW," he yells into the crowd, "THE TIME HAS COME. LET THERE BE LIGHT!" There's a quiet gasp at his small blasphemy, but the light comes on and the theatre rests in utter silence. Then someone gasps loudly. And finally, a barrage of applause hits Arlo's ear.

He is euphoric!

For the first time, ever, he leaves the lamp on. People start yelling questions from the audience, and Arlo starts strong. Answering without answering, not giving away any of his secrets. But then… the wood of the stage starts vibrating. Arlo looks towards the lamp, and he's not sure if he's imagining it or not, but behind the light, from the rods themselves, it seems like there's *something* coming off it in waves. He steps towards it.

The woman in the plaid dress from earlier screams out from the audience, "*My head! My head feels as if it's on fire!*"

Distracted, Arlo looks at the audience again. More people's voices are joining hers, screaming about pain in their heads. People are clutching their ears. Arlo's own head is filled with thoughts of violence and anger at the audience around him, but there's an infinitesimal part of him that knows he needs to get to the lamp. He tries to step towards it, but there's a strange pressure against him and he can't move forwards. He grunts, his arm outstretched, but he's still too far. The stagehands have fallen to the ground and are rolling, palms shoved up against their ears.

Then, all of a sudden, everything goes quiet. Arlo stops struggling; the audience is silent as death. He looks out at them, and they're wide-eyed and waiting. And then Arlo's memory goes completely blank.

"This is basically where our family story ends." Addison wipes his hands together like he's dusting off an invisible layer of narrative.

"This is horrifying, by the way," Spider-Man says

from where he's hanging, upside down from a web stuck to the ceiling.

"Tell me about it," Brewster mutters. But Addison's not finished.

"My grandmother, rest her soul, spent *years* trying to figure out what happened. Because no one there who lived to tell the tale ever told it. Not a single soul who left that place ever spoke of it again." He takes a deep breath and makes to wrap up his story.

"When Arlo eventually comes to, it's an hour later. His lamp stands before him, the glass of the bulb completely shattered, the power cord frayed. He cries out. Then he hears the moans coming from the audience. He turns from his point on the stage and sees a *mess* of humanity. Women have blood under their nails from scratching earrings out of their neighbours' ears. Men who have never lifted a finger in their lives have bruised and bloodied knuckles from trying to steal each other's gold watches and rings. More than one person didn't make it out alive."

At this, Spidey gasps, horrified by what he's hearing. And pieces of it are terrifyingly familiar. Beetle's dead-eyed stare flashes in his memory. Addison makes no notice, though, and just keeps going.

"My grandmother finally found the family of a newspaper boy who had been selling papers across the street that day. He'd heard the commotion and peeked in a window and seen the carnage for himself. The way he'd described it… the most intense violence he'd ever seen, all spurred on by coveting thy neighbour's riches. Of wanting and wanting more. And looking back, what we can surmise is that… *that* lamp? The one Arlo Alredge spent months of his life making? It made people absolutely mad with want. Absolutely furious with need. They legitimately could not help themselves, like they'd been infected by something. Like it was contagious just being near the thing. Thankfully, the reaction to the lamp seemed short-lived. It ended the very minute the lamp expired. Then Arlo packed up the broken pieces, put them away, and never spoke of it again."

CHAPTER TWENTY

"That is... one heck of a story," Spider-Man says, slowly inching down so he can drop onto the floor. Brewster is looking at him strangely. "What?" Spider-Man asks, now right-side up.

"Don't you get woozy from being upside down so long?" Brewster asks, one thick eyebrow raised. Spidey shrugs.

"Nah, I think it's the whole being-part-spider thing." Both Addison and Brewster give him appalled looks. Spidey raises up both his hands, and his lenses go wide. "Kidding! Kidding!" They gawk at him. "So, what happened after that?" he asks, trying to get the conversation back on track.

Addison shrugs.

"As a boy, I read through some of Arlo's old journals. They only exist up to the day of the event; he never wrote a word after. But there was a marked difference between who he was before he started using that meteor and after."

"And it *was* a meteor, you're sure? Because it sounds like no one really believed Arlo," Spidey interjects.

"I don't know what earthly material could have had that kind of effect on a crowd, so I'm inclined to believe it was extraterrestrial in nature," Alredge answered. "On top of how much Arlo changed. That is one thing that's for sure. Before the lamp, he wanted to be known, to be remembered. After, he was obsessed with entitlement, with deserving more, with getting his due; he felt he should be in control – no matter the cost. There was so much violence in his books." Addison shakes his head, mourning an ancestor he never knew for the choices he'd made. "A shame." Brewster puts his hand over Addison's, which is resting on the arm of his chair. "I never want anyone to go through something like that because of my family again."

Spider-Man thinks back to the lamp as he remembers seeing it in the museum – he can't recall if the rods were actually inside of it. It might have been, but he's not sure.

"Sir… were the rods still in the lamp when you donated it?" Spidey asks, somewhat clumsily, knowing he needs to ask but wanting to give Addison some space. Addison flinches but takes the question gracefully enough. He pushes himself up from the chair, grasps the head of the cane that has been leaning next to him, and walks slowly past Spider-Man. He stands in front of a portrait of someone who must be an old Alredge from, Spidey isn't sure, but probably at least a hundred years ago.

"My family has hidden the elemental rods for years, unwilling to accidentally set it off by doing something drastic in an attempt to destroy it. They were understandably wary of involving outsiders, fearing the impact of it on society as a whole. After your last call" – Addison turns back to Spider-Man – "I separated the lamp and the rods, just in case. And then I kept the rods somewhere safe. But I fear it's too late. I should have done it from the beginning. It had just been so long, you have to understand, I got complacent."

He's breathing heavily now, and Spider-Man thinks that all the talking must have winded him. Brewster stands and walks over to his husband to offer his arm, glaring at Spider-Man on the way. Spidey again lifts his hands in apology.

"Hey! I didn't *ask* for a compelling, impressively told narrative!" This time Addison shoots him a dirty look. "I appreciate it." He directs this at Addison. "But I didn't *ask*." He says to Brewster again, "Soooo…"

"Sewing is an act, not the beginning to a sentence," Brewster says, his mouth tight. Spider-Man's lenses narrow, and he points two fingers at his eyes and then the two fingers at Brewster in the universal sign for *I am watching you; you are on thin ice*. Then he turns back to Addison.

"Where are the rods now?"

Addison taps his fingers against the top of his cane.

"It's in here."

Spider-Man leans forwards, as if he needs to get closer because he hasn't heard correctly.

"What?"

Addison taps the cane again.

"I said, it's in here."

Spider-Man turns away and faces the door. He puts his palms against his mask and pulls down at his cheeks in frustration. Then he takes a deep breath and twists back to look at Addison and Brewster.

"Mr Alredge, I *so* appreciate the fact that you shared this story with me. I *really* do. But – and I am *sorry* for having to say this to you, because I totally respect you – do you think that you, an eighty-five-year-old man, are the best security system for this terrifying piece of maybe-alien matter that a super villain is currently trying to steal from you?" Spider-Man's voice has got higher and higher as he goes on, while Addison's face lowers further and further into a glower.

"You think I'm *eighty-five years old*? I am *seventy*, and I am *recovering* from a racquetball accident!" he roars.

Spider-Man takes a step back just as Brewster starts to… laugh.

"I told you," he chokes out. "I told you not to keep it on your person, Addie, but *nooo*."

"I know what I'm doing!" Addison says, now more sullen than angry.

"That's what you said when you met my mother and remind me how *that* went."

Spider-Man is starting to feel a bit agonised at having to witness what is clearly some kind of old married couple's lovers' spat.

"If we could just—" Spider-Man starts to say.

"It went *great*," Addison interrupts.

"Oh, did it?" Brewster asks drily. He's seated again, inspecting the edge of his armchair in faux idleness.

"So, anyway, guys…"

"I have a plan, Brewster! I'm not completely out of touch, you know!" Addison bursts out, breathing heavily again. And Brewster jumps to his feet and is at Addison's side in a second, Brewster's arm around his shoulders.

"I only want you to be safe," Brewster says quietly. It's very sweet, and Spidey's feeling all sorts of warm affection for these two random old lovebirds. Then he rewinds and realises Addison used the word *plan*.

"Did you say '*plan*'?" he asks loudly, grateful for a way

to pull the focus back to the matter at hand. *And so we can stop talking about these old people's love lives, even if it is pretty cute.*

"My *plan*, my intent, was always to get it into your hands," Addison says with a plaintive note. He pulls a long round cylinder out of his cane and hands it to Spider-Man.

The first thing Spidey notices is that his spider-sense is quiet. The rods are heavy but somehow feel full of air. It's such a strange sensation that Spider-Man nearly drops them. There's a piece of tape around the centre, where he assumes the two pieces of the rod are held together, and there's a piece broken off one of the tips, like it's snapped apart. "You can keep it safe. I know you can," Addison says, wrapping Spidey's fist around it. "But keep it far away from you and anyone you care about – I've only had it nearby for... well, a few days, and it's been—"

Brewster picks up the sentence. "Difficult," he says. "It's been very difficult."

"Did it... Did it make you guys scary angry?" Spider-Man asks. "How bad is it?"

"No! No, not really. We believe it needs a power source to really affect people, but in the last few days, being in such close contact, it's... *Something* is happening when we get near it. It's uncomfortable to be around. I wish I could tell you more than just be careful and be safe."

Spider-Man nods, but his shoulders slump slightly at

the daunting task ahead of him. He knows he can keep the cylinder away from Sandman, but now he has to figure out where to put it.

Sandman is rocking back and forth in his dingy space. His mind runs a mile a minute.

How did that thing... What was – how did it do that to me? How did it tie me up like that? How was it so strong? Nothin's ever gotten ahold of me like that.

The lamp is still standing, quiet and inanimate, but the back of Sandman's neck prickles, like the artefact is going to come to life any minute and end him. If he doesn't get the other piece of this thing, he's going to be taken off this planet. *Permanently.* He knows it, deep inside, he can feel it.

But what am I supposed to do? I got the freakin' lamp – how am I supposed to find this other element thing?!

Sandman stands up and inches towards the artefact. He ducks down and looks at that small piece of the missing rod and shudders. It's calling to him but repelling him at the same time. Then he growls and grasps the lamp in one large hand, about to throw it at the wall, his body shaking with fury now, not fear.

His muscles tense and then relax. He takes a step back. He won't let this stop him from getting what's his.

Those rods weren't in the safe, so it could be anywhere. But I know someone who will know where it is. Addison Alredge. Might be time to take another trip uptown and twist a few screws.

It's either very late at night or very early in the morning when Sandman exits the old warehouse. There's a chill in the air, and steam is rising off the subway grates. He dips back down into the subway and flies through the system. First under the river and then onto the island of Manhattan before heading up, up, up to a street he's painfully familiar with.

Flowing into the house is old hat at this point, but when he gets to the foyer, he swerves to the right and creeps up the spiral staircase instead of going straight to the back of the home. When he makes it to the second-floor landing, he moves forwards. There's an open door on his right, and he can hear an old man snoring. Out of habit, he re-forms briefly to peek inside, but he doesn't find the right old man. This one's passed out in an armchair with a book on his lap, his mouth open, and breathing heavily. Sandman rolls his eyes. *What a loser.* He falls back into his sand form and keeps moving.

He can hear someone else in fitful sleep down the hall. His sand crawls in under the door, and there's Addison Alredge asleep in his bed like a sitting duck. Sandman moves forwards, sliding slowly up the bed valance and onto the soft blanket. He moves across the coverlet and then all at once covers Addison's mouth with a tightly packed, heavy mound of sand. Addison's eyes shoot open and he tries to scream, but Sandman just laughs.

"Ah, ah, ah, old man Alredge, you and me? We gotta *talk*."

An hour later, Sandman, back in his human form, walks whistling back into his neighbourhood in Brooklyn. It's *very* early morning now, and he passes by a crew of construction workers getting into work.

"Mornin'," he says jovially. They mumble back a few replies.

Sandman's in a good mood – he knows exactly who has the rod now. *The bug won't know what hit him.* His phone buzzes in his pocket, and he pulls it out.

FIND HIM. WE FIND IT. WE GROW.

It's *early*, but Peter's awake, lying on his bed and staring up at the ceiling. He can't stop thinking about the story that Addison told him. He'd used the word *contagious* – somewhere in the history, someone must have thought that behaviours had spread through the crowd like a virus. *Is that what happened to Beetle? And how is Sandman involved?*

The problem is, Peter can't tell if Sandman is being controlled by anything. The most interaction they've had since Spidey's chat with him in Brooklyn several weeks ago was the fight at Addison's – and they didn't exactly *talk*. Sandman *was* surprisingly vicious that day and driven in a way that Peter didn't recognise, but – *was he being controlled by something?*

Maybe Sandman has *way* bigger aspirations than Peter has ever realised. Maybe he has been wrong in assuming that Sandman was happy being a cog in someone else's wheel. And on top of all that, the way Addison had described Arlo was reminding him of something, but he couldn't figure out what. It's an itch he can't quite scratch.

He rolls onto his stomach and bangs his head into his pillow a few times, frustrated. He's about to give up and give in to sleep when his phone buzzes next to his head. He reaches over to grab it without looking and sees that it's a text from MJ.

> **HEY NIGHT OWL - SAW UR LIGHT ON, WANNA SNEAK OVER?**

Peter doesn't hesitate.

> **BE THERE IN 5**

He throws on a pair of tracksuit bottoms and sneaks out of the front door before crossing the lawn over to the Watsons'. MJ's waiting for him on her porch steps when he walks over. He immediately notices something's weird. She's not looking him in the eye, and she's *really* fidgety.

"Hey, MJ?" he sort of asks more than greets, his voice tentative and quiet in the early-morning light. She looks up at him then and gives him a worried look.

"Hey," she says. He gestures to the empty space next to her on the stair, and she nods, letting him know he's free to sit down.

He's on edge, though, and his leg starts bouncing, unease manifesting as soon as he sits. *Why is the mood so weird?* The wood of the stairs creaks with every movement of his foot.

"So," she starts.

And Brewster's voice pops into Peter's head at the most inopportune moment. He struggles to keep his features under control.

"Uh-huh," he says, hopefully not betraying the absurdity of his own brain.

"I…" She pauses, as if trying to figure out how to say whatever she needs to say. He waits, anxiety rising with each added second of silence. "I have something to tell you," she finally says.

Peter's stomach is in knots, and he's regretting the

street hot dog he grabbed on his way home. *Does MJ want to stop hanging out already? Did I do something wrong?*

He racks his brain, trying to think of what he could have possibly done, but is coming up completely blank. The only thing was leaving their date early, but he'd seen her since then and they were fine! She's biting her lip and looking at him now, and he realises he hasn't replied to her statement.

"You can tell me anything," he says, hoping it's the right call. She twists her fingers and then separates her hands, balling them into fists before laying them flat on the porch behind her and leaning back. She takes a deep breath and then turns her head so she's looking at him directly in his eyes.

"I—" she starts, and then takes another lungful of air. "I think you're Spider-Man."

CHAPTER
TWENTY-ONE

MJ bites her lip and waits. She wonders if she made a mistake bringing it up – but when she saw Peter's light on *and* when he answered her text, it felt like a sign. So, she powered her phone down and waited for him to get to her house.

Across from her, Peter looks completely and utterly shocked. *Am I wrong?* But then she thinks back to their date again – Peter disappears, and then Spider-Man just randomly shows up with Peter nowhere to be found? The same thing happened when Spider-Man showed up at their school. Peter mysteriously gone and – *oh!* – there's Spider-Man.

She found footage of the fight between Spider-Man and Panda-Mania on YouTube and watched it. Originally, she was pretty shaken and wanted to see how close she'd been to being in actual trouble – but when Spider-Man swung onto the scene, she was surprised. She always thought he was usually more of a midtown hero. Plus, she couldn't help but notice the way Peter tried to be *so* nonchalant about the *Bugle* social posts featuring Spidey – not to mention how he got all those sick photos of Spider-Man.

AND, she thinks, *how many times have I watched him sneak in and out of his house in the middle of the night?! Either he's Spider-Man, or Peter Parker has a* very *suspect night job that I'll need to tell May about as soon as we are done with this conversation.*

Peter starts running through a litany of protests.

"I—uh, what? I mean no. What? How could you even?" He laughs, the sound of it bordering on hysterical. "Spider-Man? Me? I *wish* I had that upper-arm strength, am I right?" he tries, but MJ shakes her head. She's not buying it. "Come on, how could I be Spider-Man? That dude's probably like twenty-five years old! I'm *sixteen*. Like I could be Spider-Man." He half scoffs and half laughs so it turns into a snort, and then she thinks he might have choked a little bit at the end. He clears his throat and then continues. "I can't be Spider-Man because I'm… I'm me. I'm not… you know." He gestures vaguely.

"Peter, just tell me the truth!" she exclaims. *This is ridiculous*, she thinks.

"MJ, if I was Spider-Man, why wouldn't I immediately join the football team so Flash Thompson would stop bullying me? In fact, why wouldn't *I* bully Flash Thompson?" he says, like he's got her. Like she won't have an answer for such a ridiculous question.

"Because you're a good person!" She punches him lightly in the arm.

He rolls his eyes. "Fine, why wouldn't I be rich or something? I bet Spider-Man is super rich."

"Why do you think *Spider-Man*, who clearly subsists on pizza and hot dogs, is rich?" She gives him a deadpan look.

"Okay, okay, if *I'm* Spider-Man, why do I live in Forest Hills instead of like... the middle of Manhattan with access to the coolest gadgets?"

"I don't know!" she says. "But I know you're him!"

"If I'm him," Peter finally says, a small amount of weariness in his tone, "why would I do this by myself?"

"Peter, don't pretend that I don't see what's in front of my face!" she says, feeling hurt and confused by his reaction. His eyes go wide, and he looks to the side, like he's thinking something through. She waits a few minutes, and eventually, he takes her hand. He pulls her away from her porch and deep into the Parkers' back garden, where there's an old swing set. She's never been on it. By the time she moved here, she'd already outgrown the playground. From the look of it, though, Peter hasn't been on it in a while, either. The chains are brown with rust, and black rubber seats are old and cracking in some places. But Peter plops down onto one and signals for her to take the other. She follows suit and falls back into the swing. They kick and swing back and forth for a minute or two. But MJ has visibly relaxed. She can wait for Peter to think through whatever he needs to.

Finally, he drags his feet along the ground and slows to a stop. He twists the swing towards her.

"Okay-you're-right-I'm-Spider-Man." He says it all in a rush, and it sounds like one word, like he's afraid he won't get it out if he breathes or pauses between the words.

MJ can't help it; she smiles wide and open-mouthed and lets out a squeal. "I *knew* it!" she says, and fist-pumps once. "I *knew it*! Of *course* you're Spider-Man, I mean, *obviously*."

Peter lets out a gasp of horror, and his face has paled. She realises what she's said and immediately backtracks.

"I mean, okay, it wasn't *easy* to figure out. Not obvious. Honestly, I didn't put two and two together until you disappeared on our date and Spider-Man just *happened* to appear. Then I saw a *Bugle* photo that went up that day, and there was something stuck to your boot and..." She grins ruefully. "It was a receipt from the bodega we went to. That cinched it. So, really," she continues, "there's probably no one else in the world who could have figured it out but me."

"Of *course* that's the photo they used," Peter groans. "I didn't realise because I honestly didn't even look at it. Having to read mean captions about yourself is not a good job, turns out." But his heart's not really in the complaint. His brain is going full tilt. *MJ knows I'm Spider-Man. What do I do? What does this mean? Is she safe?* MJ's voice cuts through his spiral and pulls him back into the moment.

"Is that why you wanted to get better at, like, social media or whatever?" she asks.

"Yeah... I was tired of being the butt of the *Bugle*."

She laughs a little at his expression. He squints at her, like it will help him look inside her brain. "Are you sure you're okay with, you know, all this?" he asks. Her eyes grow big in the brightening day, and she looks at him like she thinks he's messing with her.

"Yes! This is *awesome*. Like... you help so many people, just because you're, well, like I said... you're good. That's *awesome*," she repeats. She says it so matter-of-factly that Peter's momentarily taken aback by how thankful he is that MJ's the one who figured it out. And MJ's the one he gets to share his secret with.

Oh man! I can share this with her – I have someone to talk to*!*

"Hey, MJ—"

"Hmm?" she asks, concentrating on pumping her legs so she can swing.

"Can I ask you a question about a case I'm working on?"

She immediately slows to a stop and looks at him, brow furrowed and chin up. She pulls her swing closer to his.

"Case, like… a Spider-Detective?" she jokes. He pulls a face and pushes her away, but she just comes back and knocks against him. There's an uncanny ease to their interaction. MJ is being totally normal – *like I'm not a complete weirdo for putting on a suit and swinging around New York*. He's laughing quietly with her, and he feels a sense of rightness.

Plus, I've gotta admit, it feels good to have someone I can be completely honest with. It's been a really long time.

"Yes, like a Spider-Detective," he finally says, the corner of his mouth quirked up in a half grin. "You remember that guy Sandman?"

MJ thinks for a second, slowly twisting back and forth on her swing, a finger to her chin.

"Yeah, I think so? He's one of those super-bad guys, right?"

"Yeah, that's him. So, a while back…" And Peter tells her the whole story. About the MOMI, the lamp, Beetle,

Sandman, Addison, all of it. He just blurts it all out like a big pile of please-help-me-with-my-problem. By the time he's finished, though, it feels like there's a huge weight off his shoulders in just being able to *tell* someone.

"So where's this supposed alien thing?" she asks when he's finished talking. He pauses, not sure if he should even say it out loud. When Addison had handed it to him, he knew he couldn't bring it home. He couldn't endanger Aunt May or his neighbourhood that way. It needed to go somewhere where it couldn't affect anyone. But where would it be safe?

Then he had remembered the walks he and Uncle Ben used to go on. Something that a lot of people didn't think of when they thought of Queens was just how much of the borough was covered in cemeteries. And those cemeteries made for *excellent* walks when your uncle wanted to be all philosophical. In one such cemetery, there was an old crypt. It was so old the family name was completely illegible. It really grossed Peter out, but then Uncle Ben had showed him a loose brick on the side of the tomb and behind it were years of random paraphernalia left there by kids of the Parker family. Old buttons, a bubble gum wrapper with a joke on it. The only people who knew about it were in their family – which now meant just Peter and Aunt May.

"I mean, maybe you shouldn't say it," MJ says, realising his hesitation. "It's probably better. The less people who know, but I actually just thought of something else…" she says, pensive. "So… Beetle was acting super strange and vicious? What about Sandman?" she asks.

"Beetle *definitely*, Sandman… it's tough," he admits. "I haven't had a lot of interaction with him, but he's always mad? I guess he seems a little more… I dunno, driven? Ambitious? But like, viciously ambitious. Like he doesn't care who he hurts?"

MJ looks at him for a second and then raises her eyebrows like he should be making a connection. *But what?* He gives his head a tiny shake.

"Doesn't that sound like something you've heard before?" she asks. "Because between Beetle and Sandman, it sounds a lot like what I was feeling and seeing before I stopped using my phone so much." She jumps up and starts pacing. "I wonder if something's affecting Sandman the way it was affecting me? Oh my gosh!" She stops suddenly and stares at Peter, looking like she's about to yell out the word *Eureka!* "Peter! Didn't you say Sandman *and* Beetle were at the museum that day, too? The day the weird alien element thing was there? Do you think…?" she starts.

Peter slaps a palm against his head.

"You know what, you must have all been there when the lamp accidentally got turned on!" *That* is what he had been thinking about when he was going through Addison's story again. "MJ! You're a genius," he says, but then stops short when he sees the look on her face. She seems anxious now, instead of victorious like she had seconds earlier.

"Peter... do you think it's in our phones?!"

Oh no.

"Do you have your phone on you now?" he asks, suddenly very worried. If that thing is in her phone and it heard them talking...

"No!" she says quickly. "No. I left it under the blanket on my porch. And it was off the whole time you were there. For one thing, I've been trying to be, you know, like, more *here*," she says, waving at the empty space between them. "But for another, I've been suspecting something was up with my phone for a while. But I thought it was some big corporate-overlord thing... not alien meteors!" Peter lets out a huge sigh of relief. MJ slaps a fist against her open palm. "Okay, I have research to do."

Peter blinks, surprised. "What?"

"Well, if this happened to me and to Sandman, maybe, I *bet* there were other people there that day who went through the same thing. I saw a little bit of it when I was looking it up ages ago – I'm sure I could find those examples again. And maybe then we can figure out *how* this thing is... doing whatever it's doing."

"Creepily infiltrating brains?" Peter asks, caustically. But then he shakes it off because MJ is going to *help him*. "It's also a super-small window of time. Addison's sure that the rod needs power to work, and the museum employee told me it was only on for fifteen seconds. And you were only there for—"

"Like, ten minutes! Tops! That is going to really narrow it down!" MJ is nodding her head, clearly already thinking about how to move forwards, and Peter bites the inside of his cheek to stop the grin on his face from looking manic.

"You are the best," he says. He gets up from where he's been swinging lightly and stands in front of her. He takes her hand. "Seriously, thank you so much. This is… It really means a lot," he finishes, faltering a little at the end. MJ's cheeks redden and she looks away.

"It's not a big deal."

"It *is* a big deal!" he disagrees, vehement in his opposition. She just smiles and pulls her hands back. She pushes her hair behind her ears and looks away again.

"I better get back. I'm gonna be a *zombie* at school today." And then, before Peter knows it's happening, she's kissed him on the cheek and taken off. "Bye, Peter!" she calls.

He lays a hand against his cheek where she kissed him, and he knows he's grinning like an idiot and that his life just got a little more complicated, but in this moment, nothing matters except Mary Jane Watson.

Peter still hasn't stopped smiling when he walks into the *Bugle* a few days later. Or at least, he doesn't think he has. He hums as he walks by Tommy and Rodrigo, singing a bit of a song as he taps his security card on the entrance to walk through, and straight-up *belts* a verse in the lift.

Unfortunately, that good mood evaporates pretty quickly when he steps out onto the seventeenth floor.

"You want me to do *what*?!" J. Jonah Jameson's voice carries all the way to the lifts. Peter hitches his bag onto his shoulder more tightly and takes a deep breath. He wonders if the employees sent Jonah the letter.

"Be nicer about *Spider-Man*?!"

It looks like the *Bugle* staff *did* send him the letter. Peter wonders if he should just go home and call in sick. *No! If I can fight Electro and Scorpion, I can handle J. Jonah Jameson.* He taps his card against the reader next to the glass doors and walks onto his floor. When he makes it to his desk, Jameson is red-faced and panting. Peter is sure that if this were a cartoon, there would be actual steam coming out of Jameson's ears. He's surrounded by several people, including Sushant, Kayla *and* Mr Robertson. Peter notices that Ned Leeds is conspicuously absent. The younger employees seem nervous but confident. Peter sits quietly at his desk, not really wanting to get involved. This feels quite literally way above his pay grade.

"You signed off on this?!" Jameson is demanding of Mr Robertson.

"Jonah, they're not wrong. It's impacting the *paper*, and I *know* you care about that. When we editorialise about Spider-Man's actions, it's a bad look. We should be reporting the facts," Mr Robertson replies, his voice even and steady.

"Who says these aren't facts?!" Jameson growls. He's trying to pace back and forth in the small space, and the staff keep moving around him. If he wasn't so worried about being noticed, Peter would probably laugh.

"I sent through all of Peter's captions, which accurately state what Spider-Man was doing at the time of the photos," Kayla speaks up. Peter is both gratified and *horrified*. Jameson spins around to look at him. Peter's never been so nervous in his life, which says a lot about this particular moment, considering what he spends his nights doing.

"That kid?! He's a *kid*! He probably thinks Spider-Man's just a do-gooder in a mask. If he's such a do-gooder, *why's he gotta hide his face*?!" Jameson asks, and Peter realises it's directed at *him*.

"Um…" he says eloquently. "Maybe because… he's trying to keep… his family safe?"

"PSHAW!" Jameson yells. "You're all fired! Get out of my sight!"

Mr Robertson sighs, rubbing at his temple. The fluorescent light above him flickers once and then comes back steady.

"No one's fired. Jonah, please listen to reason. Did you read past the first sentence of the letter?"

Jameson mumbles something in response, and Robertson answers again.

"Then *read the letter*, Jonah."

Jameson throws up his hands.

"Fine!" he yells. "I'll read the letter and then give you my *honest opinion*." He storms off.

Mr Robertson turns back to the crowd of employees and shrugs his shoulders. "Believe it or not, that was a success. He'll read it, and he'll come up with a solution."

Peter hears Kayla scoff, in obvious disbelief. He's kind of with her right now – he's been in the same room as J. Jonah Jameson a few times, and he cannot see that man changing his mind.

CHAPTER TWENTY-TWO

There's a commotion going on a few streets south of Spider-Man on 2nd Avenue. Kids running in the opposite direction were yelling about broken windows and massive amounts of *sand*. Spidey's swinging and zipping as fast as he can down the avenue. If it's Sandman, he's got to get down there and see if he can subdue him. *Maybe even get him some help if my and MJ's theory is right!*

The screams and sounds of demolition get louder as he gets closer. He finally drops onto the scene, and it is utter chaos. People are running; there's dust and smoke everywhere. Spider-Man webs himself up to the top of a traffic light.

"SANDMAN!" he yells out. "FLINT, WHERE ARE YOU?! COME OUT!"

He hears a voice chuckling from somewhere below him. It's not a happy chuckle; it's dark and desperate. Spider-Man jumps off the pole and barrel-rolls in the air to land on the ground, crouched and ready to fight. Flint Marko towers before him, massive and almost amorphous in his visage. "Yer gettin' predictable, bug," he says, quieter than Spidey was expecting.

"Well," Spider-Man says, unsettled but trying to find his footing. "You're getting lazy, Marko. What are you doing here?"

Sandman sends a huge sledgehammer of a sand fist his way, and Spidey launches up and over so he's on the other side.

"Get out!" Spider-Man waves at people cowering behind some rubbish bins. "Go!" They take off down a side street, running as fast as they can.

"I ain't doin' nothin, brat. Just mindin' my own business, and you show up to give me trouble! Like clockwork!"

Sandman doesn't sound scared or frustrated; he sounds confident. He sounds like he's been waiting for Spider-Man to show up. It's throwing Spidey off his game. He shoots a mass of webbing at Marko, who just morphs around the stuff, letting it go through and hit the wall behind him.

"Try again, twerp!" he calls, a cutting laughter

breaking into his barb. So Spidey does – he flips and *thwip*s, but Marko just keeps dodging and throwing out that maniacal laughter. Then, as he's coming in for another hit, Marko throws out his huge hand and wraps it around Spidey's middle, squeezing and squeezing.

"Erm ahhh," Spider-Man grunts, fingers scrambling to claw underneath Marko's tight grip, but finding nothing but sand. *"Can't… breathe,"* he gasps out, and Marko gives him a toothy smile, before flinging him hard into the side of a building. Spider-Man drops to the street on his stomach, pressing his hands into the ground. *I've got to get up!* He pushes and finally stands, bending his knees, ready to leap forwards again at Marko, whose huge sand torso leads into a massive head and arms poised to fight. But what he says next stops Spidey in his tracks.

"I found that thing you was hidin', Spider-Man. I got it *and* the lamp, and everyone's gonna be sorry soon. And I'm gonna get what's mine." And then he drops into the rest of his puddle of sand and flows into the 2nd Avenue subway station. Spider-Man shoots a web at the entrance and pulls himself forwards as fast as he can, but he's not fast enough. By the time he jumps down the stairs and through the turnstile, Flint is long gone.

"MARKO!" he yells into the tunnel, heedless of the surrounding foot traffic. "IT'S CONTROLLING YOU!" But he has no idea if his message was heard or not, and now he's panicking. *Marko can't have the conducting rod! How could he have found it?! I've got to get to the cemetery! It has to be there!*

An eastbound train flies into the station, and Spider-Man webs himself to the roof of it, crouching and waiting for the train to get above ground and back into Brooklyn. The minute it leaves the Delancey-Essex station and crawls up into the daylight from the dark tunnels, he launches into the air, swinging from the rafters of the Williamsburg Bridge into Brooklyn and turning north. He ignores the cries of people walking along the bridge below that spot him, intent on getting to the cemetery as soon as possible.

How did Sandman know I had the element? How did he find it?! The only other person who knew was... *Oh no.* He needs to check on Addison Alredge and Brewster, too. He zips along towards Queens, flying over coffee shops and bodegas, restaurant pop-ups and dog parks. There's a running refrain of *gotta get there, gotta get there, gotta get there* in his head while he flings himself up Flushing Avenue.

After what feels like hours, he finally makes it to the gates of the cemetery, running full-speed to the small mausoleum. He slides to a stop in front of the loose brick and yanks it out of the wall and... *What?*

The rod is still there, folded along the tape into two pieces, shoved deeply into the hole. *What in the—?* But before he can finish that thought, his spider-sense buzzes so badly he nearly falls to his knees.

Sandman had been looking for Spider-Man day and night, and now that he wanted to find him, he was nowhere around. Flint even went so far as to scope out the entrance of the Café With No Name from around the corner in hopes of running into someone who might know – but with the Maggia family's hit still on his back, it wasn't worth the risk to go inside.

But that mysterious voice calling the shots was very clear – if he can get near the thing, they'll be able to feel it. *Some kinda psychic connection*, he thinks. Like he can feel that small piece at his place. He shudders a bit, remembering what they could do to him so close to that small remnant. It made them stronger.

But that was irrelevant right now. He needed to find it, so he came up with a plan.

He drew Spider-Man out, and then he made him think Sandman *already* had the elemental rod. Spider-Man rushed off immediately, and all Sandman had to do was follow him! *Never had an easier score in my life.*

He follows Spider-Man all the way up into Queens and into a cemetery, where Spider-Man starts running with purpose. It was such an *easy* follow. Spider-Man was so distracted by what Sandman said, he didn't stop to *think*. So now, Sandman sees Spider-Man standing in front of some crypt holding the very thing he's been looking for, and Sandman puts his fists together and just *blasts* forwards a column of sand.

"FOOLED YOU, BUG!" he screams as his sand completely envelops Spider-Man *and* the tomb. It's pretty gross; he can feel every part of the old stone. He can also feel the uncomfortable alien-ness of the rod as he pulls at it. But Spider-Man's not letting go. Sandman pulls enough of his sand back so Spider-Man's head is free.

"Let—go—let—go—let—*go*!" Sandman shouts, punctuating each word with a huge sand fist slamming to Spidey's head.

"YOU—LET—GO!" Spider-Man yells back, and Sandman is more furious than he's ever been. *I'm so close.* He tightens a thick stream of sand around Spider-Man's chest and another around the rod, and then he rips the two apart with all his strength. He flings Spider-Man as hard as he can, and Spidey flies so far away Sandman can't even see where he lands.

But Sandman doesn't care because he *has it*. He shrinks back down and re-forms into his standard self. He holds the rod in his hands, and a toothy grin cuts its way across his face.

Sandman has never been known for his plans, but this was a good one. This was a plan that worked.

When Spider-Man comes to, it's dark outside and he's somewhere on the western edges of an entirely different cemetery. He's lying on his side against a headstone. His mask is ripped and one lens is broken, giving the world an off-kilter, uneven look. He shakes his head and then immediately regrets it.

"*Blargh*," he says. And then groans. He brings a hand up to his head and then looks at his fingers to check if there's any blood. He grins shakily when he sees that they're clean. It looks like he managed to make it through without actually needing any sort of bandaging. A plus.

He puts one arm up and rests a hand against the top of the tombstone, using it to pull himself up.

"Thanks" – he pauses to read the lettering – "Mrs Lucas. Appreciate the help." His voice is rough with pain, and he winces when he stands. This is going to take him a minute to recover from. Then he remembers what happened. *Oh no*. Sandman has the lamp *and* the rod, and Spider-Man has no idea what he's going to do with it, but he knows it won't be good. *I can't believe I let Flint Marko of all people trick me so easily! I led him right to it!* He puts his head in his hands and screams into them, muffling the sound.

Whew, okay. I needed to get that out of my system. He's going to fix this because he *has* to fix this. What does he need to do first? He needs to get home and call Addison and Brewster and make sure they're okay. He needs – okay, maybe *wants* – to talk to MJ. In this case, he knows two heads are better than one. He has no idea what Flint might be up to or what his next move will be. Okay, Peter's got to get back to Forest Hills. He limps forwards onto the path between graves and tries to get his legs back into his normal rhythm, walking a few steps before breaking into a soft jog, and then finally a run to the exit. By the time he makes it to the gate, he's ready to *thwip* some webbing to a streetlight and go swinging.

Peter gets back to his neighbourhood, and he bypasses his house completely, swinging straight to MJ's. Her room is dark, but he taps on the window. There's no response, so he waits a beat and taps again. Finally, there's a shifting in her room; he can see a foot poke out from her bedding in the moonlight. Then she's standing in front of her window, in a pair of polka-dot pyjamas, rubbing her eyes and her hair a complete mess. When she sees it's him, her eyes go wide and she slams her curtains closed.

"Uhh…" he says, unsure of what's happening. But a minute goes by, and she's opened the curtains again. Now her hair's up in a ponytail, and she looks a little more awake. She unlocks her window and pushes it up.

"Peter? What are you doing here?" she asks, moving aside to let him crawl into her room. He drops in, and she gets a good look at him, her mouth opening into a small O as she takes in his battered appearance. "What *happened*? Are you okay?!"

He puts up two hands so she'll pause.

"I'm okay. A little sore, but I'll be fine by tomorrow morning," he starts. "Well, maybe everything except my dignity." He laughs and then grips his ribs. *Ouch.* "Oof." He tries to sit but ends up collapsing into her beanbag and pulls off his mask. She grimaces at the sight of his face. "That good, huh?" he asks with a pained smile.

"I mean... there's no blood?" she says, kind of asking.

"That's my bright side, too!"

"Your life is *weird*."

He nods. "Unfortunately."

"Do you want some aspirin?"

This time he shakes his head no.

"No, I'll be okay soon – perk of the powers." Then he pauses, wondering how to start. "Do you have your mom's laptop in here?" he asks finally. She looks around at her desk and sure enough, the notebook is sitting there.

"What do you need?" She opens it and boots it up. Peter rises slowly and makes his way to the computer, opening an incognito tab and signing into his free phone number. MJ shoots him a questioning gaze, but he just dials Addison's number and crosses his fingers when it starts ringing.

Ring
Ring
Ring
Ri—

"Hello?" a tired-sounding voice answers, and Peter recognises Brewster's gravelly tenor.

"Uh, Mr Alredge – it's, uh, Spider-Man."

MJ is looking at him, hand over her mouth, trying not to breathe out a sound, he assumes.

"Spider-Man! Oh, thank goodness. We were trying to call you, but Addison lost the phone number you gave him, and we didn't know what to do. He was attacked by Sandman; he knows—"

Peter cuts him off.

"Is Addison okay?!" he asks.

"Yes, yes, he was a little worse for wear, but nothing some rest and good eating can't fix. And a short stay in the hospital," he adds, conceding that it was worse than he was letting on.

"Okay—okay, did Sandman say anything or do anything else?"

But there's nothing Brewster can tell him. Sandman

tortured Addison for the information and left as soon as he gave in, but Sandman had shared nothing of his plans. Peter thanks Brewster and wishes Addison well before hanging up.

"This is going to take some getting used to," MJ says from behind him. He turns around.

"Huh?"

"I mean… this." She gestures at all of him. "You know, the suit, the two-in-the-morning chats. The— What is it?"

"Ugh, I should have changed. I'm sorry. I just—"

"No! That's not what I'm saying – it's just going to take some getting used to. Not in a bad way," she adds, clarifying. "In an *oh-now-I-know-the-secret* way." She smiles. "Seriously. Now what is going on? Why did you show up here on the verge of collapse and call that old rich guy before you even filled me in?"

"MJ, Sandman got it. He got the element." Peter can't help it and his voice cracks, but he just clears his throat and continues. "He tricked me and followed me to the hideout and then—" He tells her what happened, not sugar-coating any part of it. "So now I'm here," he finishes. "Because I don't know what to do next."

"Oh, we will figure this out." Peter looks up at MJ, surprised by her fierce tone. She has a scary sort of grin on ̶ace. "Some random bad guy can't beat *us*. I told you," ̶s, "I've been doing some research, and I think I ̶ *how* whatever this alien thing is actually works."

CHAPTER TWENTY-THREE

MJ's original plan was to tell Peter about her research payoff in the morning because it had *just* happened that night. But then he tapped on her window and climbed through, groaning in pain and hugging his side, and all of a sudden, Peter's side job became *very* real. She maintained an even and light tone and hoped that she was keeping her anxiety off her face. He's looking at her expectantly now, waiting for her to share what she knows. MJ takes a deep breath to settle her nerves. *This is the job*, she thinks, taking in Peter's torn suit and his scuffed chin. There is a deep purple bruise forming above his right eye. *This is what it really means. And I can help.* MJ lifts her own chin and begins.

"I finally found the accounts for the people who were at the museum at the same time as me—"

"How'd you find them?" Peter asks, voice still shaky. MJ bites back the urge to ask if he is okay again and answers his question instead.

"I went back to the museum, and I told the security guard I needed to see if my grandpa was there at the museum on the day of the break-in because he lost his smart watch. And I was going to be in *so much trouble* if I didn't find it because I was supposed to be watching him!" She widens her eyes in faux innocence and puts a hand against her chest. "And then he let me see the security logs to check."

"I know I've said it before, but I'm saying it again, you are *amazing*."

"Anyway" – a smile cuts across her face while she goes on speaking – "including me, there were ten total people in the museum while I was there. Now, three we know: me, Sandman and Beetle. That leaves seven. I saw two little kids, like, too little for phones, while I was waiting for the bathroom. That leaves five. So, I did a search for hashtag MOMI on Instagram and Twitter for that date and time period." She pauses here and lets the drama build before adding, "I found *five accounts*."

Peter clenches his fist and hisses out a quiet *"Yes."* It brings a sense of normality back to the room.

"It's not all good news, though," MJ continues,

explaining what she discovered. Three were defunct accounts – no longer updating. She didn't want to think too hard about what that might mean. The other two? For days afterwards, their content was disturbing. But all of a sudden, it changed back to normal. In one case, the person had dropped their phone on the subway tracks and had to get a new one. In the other, they got grounded and their phone was taken away. It sounded exactly like what she went through, up through to when she deliberately disconnected from her phone.

"Do you see what this means?" she asks Peter, who has been listening intently.

He lights up. "You were right. That whatever this thing is… is *in the phones*."

"I think it's even more specific, it's in their Wi-Fi antennae – that's the part of the phone that looks for a Wi-Fi signal. Anyone who logged on to MOMI's Wi-Fi when that lamp got turned on. Whatever this thing is, it's using a gigahertz frequency is my guess. Meaning radio waves." She picks up her phone, powered down now as it had been since she figured everything out. "And we know whatever it is probably needs to be *close* to the element based on the fact that you got hit by some invisible force at the museum but haven't been touched since." She continues, tossing her phone from hand to hand. "So, they must have a way of literally solidifying radio waves or even" – she shakes in anticipation of this next part – "using those waves to control minds on some level. And they're using the power inside our phones to do it, piggybacking off the signals put out by our Wi-Fi antennae."

Peter's eyes are darting again, MJ notices. *He does that a lot when he's fitting pieces of a mental puzzle together.*

"Whatever Sandman does with the lamp… he can't do it to more than a small room's worth of people," he says slowly. "The people outside the theatre in Addison's story weren't affected when Arlo turned on the lamp, because there's nothing in the lamp to amplify the signal like there is in an antenna. I don't really get how the lamp, or the rod, whatever plays into it?"

"I *think* the rod is where the waves are actually coming from, like, it's the conductor that gives them existence. But I don't see what Sandman can do… unless…" MJ says, pausing as a horrified thought comes to her… "He has some kind of amplifier. Like a router or a satellite, whatever it is that can take the small radio wavelength that the arc lamp powers and send it out to a bigger audience."

Peter's face pales.

"You're right. We have the technology now that could help him send this thing far and wide, bouncing it off other amplifiers and… this could affect the whole world!" He starts pacing, wringing his hands. But then he stops. "But… now we know what he needs! How many of those, like actual, massive signal amplifiers, can exist in New York City? He's going to want to affect as many people as possible, because how many shots is he going to get at this? He can't risk having to… demo this thing."

"But how are *we* going to find it?" MJ asks. "I wouldn't even know where to begin looking."

Peter's got a gleam in his eye.

"I… actually do."

Peter and MJ take the bus together the next morning. He makes sure to be on time – he *almost* doesn't make it but jumps onto the stairs just before their bus driver, Ms Betty, closes the door. She gives him an aggrieved look and gestures to the back.

"Thank you," Peter gasps out before walking down the aisle and plopping in the seat next to MJ. She laughs.

"I'm going to start calling you when I wake up so that *you* wake up."

"That is so much more appealing than my horrible phone alarm," he replies.

Then she takes his hand, and he's gratified all over again to have her in his corner.

"So, we'll just ask Dr Shah as soon as we get into class. Is that too obvious? I'm very new to this covert-ops thing." She grins. "But it *is* exciting."

"I think we can ask him as soon as we get there," he says, not hiding the mirth laced into his tone. "You know," he says, "I am *really* glad you know."

"You've said," she answers, but her voice is pleased. "I am also *really* glad I know," she teases.

They spend the rest of the ride in easy banter, but there's an underlying anxiety to it. In the back of his head, he knows somewhere Sandman is sitting with the elemental rod and the arc lamp, waiting to unleash them on the world.

They walk into class together, fifteen minutes before the bell's set to ring, and go straight to Dr Shah's desk. He looks up from the lab report he's marking when they approach.

"Ms Watson, Mr Parker – very impressed to see you here ahead of the bell," he jokes lightly. "What can I do for you?"

"Peter said you know about that arc lamp that was going to show at the Museum of the Moving Image? I *almost* got to see it!" she says. "I was actually there the day before they were unveiling it. That's when I read about it."

"Oh, yes!" he says, lighting up. "I told Peter, but it was a very exciting proposition. I was just corresponding with a colleague about this – the same one I recommended to you, actually, Peter." *Dr Monica Diaz*, Peter remembers. "She and I were talking about the potential for an electromagnetic wave-based ionization project. Because in theory what the lamp, with the alien element, does is..." He trails off, noticing that Peter and MJ are staring at him blank-faced. *An electromagnetic what, now?* Peter's head is spinning. Dr Shah lets out a bark of laughter. "Sorry, sorry, I've gotten too used to the scientific chatter again. Basically, it operates on a frequency we don't have access to, generally, and its electromagnetic waves literally detach electrons from atoms and molecules *just* by using energy. So, in theory, what this arc lamp could do, outside of creating a very bright light, is create a strong pattern of electromagnetic waves that affect organic chemistry. Or any chemistry, really."

"But why would someone want to do that?" Peter asks.

Dr Shah leans back in his chair and it squeaks loudly, but he doesn't react, clearly used to the grating sound. He puts his hands behind his head and thinks for a moment.

"A multitude of reasons, really. In science—"

But Peter interrupts impatiently. "Sorry, but could it affect someone's actual body, or like, the chemicals that make up their body?" he asks, all circumspection forgotten. Dr Shah frowns, visibly considering the question. Behind Peter and MJ, their classmates are slowly trailing in, and the room is beginning to fill with chatter.

"Well, they pretended to try it in medicine about a hundred years ago and it did not work *at all*," Dr Shah says deliberately. "And I don't think it ever will. But the thing is, if the waves are created by an element we've never seen before?" Dr Shah shrugs. "Who's to say what it can and can't do? And what people have been theorising about this element for over a century is that it could change the way we think about electromagnetic waves because of the frequency. Beyond *gamma*. It's like moving from 3-D to 4-D to 5-D."

Peter's head hurts.

"So," MJ starts, "if it was a *really* powerful mysterious-frequency wave, it could literally change the way someone thought."

Dr Shah nods. "Yes, I guess so. But you'd need something to massively enhance the signal, like *massively*," he says. "Especially if the goal is any kind of long-term change. No way a tiny arc lamp can do that. I don't care how powerful the mysterious element is. And there's nothing powerful enough…" He hesitates.

Peter notices the pause and urges him on. "Sir?"

"Well," he says, pausing again. "It's nowhere near ready, but the Empire State University research team I used to be on did start looking into what it would take to create a large-scale EASER. An electro – you know what, basically it's a *humongous* amplifier. Imagine there was a satellite big enough that you could watch shows from Japan on your television with just an antenna."

The blank expression slips back onto Peter's face again.

"People used antennae to watch TV?" he asks. He

looks at MJ, and she just shrugs back at him. Dr Shah seems mildly appalled, his jaw slack for a moment.

"Okay, well, now I feel old *and* out of touch. It would just mean it could take a small radio or electromagnetic-wave signal and give it a much larger radius."

This all sounds exactly like what Marko would be looking for. Peter is sure that if his spider-sense reacted to clues, it would be going bananas.

"But I believe it's very far from working. Last I heard, they'd barely gotten it to recognise the waves at all, let alone amplify them."

The late bell rings as Dr Shah's finishing his sentence, and he claps his hands together.

"Well, I hope that helps or was informative at least?" he asks.

"Very!" MJ supplies as Peter's brain is going haywire. "Thank you, Dr Shah!" she says brightly, grabbing Peter's hand and pulling him to his seat.

"That's what he's going to use," Peter says without letting go of MJ's hand.

She nods. "You're probably right. I think you're going to have to check it out. But let's talk after class – man, this life is *intense*."

He cracks half a grin in response. MJ squeezes Peter's hand and then lets go, heading back to her seat.

"Okay! Class!" Dr Shah calls from the front of the room. "Let's get started."

During lunch, MJ and Peter sequester themselves in the library, hunching in front of one of the computers. They look up anything they can on the research team Dr Shah mentioned, and 'EASER', though their search results keep bringing back 'easier', which is not as helpful as the search engine might think. After twenty minutes, Peter rubs his eyes.

"I'm still so beat from last night. Why can't any of this be *easy*." Then he stops. "Ah, sorry. I'm usually just complaining… to myself." He ends the sentence weakly.

"No, I'm with you. I am *tired*, though granted, I didn't get thrown halfway across Queens, but I did have a cute boy knock on my window in the middle of the night." *Cute?* Peter grins. He would need to get used to being so happy and so anxious at the same time. "And I still need to finish my English essay before tomorrow," she goes on, pretending not to see Peter's giant smile. "And I am *so glad* Maia and Randy offered to do the PowerPoint for our OSMAKER thing—"

"Who knew someone could love doing PowerPoint presentations!" Peter exclaims.

"Their interests are truly varied." MJ pauses and then types something else into the search bar. "Let's try 'Electromagnetic amplifier Empire State University research'." Peter holds up his crossed fingers.

She hits enter.

"There's something!" She leans in closer to the screen. "This is an article from… last week. From the *Bugle*. 'Rival research team spy leads to relocation'," she reads aloud. Peter leans over to read along silently. "'The Empire State University research team, while working on their recently proposed EASER, had to relocate to a secret lab this week after finding out that one of their fellow researchers was in fact a *spy* from a rival group of scientists'!"

"Who knew science was so *dramatic*?" Peter asks playfully after they finish the article.

"That's got to be *the* amplifier, right? If it's such a big deal. The article even quoted Dr Shah's friend! And someone named Dr Dewey Ponce, which is an *incredible* name."

"But it's too bad it doesn't say *where* the thing is," Peter groans. But then he sits up straight and reaches across MJ to scroll back up to the top of the page. "There!" He points to the writer's name: *Kayla Ramirez*. "I know her!" he blurts out. "She's… kind of my boss? At the *Bugle*."

"That's perfect! You can ask her – she must know something they didn't print."

"I have to head there after school anyway. There was a 'billing error' with my last paycheque, and the people who do that part of the job – I don't know what they're called – they don't come in on the weekends, I guess. Grown-up jobs are weird."

"Well, it's a good excuse to be able to ask Kayla the questions you need to – that sounds like the universe doing you a solid," she suggests.

"Then we should be extra suspicious because the universe is *always* playing a bad joke on me, I swear. You know what?" He leans towards her and faux-whispers, "I bet Panda-Mania shows up again."

Peter takes the lift from the fourteenth floor up to the seventeenth. He'd just been to Accounts Payable, whatever that was, to find out what went wrong with his paycheque that week – Jameson forgot he was paying Peter and just hadn't signed the cheque. *Cool. Now that's dealt with, I can go find Kayla.*

When he gets there, she's chatting with a dark-haired young white woman that Peter has seen around the office once or twice but hasn't met.

"Do you think he's read it yet?" the young woman is asking Kayla. Kayla just shrugs.

"No idea – but there's nothing we can do until then. I've stopped posting any Spidey stuff on social—" She sees Peter come in and waves. "Despite getting excellent material," she adds, smiling at him. She mentioned it to him the last time he was there that he could continue sending photos and captions, but they'd put a moratorium on posting until Jameson responded to the employees' letter. Peter just shrugged, happy to continue to do his job regardless. "Peter," Kayla says now, "this is Betty Brant. She's not usually here on the weekends."

"Hi," Peter says.

"Hi, Peter, nice to meet you finally. The weekday crowd has been loving your photos!" Betty says. Betty directs her next comment to Kayla, and Peter takes a seat at his desk waiting for Kayla to be free. A few minutes later, Betty waves at him as she says goodbye to Kayla, who turns to Peter as soon as Betty's out of earshot.

"So, what are you doing here on a weekday?"

"Mr Jameson forgot to sign my cheque," Peter tells her. Kayla laughs and repeats what Peter said, only she air-quotes around the word 'forgot'. Peter makes a wry face and shrugs. "We got it sorted out, I think. At least, this time," he caveats.

"I appreciate you coming to say hi – I think I saw Randy upstairs with Robbie, actually."

Peter raises his eyebrows; he and Randy must have got on the same train without realising it. He makes a mental note to text him when he's done and see if he wants to head back to Queens together – that is, if he doesn't get the intel he needs here and has to start looking *immediately*.

"Oh, I didn't know, dang. Missed out on a subway buddy," he jokes. "I, uh, wanted to ask you about an article you wrote last week."

She was looking at something on her screen while talking to him but turns her chair around at this.

"Of course – which one?"

But as Peter's about to answer, J. Jonah Jameson's voice echoes through the hallways.

"*RAMIREZ!*"

Kayla bolts up from her chair as Jameson rushes over to her desk.

"Here's what we're going to do," he says before she can say anything. "We can have some" – he grits his teeth and in a weird coincidence air-quotes the word – "'balanced' coverage of Spider-Man. By which I mean you, and he" – Jameson leans over to glare at Peter, who just ducks his head – "can make your case for however you wanna caption the photos on our Twistagram."

Peter holds in a very inappropriate snicker.

"*However*," Jameson continues, "I reserve the right to veto everything and disagree. And the opinion pages are *still mine*. I've talked to Robbie about everything else."

Kayla beams.

"Thank you, Jonah! This is going to be so good—"

Jameson cuts her off.

"It was a good letter," he says begrudgingly. "You've got talent. I'll talk to Robbie about bumping you up a title—"

"And a pay raise?" Kayla asks, voice innocent and

saccharine. Jameson makes an inarticulate noise and storms off back the way he came.

"He is *terrifying*," Peter says as soon as he's out of sight. Kayla shrugs, staring at the direction Jameson had walked off in.

"He is what he is." She looks back at Peter. "Now you wanted to ask me about a story?"

"Oh! The one about the spy at Empire State University."

"Oh man, that is *such* a good piece." Her whole face lights up. "Ned was so jealous that I got it and he didn't. But – don't tell him I said this – I'm a better reporter." Peter chuckles in response and mimes keeping his lips zipped. "So what do you want to know?"

"Do you know where they ended up moving? I'm kind of dying to see that EASER thing they're working on. We're doing some similar stuff in class. My teacher used to work on their team," he half fibs.

Kayla takes a second to consider. "I don't think they're going to let a kid in there, no offence," she adds at the end, cushioning her statement. "I can try and look at my notes, though."

He shrugs. "It can't hurt to ask, my aunt always says."

"She's not wrong," Kayla replies. She's turned back to her computer and is scrolling through a bunch of files. She finally finds what she's looking for and double-clicks the file open – it's written in a shorthand that Peter cannot read, even though he can see the screen clearly.

"Hmmm, you know what, they didn't tell me the exact place – just that it's somewhere out near Citi Field in Queens."

It's not exactly what he needs, but it certainly narrows it down.

"Oh, hm, I'll ask my teacher; he might be able to figure it out from there!" Peter says, and thanks her for taking the time.

"I got you, Peter," she grins. "You're a good kid; it's no trouble. Ask me anytime."

CHAPTER TWENTY-FOUR

Peter missed Randy by the time he left the *Bugle*, so he takes the train home by himself and considers how to approach what he knows. He's itching to get to Citi Field and look for the Empire State research team. Then he can start keeping watch. But he also wants to talk to MJ. He jogs up the stairs of the 71st Street–Forest Hills station and starts the walk home. It's early evening, and the sun has just about set by the time he turns the corner onto his street. He swings by his house first to drop off his backpack.

"Hey, Peter!" Aunt May calls from the utility room in the back of the house. Peter toes off his shoes and drops his bag next to the stairs before going to see her.

"Hey, Aunt May," he says, joining her at the washing machine to give her a kiss on the cheek. "What's up?"

"Taking a break from some grant proposals to get this laundry into the dryer. How was your day? Did you get the *Bugle* thing sorted out?" she asks, moving a few towels into the tumble dryer.

"I did!" he answers, and then tells her about what happened with Jameson and the letter.

"That's fantastic news." She's stopped loading the dryer and is listening, rapt with attention. "And a good lesson to learn: don't compromise on your integrity." Aunt May's always given him good advice, but in that moment, she reminds him so much of Uncle Ben with his short pearls of wisdom that Peter steps forwards and hugs her tight. She starts but then quickly wraps her arms around him. "Well, thank you for this, though I'm not sure what I did to earn it." She laughs.

"Just by being great, Aunt May." He steps back and then adds, somewhat awkwardly, "I'm, uh, gonna head over to MJ's."

This time Aunt May's smile is all too knowing, and Peter groans when she says, "Okay, Peter." Because he can *hear* everything she's not saying through her tone.

"*Okay*, Aunt May," he says back, hoping she can hear everything he's not saying as well. She just laughs again and sends him on his way.

Peter's at MJ's fifteen minutes later – her mum and aunt are home, so they're sitting on the swing on her porch and he's filling her in on what Kayla told him about the research facility.

"Citi Field?" she asks. "Hmmm." She pulls out a phone, and Peter notices it's not her old one. He gestures at it, a question on his face. "Oh," she says, "turns out we were due for an upgrade, so I asked my mom if I could have it as my birthday and Christmas present combined, and she said yes. I dropped the old one in a cup of soda."

"Oh, that's great – do we think the soda will stop it?" he asks, unsure.

"I hope so. But just in case, I taped a bunch of magnets to it, put it in a Tupperware filled with water and vinegar, and hid it under the porch," she replies. Peter is suitably impressed. She notices his expression and smiles. "It's probably sort of excessive, honestly, because I think once we deal with the rod, it won't matter. I'm pretty sure that's what's powering it, so without a source, it'll disappear." Then she opens the maps app on her new phone and starts navigating to Citi Field. She scrolls a bit and then stops. "Hey, would it be too on the nose for them to move to the New York Hall of Science? It's, like, across the street from Citi Field." Peter leans over to look. "It can't hurt to check it out, right?"

"Well, I guess I know where I'll be tonight."

"Just make sure your phone is off when you get there." MJ turns to him as she says it, and he nearly jumps when he realises how close they are. For a second, he's staring into her eyes and thinks they are such a beautiful, unique green, he's not sure it's a colour that's been invented yet. He leans closer.

Just then, the porch light turns on and the Watsons' front door opens. Peter and MJ jerk apart as MJ's aunt comes out onto the porch carrying a tray.

"I brought you guys some snacks and a drink!"

Peter sighs. The universe is definitely laughing somewhere.

Dr Dewey Ponce has been *most* helpful to Sandman. He is easy to find, and once Sandman gets inside his home, he is quite amenable to offering up some information. Last night, Sandman had got back to his temporary home in the warehouse with the element in hand. It took him hours to connect the rods correctly, and once the lamp turned on, a light hit his eyes and Sandman had never felt so powerful and bloodthirsty in his life. He felt *great*. Then the light flickered once and dulled.

"No! You can't break!" Sandman shouted, but then stopped. The lamp was still vibrating. He could hear them, the ones who found him.

We are

    WE ARE

    WE ARE

The voice – *or maybe voices?* – reverberated in his head. At first, he couldn't handle it, he almost fell, knees buckling at the shock of hearing it bounce around inside him.

YOU

    YOU

        YOU HELP US

    WE HELP YOU

SANDMAN

        WE

"Who are you?" he'd asked.

The Faithless

    We are the Faithless

We are

We are home

Must help us

Must do our work

Cannot help

Weakened

Share us share us share us share us

And then they told him everything they needed. He'd share their voice with the world. He just needed a loud enough speaker to do it. And that's how he found Dr Dewey Ponce.

Spider-Man crawls into the New York Hall of Science through an open window in the inverted glass dome over the front lobby. His phone is powered off and pressing against his hip. He imagines that whoever left the window open didn't think of someone being able to stick to walls wanting to get inside a science museum. He drops slowly, sliding down his web to the floor below, and walks in a crouch. It's quiet, which makes sense for a museum in the middle of the night. He's far enough in that the entrance lies shadowed behind him and he doesn't have to worry about anyone seeing him through the doors.

Spidey looks around the lobby – he notices a large black stain across the floor, etching along the white tile in spurts. *Like a kid with gigantic rubber shoes scuffed the floor. Strange. Maybe facilities hasn't gotten to this room yet? Although that means I might have to deal with innocent bystanders. Ugh. This is going to be hard enough!*

He sees a large board with a map of the museum on it and heads in its direction. Once there, he can see the full layout. *There are a lot of exhibits in this thing!* He doesn't think they're going to build a massive electromagnetic wave amplifier in the Rocket Park Mini Golf or the 3-D theatre. His eyes rove over the map, reading and discarding areas as he gets to them, but then there's an asterisk next to the Great Hall. It says: *Closed to the public until further notice.*

If the research team relocated here, that's where they've got to be, he thinks. He webs up to the ceiling and starts crawling in the direction of the Great Hall. That's when his spider-sense starts vibrating, slowly but insistently, in the back of his head.

Something's wrong. He moves across the ceiling, inch by inch, the buzzing in his head getting louder with each small movement forwards. Finally he gets to the two doors of the Great Hall. Dropping onto the floor, he sees that the lock has been broken, smashed to bits, and the handle has been torn clear out of the wood. There's movement coming from inside – Spidey can hear shifting and the sound of something heavy being dragged. He thinks of the black marks on the ground near the entrance. Someone brought *something* in.

Ever so quietly, he crouches on one side of the double doors and inches the one with the broken handle open to peek inside. The walls are curved and covered, floor to high, high ceiling, in small squares made up of even smaller pieces of coloured glass that give the effect of rows upon rows of tiny stained-glass windows. It's likely a vision during the day, but now they just reflect the low light of tabletop lamps scattered across a few makeshift desks. To the side, there's a huge rectangular device that Spidey can't quite make out. Closer to the door, a recognisable silhouette is being dragged towards it. *The arc lamp!*

Spider-Man pokes his head in the space between the open door and the one still latched. He's low to the ground and moving cautiously, looking first to the right and then to the left. It's clear, but there isn't too much that he can hide behind, just those few desks. The Empire State team has created something of a provisional lab for their experiment; there's equipment all over the place in addition to the few random desks – but it's not a ton of coverage. He looks up at the high ceiling, knowing it may be his best bet.

Inside, the arc lamp is still moving forwards, and as Spidey steps slowly in, the hulking form of Sandman comes into shape ahead of it, dragging it behind him. Now Spidey can see he's got a generator in one hand and is holding the arc lamp with the other. Spider-Man can't tell if they're connected or not.

Sandman keeps walking towards the massive shape that turns out to be Empire State University's EASER amplifier. *Gotta stop Marko before he gets there!* Spidey presses his fingers against the wall and starts crawling up and up, turning left when he's high enough to track the progress of Sandman and the lamp. Now that he's closer, Spidey can hear Sandman muttering to himself.

"Gotta get this done, gotta be fast. Gotta get it loud, share the message. Gotta share the message."

Well, that *doesn't sound good.* Spider-Man moves his feet up, so his knees are bent under him and he's got leverage to jump. Then he sticks out one hand, takes aim, and shoots. He blasts the arc lamp backwards with a powerful web shot and it falls to the ground with a large crash. Sandman whirls around and screams with rage, dropping the generator in the process.

"SPIDER-MAN! NO!" He sends a huge hammer

of packed sand in the direction the web shot from, but Spidey's already moving, flipping away from the wall and towards the lamp. He has to make sure it's broken!

Sandman finally sees him, and a huge column of sand blasts his way, forcing Spidey to change course before he can get to the arc lamp.

"I don't think so, *bug*!" Sandman yells, moving his column of sand back and forth like it's a water hose spraying out a thousand metric tonnes of pressure. Spider-Man realises that the EASER is his best defence against Sandman in this enclosed space. He jumps up high again to a spot behind the unfinished amplifier.

"Flint!" he calls out, stuck to the wall behind the machine. "There is *something* controlling you! It got in through your phone!"

"I ain't bein' controlled, Spider-Man! I *want* to be here! These guys are gonna give me everything I've ever wanted!"

Spider-Man groans. *Great. He's been indoctrinated.* Spidey climbs up a few feet and peeks over the edge of the EASER. Sandman is standing in the centre of the room, shoulders heaving. The lamp is still lying on its side a few feet away. Spidey can see now that it's clearly connected to the boxed generator beside it. He tries to reach Sandman again.

"You don't have to do this!" he says, letting the sound carry in the big room. "I know it's hard, but try to resist it!"

Sandman's face shifts into something cruel and menacing.

"I don't *have* to do this, Spider-Man; I *need* to! Why can't you get it through your thick spider skull?! Everything will be great if you just let me have this." His voice is growing louder and louder with each passing word until finally he's roaring. "You ruin *everything* – I won't let you ruin this!"

All of a sudden, a stream of sand explodes from the floor, and Spider-Man realises he's let Sandman distract him so he wouldn't notice the pile of sand slowly building below him. He flips forwards over the machine, directly into Sandman's path. His lenses go wide as Sandman pulls the sand back into himself and grows to twice the size he was before. Spidey webs himself to a wall, twisting and turning in the air.

How am I going to beat this guy? Peter knows he can't talk sense into Marko, and he can't just *punch* him. His mind is racing as he skitters across the wall, moving as fast as he can to get out of Sandman's range. He looks back once to gauge how fast Sandman is coming and is surprised to see that his absence is being taken advantage of. Sandman has made it to the lamp, his hand reaching towards the generator. *Or is he pulling his hand away? Did he already turn it on? No!*

Spider-Man *thwips* out a web and holds on to the line, swinging forwards, feet-first. He flies into a solid

Sandman, who is too focused on his mission of connecting the lamp to the amplifier to morph around the blow in time. So when Spidey's feet connect, Sandman soars forwards, his inertia stopped only by his face meeting hundreds of small glass squares.

"Flint! I know you can't help it. I know that thing is *controlling you*. And if you stop now, I'll tell everyone you couldn't help a lot of this!" Spider-Man runs towards the lamp and is horrified to see it's powered up with a small light emanating from it. A few feet before he reaches it, he slams into an invisible *something*. *Oh no*. He doesn't know if he can take on an invisible ghost *and* Sandman. But the thing just pushes him away, hard.

It doesn't seem to follow him.

Sandman gets to his feet and wipes an arm across his face. His expression is set in a sneer.

"Oh, I *can* help it," he says. "I *want* to help it. You got no idea what's comin', bug."

And then he pushes two arms out into a long arc of sand heading straight towards Spider-Man, blasting him hard to the far side of the room. Spidey stands up dizzily and sees Sandman make it to the lamp, righting it into standing position. He's got two thin wires in his hand and is moving to twist them together. Spider-Man shoots two lines of webbing in Sandman's direction, a desperate ploy. He knows he's too far away. Sandman gets the wires entwined, and Spider-Man, running forwards, can see they're linking the arc lamp to the EASER.

"FLINT! The EASER doesn't even work! They haven't figured it out yet!"

Sandman laughs without any humour in it.

"That's what they *want* you to think, Spider-Man, but I talked to a Dr Dewey, who let me in on a little secret."

Under his mask, the blood drains from Spider-Man's face.

CHAPTER TWENTY-FIVE

Oh no, oh no, oh no, oh no. If the EASER is functional, Spider-Man cannot let Sandman turn it on. Spidey knows he's strong, but what if it makes that thing that's helping Sandman even stronger? Plus, Spidey's not sure he'd be able to stop reacting to whatever waves an amplified version of what that lamp might let out. *So what if you do?* a small voice inside him says. *Take control, take all of it, take Sandman down and you'll be the hero everyone loves.* Spider-Man shakes the voice out of his head.

No!

He runs forwards and jumps the last ten feet, fist-first, just out of sheer desperation, and he blows through

Sandman's form. But it doesn't do anything, and Sandman still heads steadily towards the EASER and the switch to power it on.

Spidey's panicking now. *How am I going to stop this?* On the ground, he spies the metal wire, bright orange against the dark of the floor. He shoots a thin line of webbing towards it and yanks back hard. He hears the gratifying scrape of the wire being pulled away from a conducting rod on the side of the EASER. Holding on to the web, he flies forwards, pulling it behind him. Sandman spins around, wailing wordlessly. A huge fist follows Spidey, but then instead of hitting him, it overtakes him, flying past and crashing into the wall.

"Ha! You *missed*!" he calls back, laughing.

"WASN'T AIMIN' FOR YOU, WALL-CRAWLER!"

And Spider-Man realises his mistake too late. All the hair on his arms goes up, and *something* yanks him to the ground, hard. Then the chunk of the wall that Sandman hit fractures down on top of him, and Spider-Man is flat against the floor. The weight is heavy on his back, and he moans at the pain in his hips and his ribs. He's lost the web attached to the wire, and his advantage with it. He pushes himself up on his hands and pulls himself out of the mess of glass and rock. A trickle of blood drips down his bicep from where a glass shard has cut his suit open, and there's another tear along his calf. He is in rough shape.

But he sees Sandman advancing on the EASER again, pulling the wire behind him. The light in the lamp is blinking weakly. Spider-Man doesn't feel anything in the air anymore, and he remembers the museum and how the threat had just dispelled. He doesn't think whatever it is has another hit in it. He's got to focus on Sandman now.

Spidey lifts his arms up straight and in front of him and presses his fingers against the buttons on his palms. *I'll sling myself over!*

Or I would, but I'm out of web-fluid! What am I going to do now? Not only is he out of web-fluid, but there's nowhere with enough water to immobilise Sandman right now. *Come on, think! What are your other options?* His heart is racing, and he can feel himself falling further into a panic. He steps forwards and hits a soldering iron with his toe.

A *soldering iron* – in the middle of an exhibition? *Wait!* Spidey slaps a hand against his forehead and then winces, finding another small cut. *This is a lab!* Spider-Man looks to his right at the desks of all the researchers. He rushes to the first one and looks at the equipment there – a lot of wiring and soldering tools, but nothing that will help him. Same with desk number two, but there, three desks back, is something he might be able to use.

There's a heavy tank, with OXYACETYLENE written on the side, and a thin nozzle coming out of the top, along with a release button. HIGHLY FLAMMABLE, he reads on the label. There are knobs for temperature and fuel gas flow. Spidey turns them both all the way up. *What happens when you combine a flammable gas with a whole lot of sand? Time to find out.*

He picks the tank up easily and grabs an antique-looking metal striker sitting innocuously in someone else's workspace. Sandman is almost at the EASER now, so Spidey runs and jumps forwards high in the air, landing a few feet away.

"Hey, SANDMAN!" he yells, one hand holding the nozzle in Sandman's direction with a finger on the release button, and the other hand gripping the metal striker. Sandman turns to Spider-Man, an incredulous look on his face.

"Again with this? What, you gonna turn me into a balloon or somethin'? I *won*, Spider-Man. Figure it out!" And one of his hands turns into a long pillar of sand, rushing towards Spider-Man. But this time, Spidey presses the release button and squeezes the metal striker. Nothing happens.

"Come on, come on, come on, come on, *please, please, please, please.*" He tries again, still nothing.

The sand is rushing towards him, and he steps back.

"COME ON." And he gives it one more squeeze. This time, a spark jumps out and ignites the gas. A long stream of flame hits Sandman in a small but bright explosion.

Sandman screams in pain.

Spidey keeps up the pressure, though he's flinching at every pained sound Sandman sends out. Sandman has started to crystallise, the heat turning his sand solid and shining brightly in the steady light of the flame.

"*Stop!*" Sandman cries, and Spidey waits for Sandman to relent, to agree to stop, but instead he just says, "I need to do this." And Sandman tries to reach forwards with one hardening arm. It loses mobility three feet away from the EASER. The crystallisation spreads and makes its way up Sandman's body, spreading too fast to follow now. But Sandman makes one last effort and shoots a stream of sand forwards towards the EASER, forcing Spidey to jump up and flip over the hardening form of Sandman. He holds the fire steady as he goes so that he hits every part of sand that he can see. Until finally Sandman is completely and utterly stuck as an unmoving glass statue.

But that's not completely correct, Spidey realises, as the force of Sandman's attempted Hail Mary causes him to teeter back and forth, slowly rocking until he crashes backwards towards the arc lamp. Without any web-fluid, Spider-Man's only recourse is to rush forwards and try to hold the statue-like Sandman, but he doesn't make it in time. He hears a *crunch* as a heavy glass Sandman lands directly on top of the arc lamp, smashing it to bits.

Sandman will be fine, he thinks. Spider-Man knows that all Flint Marko needs to survive is a single grain of sand, but it doesn't make it any less bleak to think about as he looks around at the broken pieces of glass and lamp on the ground before him.

The EASER looks fairly untouched, for which he's thankful. The museum is not so lucky. There are scorch marks all over the flooring and some of the walls – and of course there's the huge hole in the side of the building. Spider-Man hadn't noticed during the fight, but now he can hear an alarm going off across the building, and sirens blaring in the background, police on their way to see what's happening.

That means he only has a few minutes. He pushes the vestiges of Sandman's form off the lamp, grunting in pain as he does so. He may have the proportionate strength of a spider, but glass Sandman is *heavy* and Spidey's bones are aching already. Underneath, the Alredge arc lamp is completely demolished. Spider-Man pulls the metal apart searching for the element, but all he finds is a pile of black dust in the shape of the long, thin rod. He picks up the gas tank again and points the flame directly at the remnants. The minute it hits, the powder and bits of rock start bursting into flame and evaporating away into the air.

Was that all of it?! The sirens are getting louder as they get closer.

"I really hope this isn't a terrible idea," he says, doing one last search for any of the dark powder. The area is clear, he thinks. He hopes.

Then he riffles through a desk again for a paper and pen and some tape so he can leave a note for the authorities. He writes something out and tapes it to the glass mass that makes up Sandman.

Please take to the Raft. Will need some rehabilitation. :)
—Spider-Man

Peter makes it home an hour later. He's hurting and tired and anxious when he crawls into his bedroom. He *really* hopes he got every bit of that element. And he hopes that this will be the end of it. Pulling off his suit, he shoves it into the back of his wardrobe. He'll need to repair it and the mask later. *That's a problem for future me.* Right now, all he wants to do is fall into his bed. Instead, he sticks a plaster across his forehead and on his arm where he was cut by the glass, and then he winds a long bandage around his middle to support his ribs. With that taken care of, he moves to drop into the welcoming warmth of his bed. But before he can, he sees his phone light up bright and insistent in the dark. He sees Mary Jane Watson in the little notification box, and he swipes it open.

> **ARE U OK???????? JUST SAW UR LIGHT TURN ON**

He types a few words and hits send. He gets a thumbs-up back a moment later.

In five minutes, he's tapping at MJ's window again, only this time instead of his broken suit, he's in his Weinkle's Daycare T-shirt, a pair of pyjama bottoms and some fuzzy socks. She comes to the window and slides it open, eyes wide. She's in those same polka-dot pyjamas.

"What did you mean by long story? Are you okay?! Tell me *everything*!" she says as soon as he's inside. He sees her take note of the plaster across his forehead and the way he gingerly holds his side. He sits down on the floor, his back against her bed, and she joins him. He takes her hand in his while he starts his story.

"You were totally right – it was at the Hall of Science." And then he tells her all about it – the desperation Sandman had, the ugly way the fight ended. Burning the element. All of it. "I wish I knew what they'd promised him, and I wish I could say that it's all over, but—"

"It is. You did the best you could," she supplies. "Seriously, I don't think I would have done anything different. The thing's destroyed, and its influence should be, too. Now we just cross our fingers and hope."

He rests his head against the edge of her mattress, looking up at her ceiling. There are little glow-in-the-dark stars all over it. He grins. This is what he was waiting for: a quiet moment with MJ.

"Well, I think it's over, so maybe now we can focus

on…" He pauses, wondering how to ask what he wants to ask.

"Our… OSMAKER project?" she asks, like she can't believe that's what he would bring up right now. He gives her back an equally disbelieving look.

"What?! No! I—uh, I mean. We can focus on, uh…" *I just beat a ten-ton pile of living sand. I can do this.* He takes a deep breath. "If you want to be my girlfriend?" he rushes out.

MJ's face goes tomato red, and her eyebrows seem to go all the way up to her hairline. "OH," she says, and then more quietly, "Oh."

She thinks for a few minutes, and Peter's wondering if he's ruined everything by talking about it *now* – all busted up after a fight with a super villain. But then MJ laughs and looks him straight in the eyes and says, "Of course, Peter Parker."

Peter, he's embarrassed to admit, reacts with a quiet exhalation of *"yes"* and a fist pump that ends up hurting his ribs again, so he lets out a slight yelp of pain.

"Oh my gosh, are you okay?" MJ asks, and Peter nods.

"Yes! Yes. I mean, yeah, yes, I'm okay! I'm just excited and happy and—" Before he can finish, MJ is moving forwards, and finally, *finally*, Peter kisses Mary Jane Watson, and he has to admit, it was worth the wait.

EPILOGUE

In the month and a half since Peter and MJ *officially* started dating, Peter's life has been mostly good. He's had his normal Parker Luck, but as far as he can tell, there have been exactly zero attempts by some random evil alien overlord to try and run the human race into a self-destructive frenzy. On the other hand, that annoying dog did get stuck in the tree four more times.

Today, Peter and MJ are walking down the hall to Dr Shah's class holding hands, and everyone's got so used to it that the only comment they get is a disgusted *"Ugh"* from Flash Thompson.

Peter considers it a win.

"Did you see the new *Bugle* posting about Spidey?" MJ asks.

Peter shakes his head. He sent over a few pictures last night, but he wasn't kidding when he told MJ he stopped looking. It *never* made him feel good, even with JJJ's 'attempt' at neutral reporting. So he focused on his own Spider-Man account – which MJ has been helping with. He has two thousand followers now.

"It was actually nice enough that, uh" – she lowers her voice – "the you-know-who account could share it if you want."

Peter opens up the app on his phone and toggles to the *Bugle* page. It's a shot he sent of Spider-Man helping an old woman across the street. The caption is one that he wrote.

It's not all crime fighting and butt-kicking
for New York's Spider-Man!

He grins but then quickly shifts to a grimace when he scrolls down to the very next posting. It's a screenshot to Jameson's latest opinion piece, with a caption directing people to the link in the page's bio.

SPIDER-MAN:
MENACE OR TRIPLE-THREAT MENACE????

"Well," MJ says, shrugging, "We can't fix *everything* immediately. Like, J. Jonah Jameson is probably always going to be a... a *Bugle* butt!" She says it with such vehemence that Peter laughs hard enough to snort. He's wiping his eyes when they make it to Dr Shah's classroom.

"Oh, don't forget," she says as he follows her inside. "You signed up to volunteer at the Queens food bank with me tomorrow morning."

He nods, looking forward to it. They separate to go to their desks, but MJ gives him a clandestine smile before she walks away and he tries to keep the sappy grin off his face, but he's not sure he succeeds.

"Okay!" Dr Shah says from his desk when the late bell rings. He's holding up a stack of papers, and Peter remembers it's the day they're getting their project grades and finding out who's going to represent Midtown High in the OSMAKER competition. He looks back at Maia, Randy, and MJ. Maia's got her fingers crossed on both hands, Randy mouths, *We've got this*, but even he looks nervous and MJ just shrugs like, well, it's out of their hands now. Peter's own expression is one of nausea.

He looks back up at the front of the class, where Dr Shah has started passing out papers.

"An admirable job from everyone," he says, "but one group truly went above and beyond in their idea, pairing technology with an unexpected subject."

Peter leans his forehead in his hands, his fingers pressing slightly against his brow. That could be *literally anyone*. Flash's group did something about tech and fast-food restaurants.

The class is loud, everyone talking about their grades as the papers are passed out. Finally, a stack of papers lands on Peter's desk, and he looks up to see Dr Shah smiling. Peter looks back at the paper, and there's a bright red A circled at the top of the page, along with a big red star. *Does that mean—*

"The group that will be representing Midtown High in Norman Osborn's OSMAKER competition is Team Five: Maia Levy, Peter Parker, Randy Robertson and Mary Jane Watson! I can't wait to see this organising app come to fruition."

The group jumps up, and Maia actually *whoops* with excitement. Peter catches MJ's eye, and they grin widely at each other. Then Randy catches them all in a hug, and Peter laughs, jumping along with his friends.

Maybe the future is looking up, after all!

We are broken

But not defeated

But not defeated

We are more free

than we ever were

Home this is our new home this is

Sandman was our mistake

We will choose better next time

Dr Samir Shah picks up his phone from where it's vibrating on the table. There's a message from a number he doesn't recognise.

> **HELLO, DR. SHAH. WE HAVE A JOB FOR YOU. . . .**

ACKNOWLEDGEMENTS

This book, though written in a hilariously short time frame, was a long time coming. It's also the very definition of a group project. To my editor, Emeli Juhlin: first of all, thank you for sending me that email in March 2019 asking if I'd want to write an original Spider-Man story and breaking my brain (in the best possible way) in the process! I am extremely grateful for your unwavering belief that we could make this book happen. It really would not have been written without you. To my agent, Michael Bourret, for always being around and available whenever the anxiety came pouring out and for the much-loved words of encouragement along the way. And to my editors at Marvel Entertainment, Caitlin O'Connell and Lauren

Bisom: thank you for your guidance on making sure that we handled Spidey's story with care. To Nicoletta Baldari for a beautiful cover illustration and creating some of my favourite Spider-Man artwork ever, and Jay Roeder for the incredible lettering. To everyone at Disney and Marvel who touched the book – design, licensing, marketing, publicity, sales, production, copy-editing – I appreciate all of your hard work so much. I can write as many words as I want, but readers would never see a page without you.

I have to thank a few people in my life – and not just because they listened to me obsessively throw out facts and questions about the web-head for months on end, but for their support, for joining me in all the exciting moments and for keeping my secrets. My Chhibblings, Heeral and Vinny Chhibber, who read pitches and drafts and provided validation when I needed it. To Swapna Krishna, Eric Smith and Jenn Northington for being just the absolute best all of the time. (That's it, that's the acknowledgement; they are truly the best). To my fellow detail-oriented nerds Jason Sanchez, Charles Pulliam-Moore, Jordan Brown and Paul Montgomery for talking me through hysterically specific spider-points. To my Saturday Morning Cartoon Day crew for quite literally getting me through a pandemic with our weekly hangs to catch up and celebrate each other and sometimes even watch cartoons: Brett Parnell, David Kinniburgh and Alice Tam (who deserves a thrice-over thanks for our weekly *Supernatural* viewings and for lending me her name for what is a very in-character character). To that end: to my cousin Samir Shah, who didn't hesitate to say yes when I told him I might "name someone in a book after him". And thank you to Brette Weinkle and DeMane Davis for also letting me borrow their names! Naming characters is hard, kids! Fellow author Brandon T. Snider, who in 2018 told me he was "putting my name in for a Marvel Press opportunity", which got me in the room to write *Peter & Ned's Ultimate Travel Journal*: I literally would not be here if it wasn't for you sending that elevator down my way. To my dog, Darcy, for being so cute and loving it makes me cry.

And of course, to Stan Lee and Steve Ditko for creating this character who means so much to so many people. Peter Parker taught us that you can do good even when life is hard. He taught us that if you have the power to help people, you should. I hope if you're reading this, you take those lessons to heart and use your great power to make the world a better place.

© Randy Fontanilla

PREETI CHHIBBER is an author, speaker and freelancer living in Georgia. Dubbed a 'Spider-Man superfan and author' by Publishers Weekly, you can usually find her writing your favourite characters or binge-reading her way through several series at once. She also co-hosts the podcasts Desi Geek Girls and Tar Valon or Bust. She's appeared on several panels at New York Comic Con, San Diego Comic Con and on-screen on the SYFY Network. Honestly, you probably recognise her from one of several BuzzFeed 'look at these tweets' lists. Visit her online at PreetiChhibber.com and @runwithskizzers.